MON OCHR OME

jamie costello

ATOM

ATOM

First published in the United Kingdom in 2022 by Atom

1 3 5 7 9 10 8 6 4 2

Copyright © 2022, Laura Wilson

The moral right of the author has been asserted.

A CIP catalogue record for this book
is available from the British Library.

ISBN: 978-0-3490-0390-0

Typeset in Dante by M Rules
Printed and bound in Great Britain by
Clays Ltd, Elcograf S.p.A.

Papers used by Atom are from well-managed forests
and other responsible sources.

Atom
An imprint of
Little, Brown Book Group
Carmelite House
50 Victoria Embankment
London EC4Y 0DZ

An Hachette UK Company
www.hachette.co.uk

www.littlebrown.co.uk

To my mother, June Wilson (1920–2021)

Part I

Part 1

One

It starts the day after they take Mr Kowalczyk.

I saw the officer helping him into the car and, even though I've never actually met him, that night I dream about it. Mr Kowalczyk, the police and the people in the street are puppets with enormous round wooden heads, bobbing along on strings. Mr Kowalczyk is wearing a black suit and tie, like he had in real life, but just before he bends to get into the back seat, he turns his head right round so it's almost back-to-front, and stares straight at me with his gigantic painted eyes.

Then the officer slams the door with a colossal bang and I wake up. It takes a moment to realise that the bang wasn't in the dream but an actual noise – the sickening sound of a massive car crash. Judging from the direction, it's somewhere near the traffic lights at the big junction.

I'm already imagining it as I stumble out of bed to look out the window: buckled metal and showers of red sparks as firefighters cut people out of the wreckage, like at the beginning of the hospital drama series my grandma watches on TV. I've no idea why Prune – short for

Prudence, which she hates – likes them, because she used to be a nurse
and all she does is complain about the stuff they get wrong.

When I pull back the curtain, I can't see anything at all outside.
It takes me a moment to realise that's because none of the streetlights are on. Odd, because it's just before dawn. I can already
feel it's going to be hot, though, like it's been every day for the
last five weeks – the kind of heat that turns grass brown and cars
into ovens, when you can't touch metal. It seems to be killing the
birds, too, because I keep seeing sad little corpses in the gutters
and under trees. Ladybirds like it, though; they're everywhere. I've
even found them in my underwear drawer. Prune says it's a record
heatwave for London in July.

I can hear shouting, so someone's gone out there, thankfully,
and I hear Rusty – Prune's partner – clomping down the stairs and
swearing about how he can't find the torch.

I'm expecting to hear sirens and see flashing blue lights any
minute, but nothing happens. I keep on peering through the
window, and after a while I start to see the fuzzy outlines of the
houses across the road, and the trees and hedges – dark grey, but
getting more distinct in the gloom. There are grey streaks lighting
the sky, too, and – this is when my stomach lurches – a huge lead-
coloured ball rising up on the horizon like some alien dark force
that's poisoning the air.

For a split second I truly think I'm having a nightmare, that the
bang only jolted me from one dream into another. Sometimes you
can know that you're dreaming from inside the dream, and make
yourself wake up.

This is not one of those times. I reach for the switch on my bedside lamp, but nothing happens. 'Mum!'

No answer.

'Mum?'

Where is everyone?

I stumble downstairs in darkness, imagining the air choking the streets just outside.

'Mum!'

I hit the hallway light switch. Nothing. And where is my family? 'MUM!'

I charge through the dark kitchen, swearing as my hip slams into the corner of the table, and out through the front door. I dash down the steps, round the corner into the front garden and full tilt into Mum coming the other way.

'Where—'

'Grace! Calm down. Everything's OK.'

I stare across the grey grass. The air seems OK, but in the quarter-light the trees are gnarly and sinister and the flowers look pale and slimy, as if they are growing and decaying at the same time. 'But what's happened?'

'There was a car accident. Prune and Rusty went to see if they could help.'

'The other thing.'

'What other . . . ? Oh, the electricity. It's gone off, so I just got this—' she holds up a big torch '—from the shed. Hey! Come on . . . ' She pulls me into a hug and rubs my back. 'Oh sweetie, you're all shaky. Deep breaths, OK? This isn't like you.'

'Stop it!' I try to wriggle free, but her arms are like clamps.
'Mum, we've got to—'

'Shh, it's OK . . . it's OK.'

I let her hold me, face pressed into her shoulder, away from the
familiar street that suddenly looks so eerie, then force myself to
look again.

It's getting lighter, and the edges of things are becoming sharper.
The sky's changed from soot to charcoal, and now it's turning a sort
of pebbly colour. The clouds look as if they're boiling over, like milk.

The fact that Mum is calmly rubbing my back, as if nothing is
wrong, might be the strangest thing of all.

'What's happening, Mum?'

'Nothing, love. Or nothing that can't be fixed.'

'Then what's that?'

'What?'

'*That.*'

I break away from her and point at the lead-coloured disc
emerging from a layer of cloud that's drifting away in long lines
like smoke.

'What are you talking about?'

'*Look.*'

'That's the sunrise.' She laughs. 'Happens every day. You never
see it because it usually takes a chisel to get you out of bed in
the morning.'

'But it doesn't make sense.' I rub my eyes – gently at first, then
quite hard. 'Where are all the colours?'

6

Two

Mum frowns at me, then says, 'Let's get your bathrobe,' and pushes me back up the stairs to the front door.

'It must be some freaky thing with the weather. Climate change or something.' Even as I'm saying this, I know it doesn't make sense. I mean, even in places where they have really violent psycho-weather like hurricanes, they still have colours, so how would that even work? I pull away from Mum and run back up to my room, with her following, asking if I'm OK. I ignore her questions and stare out of the window, willing the colours to appear. I can hear sirens now, several of them. The different tones merge into a blur of sound, which means there must be ambulances somewhere. I can see the junction – not the actual traffic lights but the bit in the middle, where there are three cars with their bonnets rammed together and glass frosting the tarmac.

People are trying to wrench open the doors of one car, and a woman is lying on the ground with somebody who might be Prune bending over her. There's a man sitting on the verge with his head in his hands, and another standing over him, obviously yelling. Then I see Rusty – who is way too big for any normal-sized person to mess with – step between them and push the shouting man back with a huge palm. Three or four other people are standing around, watching or taking pictures on their phones. But none of this – men, women, cars, or anything else – has a single speck of colour.

I turn to look at Mum ... Except she's not Mum. I didn't notice it before in the half-light because I was so busy staring round the garden, but now I can see she's turned grey. Her pale freckly skin and long red hair and the blue and orange swirls on her wrap are gone. Her arms and face are sort of mottled, like lichen on a stone, and her shiny hair's a steel helmet. The bathrobe she's putting round my shoulders, which I know should be dark blue, is now slate coloured.

'Grace, what's wrong?'

'You're ...' I can't find the words. 'And everything's just ... I mean, look!'

I stare at my bedroom. It still looks familiar – tiny and cramped, with the furniture and the mess – but as if it has been carved out of stone, like a relic from some century long ago. I spot myself in the full-length mirror, and I can see that my hair's the same as usual – I get the black corkscrew curls from my dad, who died when I was six. The oversized t-shirt I'm wearing is still white, but my face and arms and legs, which are normally light brown, also courtesy of Dad, look ... I don't know, *rat* coloured.

It's horrible. Everything's dirty-looking, and just ... weird. I blink a lot and rub my eyes some more, but it stays that way. I turn back to the window, as if that might make a difference, and spot Rusty coming back down the road. His hair and beard are grey anyway, but his bathrobe, which he's wearing over his trousers, is meant to be bright red – if you added a bit of white fur, he'd be Santa's double – only now it looks practically black. Seeing him open the door of his ancient van and climb in is like watching a black-and-white film.

'Grace, please. Talk to me. I don't understand what you want me to look at.'

'Then I'm going blind,' I blurt out. 'I can't see the colours any more.'

She frowns, then starts talking in a calm, problem-solving voice. 'You haven't banged your head, have you?'

'No.'

'You're sure?'

'*Yes*. I'd remember, wouldn't I?'

'Does it hurt?'

'No. It's just . . . Mum, what's *happening* to me?'

'It must be the shock – the noise and the accident – or perhaps you've got an infection or something. Why don't you lie down and close your eyes? I'll bring you a cup of tea and if it doesn't go back to normal soon, I'll call the doctor.'

'No.' I don't want to be by myself in a grey room. 'I'll come with you.'

I stick my phone in the pocket of my bathrobe and we go downstairs – the pinky-red wallpaper on the landing looks like ash – and find Prune standing in the kitchen with her coat over her nightie. The coat's sort of like a wizard's robe and it should be multicoloured but now it's just different shades of grey.

Mum tries the light switch, and the electricity comes on. Great, but it makes everything look even worse. I stare at the fruit bowl: bananas, pears and apples, all grey and dense-looking, like if you picked one up it would weigh as much as a lump of rock. I don't want to pick one up, though. I don't want to touch anything. The kitchen – also small, because the whole flat is – looks like it's covered in dust.

'Did Rusty take that woman to hospital?' Mum asks. She's trying to normalise what I've just told her by not making a big thing of it, but the fact she's doing that is making me more scared, not less.

'Yes.' Prune sits down at the table. 'They said the wait time for the ambulance was over three hours – must be a big emergency somewhere. I thought she was OK to be moved, so . . .'

'I'll make some tea.' Mum's doing the calm voice again. 'Can you get the milk, Grace?'

I open the fridge. The electricity can't have been off long enough for everything to go bad, but it looks like it has. It's so gross that I almost slam the door shut straightaway. The bacon and the half-melon are grey and slimy; the strawberries look as if they're covered in mould and the butter might as well be putty. It all smells OK, but I can't imagine eating any of it, ever.

'Grace?' Mum prompts.

I hand her the milk. At least that still looks normal.

*

'... *Service on the Victoria Line has been suspended following reports of a major incident at King's Cross station. A southbound train failed to stop after passing two signals at danger and collided with the rear of a stationary train at a platform. So far, the driver and nine passengers are known to have died, and thirty-five people have been injured. The reason for the crash is not yet known, but it is thought to be the result of operator error. A spokesman for London Underground has said that it may take several days before full service is resumed.*'

I picture train carriages collapsing into each other in a tunnel full of smoke, passengers trapped between torn sheets of metal, bodies broken, screaming. The world around me is grey, but my imagination is a vivid nightmare of red blood and torn flesh.

'Always so quick to blame the driver.' Mum turns the radio off. 'I suppose that was the big emergency. Maybe there was a power outage at King's Cross, as well – I mean, it's not that far away.'

'Coincidence.' Prune spreads jam on her toast. It looks disgusting – a spoonful of swamp. 'As soon as Rusty's back with the van, we'll take you to A&E,' she tells me. 'It's probably inflammation.'

'Do my eyes look red, then?'

'No, but it could be your optic nerve. Don't worry, they'll soon sort you out.'

She's been saying they'll 'sort me out' and that I'll be fine ever since Mum told her about it twenty minutes ago, like she's sure of it. But she isn't.

'You'll be fine' is what people say when they can't think of anything else.

*

11

It's over an hour before Rusty comes back, and I'm getting more anxious by the minute. I wander into the sitting room and try squinting and stretching my eyes with my fingers, but everything stays grey, with the sofa – which is supposed to be dark green – a big black lump in the middle. Everything looks dirty, even though I know it's not, and it's really depressing. I go and pull some clothes out of the dryer to put on, and that's even weirder: they look like they haven't been washed, ever, but you can smell the fabric conditioner.

I better get 'sorted out', because right now, my world is just *wrong*.

Three

I'm surprised by how many people there are in the waiting room at the Western Eye Hospital. Only they don't actually look like people but a collection of statues, seated or leaning against the walls, with the receptionist behind a computer that looks like a slab of stone.

On the way here Rusty told us all – because, despite the fact they keep telling me it'll be fine, both Mum and Prune insisted on coming along – that the man who caused the accident in our road said he hadn't seen the traffic lights. The other guy thought he was drunk, which was why he was yelling at him.

The wait is over three hours. At first, Rusty tries to jolly us along, cracking jokes and telling silly stories, but nobody joins in, so he gives up and we sit on our hard plastic chairs in silence. Mum keeps reaching over and squeezing my hand, but all that does is confirm that she's way more worried than she's letting on, and by the time they call my name, I'm so anxious that it feels like someone's tied a knot in my stomach.

*

'Achromatopsia.' The doctor is oldish and looks like a garden gnome that hasn't been painted yet. He's spent the last half-hour doing different tests: getting me to look at pictures of dots and see if I can make out numbers (no) and sort a bunch of little discs into different colours (also no), and finally asking me to stare into the back of a weird-looking machine in order to have a look at my retinas, which are the big bits of your eyeballs (no idea).

'From Greek – "a" meaning "without", "chroma" meaning "colour", and "opsia" meaning "to do with sight". A description as well as a named condition, which is fairly rare and almost always hereditary – although that isn't the case here, or it would have shown up already. Besides which . . . ' The doctor frowns. 'There appears to be nothing wrong with your retinas, and you're not showing any signs of abnormal sensitivity to light, which is unusual for someone with this condition.' He clearly wants to say something else, and there's this jittery silence while he stares down at his desk calendar. I don't dare look at his face, so I stare at the calendar, too. It's got 'Kerr + Bell' written across the top, and the outline of a bell with a little cross inside, like a medical sign. 'The other possible cause is a brain injury. Have you had a fall recently?'

Like I'm ninety, not sixteen. I shake my head.

'Any injury to your head?'

'No, nothing like that.'

'OK. Well, brain injuries can also be caused by strokes . . . ' I stare at him in shock. 'Although that doesn't seem particularly likely in your case. Or . . .' he gives me a lopsided smile and then looks down at his calendar again as he says, 'a brain tumour.'

A *brain tumour?*

Mum, who's sitting beside me, clutches my hand. I don't know much about cancer, except that it killed Jake and Holly's mum. Holly's my best friend and her brother Jake is my boyfriend, and right now they're away on holiday, which I'm actually kind of grateful for, because telling them would be just . . .

I can't even *begin* to think about that. Instead, I imagine the cells inside my head dividing again and again, a single one becoming a thousand, a million, a billion, like an evil cauliflower that keeps on growing, squashing everything else to the sides of my skull. 'Does it mean I'll go blind?'

Another lopsided smile. 'We don't have a diagnosis yet. You're going to need some more tests. I'm going to refer you for a scan.'

'Are you OK, babe?'

I'm FaceTiming with Holly and Jake, who are sitting at the breakfast bar of the villa their dad rented in Portugal, where it's even hotter than it is here. I can see whitewashed walls behind them, and patterned tiles that I'm sure would be really pretty, if only I could see them in colour.

'I'm fine, honestly.' I'm trying to look happy but, judging from their faces, I'm not doing very well. 'Missing you.'

'What are you doing?'

'Oh, you know . . .' It's been a week now and no date for the scan. I've spent most of the time in my room, trying not to think about brain tumours or going blind. I tried to get some reading done for school, but I can't concentrate on anything, even Grey Netflix, for more than about a minute. 'You?'

Jake starts telling me about the jet ski and how great it is. Holl's rolling her eyes, like she's been doing ever since he got the licence and wouldn't stop talking about it, and I'm nodding away but not really listening. When he finally pauses for breath, I say, 'That's cool.' I know it's totally lame, but I can't think of anything else. Jake hasn't picked up on anything, but that's normal: he's lovely, but you'd have to have a full-on meltdown right under his nose before he'd ask if anything was wrong. Holly knows there's something, though. We've been friends forever, so I swear we sometimes know what the other one is thinking or feeling before they know it themselves, which, at the moment, makes things pretty awkward.

'You sure you're OK, hun? Did your phone break or something?'

'Yeah, sorry ... Not been feeling great, that's all. Probably just a virus or whatever. I'm going to the doctor tomorrow.' Which is a total lie, but it stops Holl asking any more questions.

It's so weird seeing the two of them like that, on the screen in black and white, like talking to an old photograph. Jake tells me a bit more about the holiday and they show me the view of the swimming pool and the beach and I say how great it all looks. And I bet it does. Normally I'd be quite jealous because I've only been abroad once, to stay with Prune and Rusty's friends in Ireland, but now the water in the pool looks like it's from a drain, and the waves of the sea look oddly solid, like a ploughed field.

I say, 'Love you, love you,' and blow kisses at them both until the screen goes black – and then I collapse onto the bed in relief.

Even if I felt I *could* talk to them – if their mum hadn't died of cancer, I mean – I still don't think I'd want to, because I don't really want to talk to anyone. Plus, it would add a whole other level of awkward to the whole Jake thing. A year ago was when it all changed. I'd known him as a friend for ages because he's Holl's big brother, but then it was like he'd *chosen* me. I was so flattered and I thought about him all the time at first, but now I'm feeling like I sort of hypnotised myself into it, because he likes me and he's popular and looks good and makes me laugh. And, because of being around a lot when I'm at Holly's, he's *there* – as in, convenient.

Urgh. I don't know. It's fine and everything – I don't *not* like him – but it just feels a bit like, what's the point? I realise that makes me sound like a bitch – doubly so because there are a lot of girls who like him. It's not something I can talk to Holl about, for obvious reasons. I'm scared that splitting up with Jake will mean losing her, because, even when she's saying he's a waste of space or whatever, she adores him and she's really loyal. Plus, I only just admitted the hypnotising bit to myself recently. Saying I loved him was … well, I kind of had to because he said it to me first. Explaining how I actually felt would have been really awkward because it's too complicated, plus I didn't know how to describe it – so it's a bit soon to be telling somebody else, and right now my head is too full of other stuff.

I find a photo of Holl and Jake on my phone, and try to remember how they both look in colour – fair hair, hazel eyes, sharp cheekbones and, by now, tanned skin from being at the beach every day – but it's almost like I'm looking at different people. That's my feelings as well, of course, but now there's a weird disconnect. It's odd, though. I mean, if Mum's past behaviour is anything to go by, being scared and depressed ought to be making me more needy, not less, but right now I just feel like I'm folding in on myself.

That didn't take long – Holly's online. I've hardly looked at my phone at all in the last few days, and I can see there's a bunch of messages from her and Jake and a couple of other friends. Holl's profile picture is of the two of us laughing our heads off at something, and seeing it faded to black and white feels like being punched.

Typing … typing …

ur not ok. tell me xx

idk but tty tomorrow after gp

I add three hearts to show it's nothing to do with her or Jake, and hope she believes me, because I really can't engage with either of them right now. Then I put the phone away in a drawer and spend the next however-long staring at the towel I've put over the mirror so I don't catch sight of myself by accident.

Mum's been googling achromatopsia and telling me about this island near New Zealand where loads of people have it from birth. OK, so it's not just me, but it's *normal* for those people, isn't it? They've lived their whole lives not seeing colours. I know she's trying to help, but I wish she'd shut up. For me, right now it's changed everything – for example, I have to ask her to pick out my clothes because I've begun to forget what colour stuff is supposed to be. I've got some birthday money left and I was going to ask Holl to come shopping with me when she gets back, but now there doesn't seem a whole lot of point.

I keep hoping it's some freaky temporary thing and I'll wake up one morning and find everything back to how it was. I dream in colour, always the same. I'm chasing a red balloon across a beach in the sunshine, feeling the warmth on my face, content. When I wake up there's that tiny sliver of time when everything's OK . . . And then I open my eyes to a grey world where everything feels hopeless.

Four

Or not quite everything, because the good news is I don't have a brain tumour.

That scan was basically a way of getting a detailed view of my brain using – I think – an enormous magnet and some radio waves. One thing they definitely did *not* warn me about was that it involves putting yourself into a tube. It's like being buried alive, but with a load of very loud clanging like someone bashing metal with a hammer, and it goes on for about forty-five minutes. Urgh. But anyway, it showed that although my photoreceptors – zillions of tiny things in the retina that turn light into electricity that whizzes up to your brain so you can see stuff – are working, there's something wrong with my visual cortex, or at least the bit of it that tells you what colour everything is.

So: they know what's happened to me, but they don't know why or what to do about it.

But also . . . and this is the *massive* news: *it isn't just me*.

There's been a bunch of stuff on the internet about achromatopsia in the last couple of weeks and loads of people having hysterics on social media. Rusty, who's so old-school that he still gets a newspaper every day, showed me an article by a journalist who woke up a couple of days ago and discovered he couldn't see in colour. People are saying the driver of the train at King's Cross might have been affected, too, and that's the reason he went through the signal. We've been wondering if the guy who caused the car crash in our road might have had it, as well. Mum, Prune and Rusty haven't said anything, but I know they must be wondering if they'll be next.

I can't work out if the fact that it's happening to other people makes me feel better or worse. Mostly, I just feel scared. I messaged Holl and Jake to say I'd seen the doctor and everything was OK – not exactly true, but as much as I can manage right now – and got all the feels back plus a load of pictures of beaches and a dinner table with huge bowls of seafood. The lobster looks bad enough – giant mutant alien cockroach – but the oysters are worse, like a plateful of tumours. I don't say that, of course – just write well jel and send more hearts to show I'm thinking of them.

'There have been a number of fatalities following multiple pile-ups on motorways near coastal areas, some stretching for over ten miles. Serious collisions have also occurred on some train lines and tube systems. These are thought to be the result of drivers being unable to see the signals properly. Reports are coming in of plane crashes at Heathrow, Gatwick and Cardiff, as well as incidents at smaller airfields in coastal areas. A light aircraft has collided with a crane in central London, and there are reports of similar accidents in Bristol and Belfast. So far, 197 people are known

to have been killed, with the death toll looking likely to rise. Motorways, railway stations and airports have been closed, buses will not be running until further notice, and the chief medical officer has said that although there is no reason to panic, people are advised to remain at home as much as possible and await further information.'

'Great idea, telling people not to panic.' Mum turns the radio off and plonks herself down at the kitchen table. 'Especially if you're basically telling them not to leave home. You're reinforcing the idea that there's something to panic *about*.'

'Well, there is, isn't there?'

'Oh, darling . . . ' Mum gives me one of those slightly crumpled can't-actually-help-but-I'm-here-for-you smiles. 'Tell me what you want for lunch.'

I never had a problem with food before, but I've hardly eaten anything for the last three weeks because it's not just lobsters and oysters that look disgusting, it's practically everything. Plus, if you can't see what colour things are, they don't taste the same.

It's only been a couple of weeks but, even though I've been avoiding mirrors, I know I'm getting skinny. Mum and I made a list of food that still looks normal because it's black, white or grey, but it isn't very long: white rice, white cheese and fish, white meat (which really means just chicken), mushrooms, cream, black grapes and olives, white chocolate, marshmallows and a few others. It's not as if I like all of those things anyway. For drinks, water's fine and tea, coffee and cola are sort of OK, but pretty much anything else looks like it's contaminated and might make you ill.

'They don't know what's going on, do they?'

22

Mum shakes her head. 'Sounds like a lot of people are having the same problem, though – or at least anyone who lives near the sea.'

'What if we went further inland? Then you and Prune and Rusty might still be OK.'

'I don't think so, love. And they said to stay put. If lots of people start driving about, it'll just mean more accidents.'

She's right, of course, but I've got that horrible jittery feeling where you know you ought to be doing something but don't know what it is. I get up and go to the front door, which is one of those stable-type things that – the flat being so small – opens straight out of the kitchen. You go along a narrow balcony, then down a flight of wrought iron steps to the back garden. 'I might go for a walk.'

'What about lunch? And it's too dangerous.'

'I promise I'll have something later, and I'll stay in the garden, OK?'

Mum sighs. 'I suppose so. Just don't go in the big house.'

We live in a pokey little flat above a double garage – which is why the front door is at the back, otherwise our outside steps would get in the way of the cars – on a road full of huge houses. By 'huge' I mean properly gigantic, with loads of bedrooms, and gyms and wine cellars and things. It's because Rusty is a caretaker. I'm not sure I'd have given him the job. He used to be a security guard, so he's got experience, but he drinks too much and is no good for anything after about 6 p.m., which is why Prune is always yelling at him. It's great that he did get the job, though, because of it coming with a place to live. That was about four years ago, and it meant that Mum and I could move in with him and Prune. It was just in time, because we were about a week away from being made homeless, and Mum's behaviour was starting to really scare me. That was when I began to hate social media. Not only is it full of bullies and trolls, but it's also rubbish seeing everyone going on about their wonderful lives when you're terrified you're about to be sleeping in a doorway. Mum doesn't earn any money from being an artist – her real job – so she decorates other people's houses, but what she gets for that wasn't enough to cover the extra rent that our horrible landlord wanted.

Some of the big houses on our road have people living in them, all super-rich like Mr Kowalczyk, who is in charge of an enormous company that makes practically everything you can imagine. Quite a lot are in the process of being done up, with scaffolding and builders and skips outside. People who can afford these houses always want to change everything before they move in – although, as far as I can see, some of them never move in at all. Other houses are permanently empty because the owners are foreign – royal families and government ministers and people like that – and they live abroad and never visit. Their houses have warning signs all over the gates, and high fences with pictures of Alsatians' heads and words like 'SECURITY PATROL' and 'CCTV IN OPERATION'.

Our big house – or rather, Mr Zhang's big house – is basically falling down because it's an investment, not a home. No-one's lived in it for twenty-seven years, which is eleven years longer than I've been alive, and there's no furniture, just collapsed ceilings, rotting carpets, ferns growing up the main staircase, and pigeon skeletons.

In spite of all that, it's still making money for Mr Zhang because the land is worth more every year. Which is sort of amazing, and – if you ask me – totally stupid.

We've never seen Mr Zhang, who lives in China, or the Russian guy who owns the boarded-up mansion next door. That house is much better kept, though, and the owner has had a ton of stuff delivered in the last few weeks because – according to Eddie, the caretaker – he's stockpiling food in all his homes in case there's a world shortage. Our little fenced-off square of garden is tidy because Prune looks after it, and usually really pretty, with flowers, fruit bushes and a vegetable patch. A gardening firm does the lawn at the front of the big house and puts weedkiller on the drive, but the outside space at the back – a whole two-and-a-half acres – is messy, with a shaggy lawn, tangled undergrowth round a pond that you can barely even see, and a totally overgrown tennis court. Right now, it all looks like a grey blur and, because there are hardly any cars on the road, it's eerily quiet.

I walk across the terrace at the back of the house, past the indoor swimming pool. It must have been lovely once, with all the mosaic tiles, marble columns and gorgeous blue water. Now it's empty except for an old mattress and the leaves that blow in through the broken windows. There's smashed glass in there, as well – some of it from the window panes and some from Rusty's empty bottles. He throws bottles into the undergrowth, too. I've found loads, but I've never said anything to Prune because what's the point of another row? Also, I like Rusty. He's got a lovely rumbly voice, like if a bear could talk, and he's a kind person, even when he's pissed.

I suppose he must realise that the bottles will be found someday, even if it isn't until they bulldoze the place, but he's like an ostrich – if ostriches stuck their heads in the next glass instead of in the sand.

Thinking about it, ostriches will look pretty much the same without colour, because they're mostly black and white and grey. Pandas will look the same, too, and zebras. And elephants. Which is better than nothing, I suppose. What happens if everybody gets achromatopsia and we never go back to normal? Even if it's all written down – that flamingos are pink, and parrots are red and blue and green and all the rest of it – will we forget what those colours actually look like?

There's a shed on the other side of the big house where Mum keeps paint tins and stuff for her decorating jobs. I go inside and spread the paint charts out on the floor: lots of little oblongs, from white to grey to black, with the different names underneath. Blue Mist, India Yellow, Cinder Rose, Sumptuous Plum . . . Right now, they're just meaningless words.

People won't want colours they can't see, so if everyone does get achromatopsia there'll be no point in decorating, which means that Mum will hardly get any work. The people who make the paint won't have much to do, either, and the people who name the paint colours won't have any work at all.

There must be loads of jobs that involve colour.

I tell myself that the government will sort it out. After all, they're the ones in charge.

Five

'Our policy is to fight this with everything we've got, and we're working hard to improve the situation.' The prime minister looks like a scarecrow with too much stuffing, as usual. He's standing behind a podium, looking uncomfortable and shuffling his notes, with the senior medical officer, who is staring down at his shoes, next to him.

'Brush your hair, you clueless pillock.' Not that Rusty should talk about anyone's appearance when he's got sauce from his sweet and sour pork all down the front of his t-shirt. We're all in the sitting room watching the press conference on television, like people did in the olden days – and even more so because I can only see it in black and white.

'How are they "working hard"?' asks Mum. 'They keep saying that, but they never tell us what they're actually doing.'

'Covering their arses.' Rusty pours himself another Scotch.

'Shut up, he's starting again.' Prune puts her arm round my shoulder and gives it a squeeze.

'There has been some disruption to your daily lives, and there will, inevitably, be more in the weeks to come, but we ask you to be patient and not to drive unless there is a genuine emergency. There are, I'm afraid, no easy options, but we are all in this together. We shall face this challenge standing shoulder to shoulder, and we shall prevail.'

Mum sighs. 'So basically, they've got no idea what they're doing but they're asking us to trust them. Well, cheers to that.' She raises her wine glass.

'I wouldn't trust *him* to take my dog for a walk.' Rusty switches off the television, eyes narrowed as if he's using a crossbow, not a remote.

'Good job you haven't got one, then.' I look down at my phone and see a message from Holl, who said she was going to watch the announcement with Jake: wtf?

smh

Everyone does a lot of head-shaking in the next few days, as the government fails to sort things out in any way. The main media story of the week is that the home secretary was caught driving his car back from a weekend at his Yorkshire cottage (those emergency holidays will get you every time) with his girlfriend (who happens to be somebody else's wife). Meanwhile, more people get achromatopsia every day, and there are more accidents, but no one seems to know why it's happening or how to stop it.

When Prune woke up yesterday morning, she'd lost her colour vision. She said she wasn't going to bother trying to get a doctor's appointment, because all the surgeries are rammed and there's nothing they can do anyway. She spent most of the day in her room, staring at the wall. I got her to come down to the kitchen this morning, and we put the fan on because they've just recorded Britain's hottest ever temperature. We're drinking lemonade straight out of the cans because that way you can't see the grey colour, so it tastes OK. Rusty's next door, watching *True Grit* for about the hundredth time, and Mum's out painting somebody's bathroom.

'Surely there have to be emergency plans?'

Prune shakes her head. 'Emergency plans are for terrorism and floods and contagious diseases, not this.'

'Doesn't this count as a contagious disease?' I ask. 'With everybody getting it.'

'Yes, but we're not giving it to each other.'

'You don't know that.'

'Nobody knows, do they? It sounds as if it's more to do with living near the water. They said on the news that it's happening in other countries, too. They were calling it the "Monochrome Effect".'

'There must be something they can do. Medication or special glasses, or . . . I don't know. *Something.*'

'You'd think so, but . . . ' Prune tails off, looking hopeless, and I know exactly how she's feeling. 'I don't think I'll ever get used to it.'

She looks up as the sounds of gunshots and galloping hooves from the sitting room are drowned by a series of thumps.

'Oh, for God's sake. What's he doing in there?'

'Sounds like he's hitting the television.' I imagine Rusty

pounding the top with his fist – the TV is a massive box because he bought it before flat screens were a thing and we can't afford an upgrade – and I've just got up to have a look when everything goes quiet and he appears in the doorway. He looks bewildered, like some big animal that's just been bashed over the head.

When Prune asks him what's up, he blinks like he's seeing her for the first time. 'One minute I'm watching John Wayne shoot the bad guys in colour, and the next . . . ' He stares round the kitchen like he still can't believe it and shakes his head. 'The world's gone to shit. I'm sorry, Prune, but I need a drink.'

I can practically hear Prune say, 'You *always* need a drink,' but she doesn't. Instead, she drags her chair over to the tall cupboard where the boiler is and stands on the seat. I didn't know she knew about the Scotch Rusty keeps up there, and, judging by his face, neither did he. He's watching her like he's worried she's going to pour the stuff over his head, but she just puts the bottle down on the table. 'What the hell. I'll have some, too.'

She goes to the cupboard, gets out three glasses and sloshes whisky into each of them. Unless two of them are for Rusty, this is a whole new level of weird. I've never seen Prune drink whisky before, either, but she is now, and she's pushing a glass in my direction.

'I don't want it.'

'Suit yourself.' Rusty puts out a big paw and claims my glass.

'I'll have that.' A voice from outside makes us all jump. Mum is leaning over the half door, wearing her work overalls.

I glance at the clock on the wall – 11.30 a.m. I'm about to ask if she's already finished the job when I see the expression on her face, and I know, without having to ask, that it's happened to her, too

The three of them sit round the table, staring into space like in one of those cartoons where someone gets whacked in the face and they just stand there with a ring of stars spinning round their head.

I decide to leave them to it. I can see that, while Rusty's being sort of normal – for him, I mean – Mum and Prune are thinking that they don't know what else to do. And that's the worst thing about it, really. When shit like this happens, you need somebody to be in control of things, and, right now, no one is. Not adults, or the government, or anybody.

I sit on the stairs. In the passage, all our coats and jackets, hung up on hooks, are like grey, dead animals. No one's talking in the kitchen, but I can hear someone pouring out more Scotch.

I think that perhaps nobody's ever really been in control of anything, and I just never realised.

I close my eyes.

Six

'D'you know what Freddie said?'

Freddie is Jake and Holly's five-year-old stepbrother. I'm sitting on a bench on Hampstead Heath with Jake. It's quite near where I live, and the two of us come here a lot. It's at the top of a slope and you can see right across London; it used to be a great view, but now it's just a lot of colourless oblongs sticking up into a grey sky. OK, so places like office blocks and government buildings and things are usually grey – to look *serious* – but, on a sunny day, with their windows gleaming, they made a really good contrast with the blue.

All around us, the trees look black and poisonous. It's still boiling hot, but the sun seems like this big lead ball of evil instead of something we need in order to be alive at all. We're both plastered in sunscreen, though, because one thing everyone's learnt in the last six weeks is that if you can't see that your skin's turning red you can get really bad sunburn and not realise till it starts hurting. Still, it's way better than when it rained – just once, for the first time in almost two months – which was so gloomy that it was practically unbearable.

Another thing we've learnt is that gradually, everyone in the world has lost their colour vision. It happened to Jake, Holl and the rest of their family, one after the other, when they came back from Portugal a week ago. The media still talks about achromatopsia and the Monochrome Effect, but everyone else has started calling it 'greyout'. First it happened in places near the sea, then in places near big rivers, and then it was everywhere. So far as we know, there's not a single person left in the whole world who can see colours – and nobody knows why.

This is the first time I've seen Jake on his own since he got back. Usually, we never run out of things to say, but when we sat down, the silence was so big and dense that it seemed like a huge block of stone plonked between us. I've already told him how I went into greyout while he and Holl were on holiday, and how I was really scared and I'd felt like I couldn't say anything. He didn't reply, but the way he looked at me was like I'd done something unforgivable. Like I should have warned him – which is totally unfair, because nobody knew the achromatopsia was going to happen to *everyone*.

Or maybe it wasn't that. Maybe he's still in shock, because he's talking slower, like he's fishing the words out of a well.

'Freddie said . . . all this was like back in black-and-white times. Like he'd worked it out, and he was really proud of himself. He was so disappointed when Dad told him that was just films.'

'That's sweet. I can see what he means, though – with history, you do think it's . . . not black and white, exactly, but sort of beige and grey because of all the castles and statues and stuff. Like maybe there was colour, but it faded away.'

'Like it will in our memories.' Jake shakes his head. 'This whole thing is just . . . ' He tails off and sits there looking hopeless, and I know exactly how he feels. You see that a lot now, people just staring into space.

I try and think what to say to make him feel better, but I just come up with a big grey nothing. I watch a dog sniffing about under the trees. It's hard to make out because of the dapple-grey undergrowth, but I think it's some sort of terrier. Dogs don't seem to notice any difference, probably because hearing and smelling are more important to them than sight – Jake and Holly's dad, who's a vet, told us that they can't see all the colours anyway. He said human beings have something called 'visual dominance', which basically means that processing stuff we see takes up way more brain-space than processing stuff we hear, taste and smell, so we tend to believe our eyes rather than our other senses. Does that mean looks really *are* everything? Not that anyone looks their best right now – just grey, and shiny from sweat.

I bet that dog is nosing after a dead bird. They were already dying, but it's worse now. They had even better colour vision than humans, because they could see ultra-violet as well as the rest. Birds that get fed by people are OK, but wild birds don't know what's safe to eat any more, and without colour they can't attract mates and breed.

I don't want to live in a world without birds. It isn't just that they're beautiful, although that's a good reason all by itself, but we need them to eat the insects and snails before they devour all the crops. The scientists don't know why insects haven't been affected, because a lot of them can see colours, too. Maybe it's because they have different sorts of eyes to us, but anyway, they're OK – at least for the moment.

I'm not going to discuss any of that stuff with Jake, though, because we'll both end up even more gloomy.

I sneak a look at my phone and realise we must have sat here for over five minutes with neither of us saying anything. I'm still trying to think of something to cheer Jake up, but it just feels like, what's the point?

'I can't even listen to music,' he says.

I lean over and touch his hand. It feels lifeless, like rubber. 'Because you're depressed.'

'It's more than that. It's connected with colours. High notes are light colours because they *are* light, like pastel-coloured balloons, and low notes are dark colours, because they're heavier.'

It's strange how we're still talking about colours in the present tense, like when somebody's died and you haven't really pro-cessed it so you talk about them like they're still here. 'I suppose. Well, a bit.'

'Definitely.'

'So,' I say, 'it's like if you write a note to someone in red pen it looks shouty, even if it just says, "Please feed the cat".'

'That's basic. But it's also more abstract, like: excitement and anger are red, calm is blue . . .'

I look at him, surprised. I get it, but the old Jake never said stuff like that. It's kind of surreal.

'Green is like . . . balance,' he says. 'Reassuring. Happiness is yellow.'

And love is pink, but I don't say this out loud.

'Purple is sort of spiritual—'

'Not if you're a Buddhist. Their holy colour is orange.'

'OK, so cultural difference. I think of orange as more like . . .' Jake screws up his face. 'Panic.'

'Why? It's a fun colour, isn't it?'

'Not in a good way, though. It's also stressful, like clowns – which are meant to be fun but are actually terrifying.'

'You've *really* thought about this.'

'That's the point – I haven't. Or I *hadn't*. I just took it for granted. Like we all did. The world's always going to be beautiful, like the sun's always going to rise. And now . . .' He slumps, gazing down at the path. 'It's gone and everything's shit.'

'Do you still dream in colour?'

'Dunno. I don't usually remember.' Jake sighs. 'It's starting to feel like a dream that we ever saw colours at all.'

I hug him, and again it's that feeling of touching something inert; human-shaped and breathing, but vacant, somehow, like everything that makes Jake *Jake* has disappeared. Then, and it's like I can feel him making this huge effort, like he thinks he ought to because it's the right thing to do – or maybe just so he doesn't have to say anything else – he manoeuvres himself round to kiss me. It's clumsy, and his lips feel stiff against mine. I'm guessing my lips feel that way to him, too, because we just hold it there, like actors pretending until the director tells them to stop.

Then Jake leans back and shakes his head with a sort of

miserable wonder. He doesn't say, 'I'm not feeling it,' but he doesn't need to. I'm not feeling it, either.

It was a greyout kiss. Any colour of kiss, even a panicky orange one, would be better than that.

Seven

I force a laugh into my throat. 'It isn't you – and it isn't me, either. It's the Monochrome Effect.'

I know that's not the whole truth – for me, anyway – but, as far as I can see, it's definitely true that the greyout is affecting pretty much everybody. There's been almost total radio silence from Holl, so I know she must be as depressed as me and Jake, and things are just as bad at home. Prune's garden has been totally trashed by slugs, so she's given up on it and seems to be spending more and more time in bed. She gets up at night, though – I hear her moving about sometimes, when I can't sleep. Rusty's drinking more than ever, and Mum's had loads of decorating jobs cancelled and she's getting more and more unhappy. She's started doing these paintings that look like violent explosions, with jaggedy black fragments going off in all directions. I think they're horrible, but I haven't told her that. Last time she started painting explosions was when I was twelve and this man she was seeing (actually he was sort of living with us) walked out on her – that was when we went to live with Prune and Rusty.

I haven't told anyone, but I'm worried about myself, too. I keep getting terrible headaches behind my eyes, with flashing white lights and zigzag lines. I think they're migraines because a girl in our class gets them and she drew pictures of what they were like, and mine are the same but without any colours. I think I'm getting one now, and I wonder if I should tell Jake. I don't, though, because then it'll be a *thing*. Also, I was one of the first people who got achromatopsia, so maybe it's moving onto the next stage or something, and it's not like they're going to be able to do anything about that, either.

Now I say, trying to convince myself as much as Jake, 'They'll find a cure. It's too important not to. After all, they've found cures for lots of other things.'

'Not cancer.' Jake and Holl's mum died when he was eight and Holl was six. I think that's one of the reasons we all get on so well, because my dad died when I was little, although not from cancer – although we've never really talked about any of that.

'Some cancers, they have.'

'But not all of them. And there's all the things that killed people for centuries, like tuberculosis.' Jake turns away from me and peers into the grey distance. 'Millions must have died before they found cures for those.'

'Have you been googling medical sites?'

'Haven't you?'

I don't answer. I have, of course, looking for anything about eyesight and headaches and blindness, but I stopped because all I was doing was scaring myself. 'We have to trust the scientists, Jake.'

'Why?'

'Because we have to trust *someone*, and there isn't anybody else.'

'I guess.'

'Look, Jake …' I'm definitely getting another headache. They always begin outside my head, like a halo, then they close in, and I want to get home before the pain really takes hold. I get to my feet, and Jake stands up, too. 'It'll be OK,' I say, and go in for a hug.

He takes his hands out of his pockets and puts his arms round me. This time it's even more uncomfortable, like some weird, meaningless ceremony we have to perform in order to go our separate ways. Then he lets go and steps away and looks at me. I just stare back, helplessly, because I really don't know what to do or say, and then it's like he just sort of gives up. He gives his head a little shake, like it's too much, and walks away.

Eight

It's a strange feeling, watching him go, as if the world's gone slack somehow, like I'd tried to beat a drum and the skin wasn't stretched properly over the top. It's not sad so much as an 'oh, well' sensation. I tell myself I ought to feel more, but I just . . . don't.

Grey emotions in a grey world.

The tightness around my head increases as I walk home. There's an old man standing outside the car park giving out religious leaflets. He's quoting from the Bible, something about how if your eye is evil then your body is full of darkness because you can't serve God and Mammon at the same time. Since the greyout, there's been loads of people saying that sort of stuff. There've been National Prayer Days as well, with big crowds in football stadiums and parks. Rusty's been going along, which surprised me because I didn't know he believed in God, but Mum pointed out that people often look for a miracle if there's no sci-entific solution on offer.

Maybe Rusty's onto something. I know what I just said to Jake, but right now I don't really feel like the scientists are going to be

41

much help. Sometimes you just say stuff because you hope it'll make you feel better.

The Bible guy looks a bit blurred, which is probably the effect of the headache. I stare at him for a moment, and suddenly it's like he's separated into two – himself, plus a fainter version standing next to him, slightly overlapping.

Double vision. That's all I need.

There aren't many people around, but someone walks into me, shouldering me aside so hard that I almost fall over. No apology – the guy just carries straight on like I'm not there, and by the time I've got my balance back he's striding off down the path. He's wearing a black suit – bit odd for a walk on the heath – and holding a phone to his ear, and I just get a glimpse of his profile as he disappears between the trees.

Even with the double vision, I know who it is: Mr Kowalczyk.

If I didn't feel so crappy I'd run after him and . . . No, I wouldn't.

I wish I would, though.

When Mum and I saw an officer helping Mr Kowalczyk into that police car, we thought they must be arresting him, although there wasn't anything about it online despite him being pretty important. Maybe it's like Rusty says, rich people almost never end up in prison.

It sounds crazy, but I have this strong, witchy feeling that he isn't on the phone at all, but talking to himself. Or God. Or . . . I don't know. The pain is closing in and I can't think any more.

I cross over into our road, where the vast mansions look not only doubled up and fuzzy, but sparkly round the edges. I've got a crackly feeling, like static inside my head, and by the time I get home all I want to do is go upstairs and lie down. Rusty seems to have gone out, and Prune's probably upstairs in bed, but I want to make sure that Mum's OK, and she isn't around, either. She might be out as well, but something tells me I ought to check round the back of the house.

The terrace is covered in corpses now – pigeons, sparrows and blue tits – and because I'm seeing everything double, it's like there's birds' bodies with their ghosts beside them. Rusty's swept some into a pile, but with the weeds everywhere, all ash-coloured, and the cracked flagstones criss-crossed with glistening slime trails from the snails and slugs, it's basically a garden apocalypse.

I'm passing the French doors from the indoor pool when I spot grey liquid seeping out from under the closed door of Mum's shed.

My first thought is that the liquid must be blood – that Mum's hurt herself – but as I get closer I can see that can't be right because it's thick and gooey. Plus, there's more of it than I thought, pooling out over the little yard at the end of the terrace.

Paint.

What's going on?

It's sticky under my trainers as I move towards the door. Everything's shifting and tilting and flashing in front of me and I'm sure I'm going to throw up, but I know Mum's in there and I need to get to her.

I open the door.

The first thing I see is paint. There's so much of it that the little room looks as if it's melting into all the different shades of grey that are splurging up the wooden walls and sliding together on the floor like thick rivers merging into a big sea. There are tins lying on their sides, lids off, and Mum is standing in the middle of it all, her dark overalls splattered, holding another tin, open, above her head. I don't think she even knows that I'm there because the next second she upends the tin and a waterfall of grey paint pours down onto the floor by my feet. Everything goes squiggly in front of my eyes, like it's dissolving. There's a pain inside my head like someone's stabbed a hot poker into the middle of my brain, and then the double vision goes away and I see – for a split second – a flash of bright, bright red.

Then it's gone.

I lurch backwards and lean over to vomit into the yard.

Nine

I *saw* colour. I *know* I did.

When I straighten up, Mum is still standing in the middle of the shed, her face a stone-coloured blank.

'Mum?' She's got a glazed expression, like a sleepwalker. 'It's Grace. What's wrong?'

She looks at me, then looks at the empty tin as if she's wondering how it got into her hand. 'I don't know . . . ' Her voice is small and pathetic.

'Why don't you come back into the house?'

'Yes.' The word comes out like a sigh. It's like she's been emptied out, too, and all that's left is this grey casing.

'Come on, then.'

She puts down the tin but she's still standing there, looking at me like she doesn't trust me. Finally she nods, like she's just asked herself a question, and starts walking towards me through the spilt paint. When she gets close I can see slow tears trickling down her cheeks, like rain on a statue's face.

'I'm sorry,' she says, and takes my hand. 'I'm so sorry.'

'It's not your fault, Mum. None of this is your fault.'

I make her a cup of tea. By the time I've done it, the pain in my head is practically unbearable, so I leave her to it and go upstairs to lie down, swaying like Rusty when he's drunk. It's a bit better when I'm flat on my bed with the curtains closed, but not much. I know I need to sleep in order to feel better – I've been trying all the painkillers we've got, but none of them make any difference – but I want to think about what I saw. I know it wasn't just a hallucination. I saw the label on the paint tin that Mum poured out in front of me. It said: *Volcanic Red*.

That's what I saw, for real. I saw red.

Ten

I spent ages googling this morning, but I couldn't find anything about people starting to see colours. Well, nothing that seemed like it might actually be true, anyway.

Mum was really upset about what happened in the shed. She came into my room at about 2 a.m. and sat on the bed, crying and saying she was sorry. She smelt like she'd been drinking Rusty's Scotch, and it took ages to persuade her to go back to her room. Then it took me ages to get back to sleep, because I had this tight feeling in my chest, scared and confused and angry, all at the same time.

I've had that feeling once before. It was when I was twelve, the time when Mum's boyfriend walked out and she started doing the weird paintings. That was the other reason we went to live with Prune and Rusty. I came back from school and found her lying on her bed, and I couldn't wake her. She hadn't wanted Prune to know she was depressed, so she'd been pretending to be OK for months. At first I'd thought it couldn't get worse than when Dad died, or what I remembered of it – her stuffing all his things into bags for

47

the charity shop and crying, then yelling at me every time I asked her something – but it did. She drifted around our flat in Dad's old bathrobe, in the room but not really there. It was worse for me, too, because Dad had already gone: that thing of thinking someone's going to leave – because if it happened once before, it could easily happen again – and you'll just be abandoned, left at the side of the road. Everyone *says* they understand this, but I'm not sure that you actually, properly, *can*, unless you lose a parent or have one walk out on you when you're young.

I sometimes wonder if maybe it was my fault because the man might have stayed if I hadn't been there. I didn't like him much, but I honestly don't think I made that big a deal of it. Mum hasn't got anyone at the moment. I'm quite relieved about that – not because I don't want her to be with somebody, but because it always ends by making her unhappy.

We've never really talked about any of this. Mum said she was sorry afterwards, but that was all. I wanted to ask her about it, but I didn't know how. And, to be honest, I've got into a habit of tiptoeing round her, so she won't get upset. I know I could have just *asked*, but I could never get the words out, and I still can't. I think it's because I've had to sort of flatten out my feelings about it, so I don't panic about the whole being abandoned thing.

Anyway.

Whatever.

It's better if I don't think about it too much.

It's also better living with Prune and Rusty, because it's someone to look after Mum, so I'm not always worrying about her when I'm out – seeing an ambulance go past and thinking, what if it's for her? Or wanting to rush home from school and dreading it at the same time.

I'm not going to tell Mum or anyone else about what I saw, though. Or not for the moment, anyway. They'd only say it was wishful thinking.

Eleven

Mum got some more pills from Dr Gupta and she hasn't done anything else crazy for the last couple of weeks. Rusty cleaned up the inside of the shed and washed all the spilt paint away with Mr Zhang's power hose, but not before a bunch of insects had drowned in it. Now there aren't so many birds to eat them, the flies are everywhere, especially the tiny ones. They film over streetlights and make everyone's windows look murky, like the sides of dirty fish tanks. There are snails everywhere, too. The earth is covered in slime trails and there are so many stuck to the window and door frames at the back of Mr Zhang's house that they look like weird knobbly decorations. And they get into our flat: we keep finding them slithering across the lino in the kitchen, trying to glue themselves to the table legs.

It's really hard to talk to anyone about Mum going mad like that, even Holly. We used to tell each other everything, but now there's this distance between us, like we're isolated in our own little grey worlds.

There's still loads of stuff on the news about 'emergency

measures' and how hard the government is working to solve the problem, but trains still aren't running and planes aren't flying. People are trying to do normal things like go to work, but they've put the dates for starting school back two weeks because of the health and safety stuff. There are notices everywhere telling you not to even think about going near a hospital unless you're practically dead, and others begging you to donate your eyeballs – when you are actually dead – for research. There must be laboratories somewhere with freezers full of them, staring up at you when you open the lid.

I've only seen Holly once since they got back from Portugal. We usually do stuff together all the time, but the greyout just makes everything so . . . meh, it's like you can't be bothered. Plus, I can't face telling her what happened on the heath with Jake. I'm meant to be meeting her there today, but she messages when I'm halfway down the road. Lotte, her stepmother, has to go out so she's got to stay at home and look after Freddie because Jake's locked himself in his room. Then she messages – greyout issues, not blaming you – so I'm guessing he's already said something.

She asks me to go over to their house but I don't think I can face Jake – if he emerges from his room, that is – and it's so hot that the air feels thick, like it's clogging up my lungs. I can feel a headache coming on, too, so I make an excuse. Holl doesn't try to persuade me, just messages ok talk soon x so I breathe a sigh of relief and head back home.

After about five minutes I'm seeing double and I feel so weird and breathless that I have to stop and lean on Mr Kowalczyk's gates to recover. They're huge, like the house is – it's one of the largest and smartest in our bit of the road. It's square and white, and the four massive pillars at the front are currently separating into eight in front of my eyes, glowing so much that it takes me a minute to realise that there's a man standing in the middle of them.

He's smart, too – suit and tie, bright white shirt, neat black hair – and for a moment I think he must be one of the staff, but as he comes down the steps and starts walking across the lawn, I recognise Mr Kowalczyk.

I'd almost forgotten about him bumping into me on the heath, but I remember it now – how I'd thought he was pretending to be on the phone but really talking to himself. I'd wondered if he'd managed to avoid going to prison, but he didn't exactly look like a man who'd got away with something then, and he doesn't look like one now, either. He's coming towards me – two of him, separating and then blurring together again. I want to move, but I can't. His face is like ashes, and when, for just a second, I see his eyes clearly, I reckon I've never seen anybody so afraid.

His mouth – the one thing in focus in the haze of his face – is moving. He's looking straight at me, but his voice is too hoarse and whispery to make out what he's saying. Seems like he's talking to himself; the same two phrases, over and over. I try to lip-read, but one of them looks as if it's 'Re Noo', which makes no sense, and I can't get the other one at all.

'Are you OK?' All right, it's a stupid question, because he obviously isn't, but it's all I can think of to say.

When he gets near enough for me to hear, I realise what he's saying is, 'Too late.'

'I'm sure it's not too late,' I say, like I've got any idea what it's too late for – although, judging by the look on his face, it's something major. 'Lots of things look worse than they are,' I gabble, 'especially right now. I mean, I don't know exactly how you're feeling, but . . .' I can hear how lame I sound, but I just feel I've got to get him to engage with me and not do – well, I don't know what, exactly, but I have this really strong sense that it's going to be catastrophic. 'Please talk to me. Maybe I can fetch someone to help.'

He stops – he's about a metre away from me now – and shakes his head. 'Too late.' Then he turns back to look at the house. He's still muttering: a jumble of words, hard to make out because I can't see his face. I think it's something about a mistake and parking a car . . . Nonsense, basically.

He turns around again, and beckons to me. He doesn't seem to know how to open the gates – they must be electronic – and I don't know, either. I'm thinking that I should definitely get away from there before he works it out when suddenly he's in front of me, reaching through the bars and grabbing my hand.

I try to pull away, but it's like I'm paralysed – a dream where you want to run but you're stuck to the spot – and he looks *so* scared. I look round, hoping someone's going to appear, but nobody does.

We're almost nose to nose, separated only by the railings, and his features are turning so blurry that it's like his head is starting to dissolve.

'What do you want?'

'I'm sorry.'

He lets go of my hand and pulls something heavy and dark – metal, but like it's melting – out of his pocket. Then a round, black hole comes into sharp focus.

'Goodbye.'

Before I can move, or even speak, he puts the end of the gun in his mouth and fires.

There's a bang and I think, for a stupid nanosecond, that it's me who's been shot. And then it happens again, the same as with Mum in the shed. A red flash: blood pouring from his nose, over his mouth and chin, as he crumples and falls.

I blink. Everything's back to grey again, and Mr Kowalczyk is lying on his back on the gravel with a dark pool spreading around his head.

Twelve

I remember people running across the road towards me, and Rusty enveloping me in a bear-hug to stop me looking. And I remember being suddenly sick, with shock, I guess. Not much else, though.

I think Mr Kowalczyk just wanted someone to say goodbye to, so he wouldn't die alone. That's what I told the police when they came to talk to me about it. I didn't know what else to say, apart from telling them that he said he'd said something about a mistake and parking a car, and that it was too late and he was sorry. I told them about him bumping into me on the heath, too – without the possibly pretend phone call, because that was just my intuition and would have sounded mad – but they didn't make a note of it.

I keep having nightmares about the gun and the blood – red in my dreams – and Mr Kowalczyk's mouth moving, like it's in close-up. I'm desperate to hear what he's saying, but I can't. I know that one of the things he said was 'Too late', because I heard it properly, but I still can't work out what the other thing was. I've even tried standing in front of the mirror in the bathroom, making the same shape with my mouth as he did, but it always comes out as Ree

Noo – and the closest word to that is 'renew', which makes no sense at all.

Mum said Mr Kowalczyk was Polish, so maybe he had an accent – or he was actually speaking *in* Polish, in which case it's hopeless. I tried putting Ree Noo into Google Translate with different spellings and got rhenium, which turns out to be this rare metal that's used for making jet engines and treating liver cancer. Rhenium in Polish is 'ren' so I suppose he might have been saying that, although his mouth did seem to go into the shape for 'oo' afterwards ... Only now I'm wondering if I actually did see that, because he was still fairly far away from me. I'm glad I talked to the police straight afterwards, because the sequence of what happened is beginning to get a bit blurry in my head. The effect of shock, I expect.

Anyway, 'rhenium' doesn't make a lot of sense – unless he was really ill, and that's why he ...? Or perhaps he was saying 'renew', like reincarnation?

For a moment, I wonder if I should tell Jake. He's really into anything that's a puzzle, but he hasn't reached out since our greyout kiss on the heath. If I'm honest, I haven't wanted to contact him, either. I just have no idea how to talk about this to *anyone* and certainly not him, with what feels like a greyout *wall* between the two of us.

I can't seem to settle down to anything, so I wander down the road and watch the security company putting up boards all round Mr Kowalczyk's garden so you can't see inside. That's not unusual in this road, but if Mr K had any family, we've never seen them.

Now, it's just a bunch of removal vans taking everything away – that sense of someone's life being dismantled, so there's nothing left. We thought his death would be on the news, but it wasn't. I couldn't even find anything about it online. I guess everyone's got bigger things to think about than just one person committing suicide, because that happens a lot these days, but it seems a bit weird, given how important he was.

The vans have the words 'FOR A STRESS-FREE MOVE' written on the back. Not very stress-free for poor Mr Kowalczyk – although I guess he's past caring. I wonder where they're taking all the stuff. I almost take a photo to send to Jake or Holly, really just so I can reach out to somebody, but then I realise again how it would mean trying to explain all the things I can't put into words.

Also – now I think about it – why the rush to get rid of all this stuff when no one's supposed to be driving if they can avoid it? It's not like it's an emergency. Guess it's another case of 'one law for the rich', like the home secretary and his trip to Yorkshire.

All over the world, governments are putting money into "research" programmes. Some companies have given money, too, but right now the research is basically just a bunch of scientists arguing with each other about what's caused the greyout and what to do about it. You see this diagram of a cut-in-half human brain everywhere: it looks like a mutant cauliflower, and there's a shaded bit at the back to show where the visual cortex is, and the special bit of it that controls colour perception. If you go online there are millions of websites with theories about what's happened, and people claiming to be able to send you a cure if you give them money.

The greyout has been blamed on pretty much everyone and everything. I've seen stuff on the internet about Islamic fundamentalists, Western decadence, immigrants, genetically modified food, chemical warfare experiments, radio waves and extraterrestrials. And while everyone's arguing about that, we've got even less money than usual, because food prices have almost doubled in the last six weeks. Mum came back from the supermarket in tears yesterday. When we found out that the Monochrome Effect was everywhere, I thought that it may be shit but at least it's fair shit because it's happening to everyone. Except it turns out it isn't fair at all, because people who can't afford food and basic necessities have it way worse – and I think rich people forget that.

Politicians keep talking about price caps and rationing, but the big food companies don't want it and anyway it would be impossible to regulate the internet, so it would be a zillion times more complicated than in the Second World War or whenever. There've been loads of protests – marches and rallies – and everyone's saying there will be massive riots if somebody doesn't do something.

Which is all very well, but there doesn't seem to be anything anyone *can* do, and it feels like all the governments have given up even trying. The food prices have rocketed because insects have eaten all the crops. Online, there's footage of air that's thick with grasshoppers and locusts and you can even hear the wings beating as clouds of them descend on the fields like hungry snowstorms.

All the governments have relaxed their rules about pesticides, and farmers are spending fortunes on them, but it's not working very well and everyone says it's going to get way worse. And that's assuming we don't all wind up growing second heads because of the massive amounts of chemicals in our crazy expensive meals.

It's just as well that no one's eating much – because it's not just me who finds it hard to eat food that's the wrong colour. More restaurants close every day and loads of people have lost their jobs. Home is no better: we tried wearing blindfolds for meals, but we kept knocking things over, so stuff got wasted.

You'd think people would start buying smaller size clothes, because of everyone losing weight, but lots of them aren't bothering. They just walk around with things hanging off them, like super-baggy is this new fashion, or cinching them in with huge belts. There is some new stuff in the shops – stripes and checks and polka dots – but it's like no one's heart is really in it. Monochrome is fine if it's a choice, but not when it's all you've got.

I've decided to wait a bit before I tell Mum about the red flashes, to see if it happens again. It's partly because I *really* don't want to worry her, and partly because of the Rule of Three: stuff being more significant if it happens three times, because then it forms a pattern. Like, if you're telling somebody a story, three is always better than two, which is why there are Three Bears and Three Musketeers and Three Little Pigs, and why you have things happening three times in a joke. The other reason – if I'm completely honest – is that I'm scared. It's worse at night. I'm frightened to go to sleep in case I have another nightmare about Mr Kowalczyk, because those are just . . .

I don't even want to think about it. I try not to, and I try to rationalise seeing a colour – tell myself it might be a good thing, even – but I just end up going round in circles.

Thirteen

'Do you think it will ever go back to normal?' It's 3 a.m. and Mum's sitting on the side of my bed because I screamed – the nightmare again – and woke her.

I know it's a silly question, but I desperately want to hear somebody say that the greyout isn't going to last forever.

'I don't know, love.' She reaches over and ruffles my hair. I hate it when she does this. It's a thing people always seem to do to kids with curly hair – more when I was little, but it still happens from time to time. I find it really annoying and Mum knows that, but I suppose she forgot.

'Hey!'

'Sorry. I suppose … Well, there'll either be a cure or we'll all just have to get used to it, won't we?'

'You don't seem to be getting used to it.' I didn't mean to say this – or not so sharply, anyway – but I was still recovering from the nightmare and I was cross about the hair thing. I mean, I've told her enough times.

'I'm trying, but . . . ' Mum shakes her head. 'I feel as if the world's died, Grace. As if I'm not properly alive any more.'

'But you won't . . . ' I can't bring myself to say it. 'You won't . . . '

'Won't . . . ?'

'You know, like before we came to live here.'

'No, love.' She looks crestfallen, then gives me a wonky smile.

'Do you promise?'

'I promise.'

I want to believe it, but I don't know if I actually do, because it's not like she can really control it – those paintings, and how she looked in the shed, blank and scary.

I don't know what to say, so I just nod. She shakes her head again, but this time it's more like she's frustrated with herself. 'I was so angry with your dad.'

I don't know what I'd expected her to say, but it wasn't that. *'Angry?'*

'Furious. For abandoning us. He never looked after himself. He'd been complaining he felt ill, tired, but he wouldn't go to the doctor.' She closes her eyes tight for a moment, and I can't tell if she's trying to summon up strength or trying not to cry or both. 'We'd been going through a bad patch – not getting on – and I accused him of making a fuss about nothing, using it as an excuse to get out of doing something or other. I can't even remember what, now. So stupid . . . I carried on being angry for a long time after he died, about how irresponsible he'd been.'

'But he didn't know he was ill, Mum – and healthy people don't expect to die in their thirties.'

'I know, love. But I didn't see it like that at the time. And it was easier to be angry with him, because then I could push away the guilt that I hadn't got on his case and marched him round to the doctor—'

'You didn't know, either.'

'I kept thinking of what I could have done differently. But then – after a few years, I suppose – it wasn't anger or guilt, it was more like being sucked into an abyss. Perhaps because I hadn't grieved properly, or . . . I don't know. It was . . . ' She shakes her head again, as if the memory is too overwhelming to even think about. 'Well, you know. You were there. And in the shed, when I lost it, it was because I suddenly got angry with him all over again: it's all right for him, he doesn't have to live through this.' She reaches out to ruffle my hair again, then stops herself. 'Were you dreaming about me?'

'Mr Kowalczyk.' I know the dreams are about her, too, even though she's not actually in them, but I don't want to say that. How I'm feeling is too confusing, and I don't want to wind up being angry with her because there's no point and it's not going to bring Dad back.

'Grace . . . ' Perhaps she can sense some of what's going on in my head, because she stops, like she's had second thoughts, and says, 'Poor man.'

'I was wondering where his family are. I thought people would come to the house – you know, for the funeral.'

'I suppose they're in Poland and couldn't travel because of all the restrictions.'

'I suppose. I used to dream about you.' I can't resist saying it, even though I just told myself I wouldn't. 'You wouldn't open your eyes. You'd be lying there, and I'd keep shaking you, but you never woke up.'

'Oh, Grace.' Her face breaks up like she's going to cry, but she doesn't, or not quite. 'I'm sorry. I never want to hurt you. I love you.'

Part of me wants to say, *But you already have. You said Dad abandoned us, and how it made you angry, but you were ready to abandon me.*

Instead, I say – not just because she said it, but because I know it's true in a deeper way than whatever else I'm feeling right now, and I need to hang on to that – 'I love you, too.'

'I honestly thought you'd be better off without me.'

'Well, I wouldn't.'

'I know that now.'

I want to believe her so much.

Fourteen

Now that the speed limits have been lowered and there are soldiers everywhere on what Rusty calls 'point duty', which basically means being a traffic light in human form, people can use public transport again and the schools have reopened. Ours looks a whole lot worse with no colours. Not that it looked great before – I mean, it's not a really *terrible* school, but it always needs loads of repairs that never get done. Last term, a chunk of ceiling actually fell down during a lesson, and nearly hit someone.

It's much quieter than before, too, with nobody really messing about or running down the corridors. It's funny how noise and colour sort of go together. Another thing I noticed, when I went into the primary school with Holl to collect Freddie, was the wall where Ms Larwood puts up all the little kids' drawings. There's usually loads of stuff up there, mums and dads and pets with trees and flowers, but now it's only a few pictures of houses and cars, and nothing that's alive. We looked for Freddie's picture, but it wasn't there. Drawing and colouring are his best things, and usually he can't wait to show you what he's done, but when Holl asked him about his picture he just looked sad and said he'd thrown it away. I fished it out of the bin when he and Holl went to get his stuff, and it was this big angry scribble of black crayon, like a five-year-old's version of Mum's explosions. It looked like he'd started trying to draw a person but then he couldn't see the point any more.

Danny Mayhew, who's in our class, was in a car crash. He's still in hospital, and his dad was killed. Jodie Hanley's mum's dead, too – she got run over. Mr Grice, who is one of those teachers you can't imagine having any kind of life outside school, got run over as well (a different car), but he's OK now. Everyone's got stories, but I'm keeping quiet because they'd probably think I was making it up or showing off. I haven't seen Jake at all – which surprises me a bit, although I'm kind of relieved. I guess he's got his own shit to deal with, like everyone, and that's fine. Then again, Holl hasn't mentioned him, and I haven't asked.

Right now, it's a special assembly. There was an announcement this morning that there will be a statement from the minister for the environment at 2 p.m., so we've all been told to go to the gym. There has been a press conference every day for ages – the prime minister with the chief medical officer or whoever – but this one is obviously a really big deal. My guess is that they're doing it because it's some hugely bad news and they don't want people to panic. I reckon everyone's thinking the same because people are usually rowdy in assembly – there's giggling and catcalls, or someone farts – but the minute Mr Metcalf asks for quiet, everyone pays attention. Mr M looks clammy-pale and wide-eyed, sort of like he's been chained to a radiator in a basement for years and only just let out. He says all the usual stuff about how we aren't to worry – yeah, right – and that the Ministry for the Environment has produced a short film, which we're going to watch.

'*Every single minute, a lorry-load of plastic goes into the ocean, causing pollution and harming marine life. Most plastics eventually break up into very small particles called microplastics . . .* ' A man with a deep, serious voice is talking over a film of seas and rivers that look like lumpy grey soup, beaches covered in rubbish, turtles caught up in nylon nets and the cut-open corpses of sea birds and whales with their stomachs full of plastic bags and bottle tops and other stuff that people have thrown away. After about a minute, Holl and I are looking at each other like, why are we watching this? It's terrible, but it's not like we haven't seen it before – and anyway, what can you expect when you make something designed to be used once, for about five minutes, out of something that lasts forever? How totally stupid is that?

'*It is now known that these microplastics are able to absorb microorganisms, including pollutants and pathogens – which are harmful substances such as bacteria, that may cause disease. Although this phenomenon was first observed in the marine environment, which appears to be most affected, we now know that this contamination has occurred in the water supply, the soil, and the air. Microplastics, with their attendant pathogens, have also been detected in human blood, and scientists are now sure that it is this contamination that has – by degrees – led to the universal Monochrome Effect.*'

The guy stops talking for a minute, and there's complete silence before someone at the back blurts out, 'Oh shit,' really loud, because this is worse than bad. Lots of people start muttering to their friends. Sonali Shastri starts to cry and Ethan Gedge says, 'So we're basically screwed.'

Ethan's right, because what this means is that we're surrounded by invisible damage. We must have got to a tipping point – the trillionth plastic bottle cap that was slung into the ocean, or whatever – and the greyout happened more quickly in places near seas and rivers, because that's where the Monochrome Effect was strongest. That's not only a million times scarier than alien death rays or evil wizards or anything else you can imagine, but also it means that we've only got ourselves to blame. There've been warnings about the harm that plastic can do for ages, but nobody did anything about it because the people who make the stuff are way too powerful. It's in way too many things, so now it's not only killing the poor sea creatures, but it's starting to destroy us as well. Looking round, I can see a few people holding their heads like they can actually feel this happening. The Fainal twins, whose parents are really religious, look as if they're praying.

The reason for the contamination, according to the voiceover, is that all the teeny-tiny bits of plastic poison are now so small that they can get across something called the blood-brain barrier. That sounds like a checkpoint with microscopic armed guards but it's actually a load of cells that stop bad stuff getting into places like your visual cortex and messing them up. The guy is trying to be reassuring, saying that, as far as they know, the only effect on humans is achromatopsia, and microplastics haven't been linked to other health issues. He's trying to make it sound like the fact that microplastics carrying bacteria or some other crap that is basically *eating our brains* is no big deal, but he's not fooling anybody.

'Haven't been linked to other health issues *yet*,' Holly mutters into my ear. 'What if we start going blind?'

'Or deaf?' says Lauren Wolf, who's on my other side.

'And the official policy' – Holl's voice is a bit louder now – 'sounds like it's "keep your fingers crossed".'

I grab their hands and squeeze, to comfort myself as much as them, because this is just . . . just . . .

Actually, there isn't a word for it.

The government will continue to invest heavily in research, and has already approved a bill that will ban the sale of single-use plastics, which will take effect immediately . . .

I'm trying to pay attention, because obviously it's important, but I'm starting to feel another headache coming on, really fast. It takes about three minutes for the screen to go fuzzy round the edges, and for the sizzly-frizzly thing to start inside my head, and a minute after that I start seeing two Mr Metcalfs and two screens.

As much as I want to see the flashes of red again – Rule of Three – I also don't want to lose my lunch in front of the entire school. I'm thinking I'd better excuse myself when the camera pans across a grey beach with basking seals that are hardly distinguishable from the rubbish, and, in an instant, a red plastic petrol can sort of bursts out of the screen.

I must have made a noise because suddenly everyone is looking at me. When I look at them, Holly's t-shirt and Lauren's hoodie and

Jamal Khan's trainers start pulsing and flashing, vivid blocks of red with light all around them. It's like someone's turned the volume up in my head to totally deafening, only it's sight, not sound. It's too much and I look away, towards the window, but three of the cars parked outside are huge lumps of vibrating scarlet, and I feel like it's actually *hitting* my brain. Then I know I'm definitely going to be sick. I can't even say anything – I just clap my hand over my mouth and charge out of the hall and down the corridor to the girls' loo.

I make it just in time.

Fifteen

'Grace?'

It's Holly. Ms Kovacs must have sent her to see if I'm OK. I'm kneeling on the floor in the cubicle, slumped against the partition with a banging headache, feeling like I might pass out any minute.

'Are you all right?'

'Not really.'

'Can I come in?'

Even inching over to slide the bolt open is a massive effort, and I flop back onto the floor feeling like I've just climbed a mountain.

Holly's eyes go wide when she sees me. 'You look terrible.'

'Thanks.'

'Well, you do. You're all sweaty and shaky. Ms Kovacs said to take you to the nurse.'

After about ten minutes I feel like I can move, and Holly helps me up and out of the block and across the courtyard. The fresh air improves things a bit, and everything's back to grey again, including stuff that I know used to be red, like the climbing bars in the little kids' playground.

'What happened?' Holly asks.

'I suddenly got this terrible headache.' I stop, not knowing whether to tell her.

'And?'

'I don't know. Everything went weird and flashy and I knew I was going to be sick.'

'Sounds like what Orla gets.'

Orla's the girl who did the migraine pictures. 'Maybe.'

'Jake was right.' Holly narrows her eyes at me. 'You've had this before.'

'What?'

'When you two were on the heath. He said you looked like you were in pain and he thought it was him, like . . . ' Holl looks uncomfortable. 'You couldn't stand him kissing you.'

'No . . . ' I stare at her, appalled. 'I mean, I have had it before, and I did get one then, but it wasn't anything to do with him. It's just random.'

'Why didn't you tell me?'

'I thought you'd start on about going blind. It was bad enough early on, when the doctor said I might have a brain tumour, and I just couldn't . . . you know . . . '

'Oh, Grace.'

She's looking at me, really sympathetic, so I decide to go for it. 'And I've started seeing flashes of red. Not like a migraine, but real. Just now, the bits in that film that were supposed to be red *were* red – and your t-shirt was, and some other people's clothes, and some of the cars outside.'

Holly looks down at her t-shirt. 'I think this one *was* red, but . . .' She frowns. 'I don't see how that's possible. You're probably imagining it because you want to see it.'

She's trying to hide it, but her eyes are disappointed, like she'd thought better of me. I have a vision of her telling Jake that I've turned into this weird fantasist attention-seeker.

It's pointless to argue, so I shut up and let her take me along to the nurse.

Ms Hendry says pretty much the same as Holly, only she seems to think it's stress-related. She asks me about my diet and if I'm sleeping OK and starts talking about how it's a difficult time, like I don't know that. She keeps repeating stuff in this really deliberate way, like she's trying to calm a horse or something. When I say that painkillers don't help, she says to lie down and she'll phone Mum to fetch me.

I must have fallen asleep, because when I wake up I can hear Mum's voice outside the door. The nurse is saying something about how she should get me a doctor's appointment, and asking if everything is all right at home. Mum tells her everything's fine. This isn't strictly true, because she's drinking quite a lot of Rusty's whisky nowadays – on top of Dr Gupta's pills – and Prune's practically turned into an owl. I can see why Mum wouldn't say any of that, though. Also, it's not as if my family are the only ones being weird. Holly says that her stepmother, Lotte, keeps the blinds drawn all the time and doesn't want them to turn the lights on, and Chloe McAndrew told us that her dad went batshit crazy and smashed up their kitchen because he thought it was the end of the world. Plus, it was on the news this morning that a man rushed into the National Gallery and started slashing the paintings with a knife. Weirdness all round, in fact.

Mum's borrowed Rusty's van. She doesn't say much on the way home, which is a relief, because I just want to sit there with my eyes closed and not have to listen to any more about how I'm imagining things. When we get home, I go straight upstairs to bed.

It's nearly dark when I wake up, but my headache has gone. Mum's in the sitting room with Rusty, watching an old film. There are a lot more black-and-white films – actual black and white, I mean – on TV now. They're easier to watch than ones that are meant to be in colour because the lighting and make-up and costumes were specially designed for black and white, so everything shows up better. Rusty watches loads. I didn't like them at first, but now I'm really into them, especially the American detective ones. Lots of people like those. There's this thing now of doing noir selfies with vintage stuff like fedora hats and trench coats, and a whole Goth explosion as well, because of all the old-school horror films. Some days, it seems like everyone in the world is wearing black eyeliner.

I put my head round the door and ask if they'd like a cup of tea. Mum comes out to join me in the kitchen. 'How are you feeling?' She looks sad and wary, like something terrible has happened to me and it's her fault. She still hasn't mentioned the thing at school, which makes me sure she thinks I'm fantasising.

'I'm OK, really. It's no big deal.'

'I've made an appointment for you to see Dr Gupta tomorrow evening. They had a cancellation.'

'You're kidding.' That's amazing. The doctors' surgeries are still rammed – apart from all the accidents, loads of people need antidepressants – and you have to wait weeks. Seeing Dr Gupta will be a waste of time, though, because it's not like he's going to believe me. After all, no one else has. But there's no point in saying that, so I just thank her and hand over a grey mug of lead-coloured tea.

Sixteen

'Look up. And try not to blink.'

The person putting drops in my eyes isn't Dr Gupta, but a man called Dr Brown. I don't think he's one of the regular doctors. He looks younger and smarter, with a suit and tie, and he seems properly interested, like he *does* believe me. He got me to describe everything that's happened and asked lots of questions. After that, he took me and Mum down the corridor to another room that's been set up with a load of optician stuff and did all the same tests I had at the hospital.

'It's atropine – bit old-fashioned, but we've run out of the other stuff. Comes from deadly nightshade.'

'Isn't that poisonous?'

'Not in such small doses. It's to make your pupils bigger so we can see what's going on when I do the electroretinogram, but it's going to make everything a bit hazy.'

I'm staring at Dr Brown's Kerr + Bell calendar – they obviously make medical stuff – and after a minute or so the little symbol of the bell with the cross inside starts to get seriously blurred.

'Now the anaesthetic.' More drops, and then, 'I'm afraid the next part's not very pleasant, but try to keep still.'

It's practically impossible not to cringe as he fixes my eyelids open with metal tongs, which I really, *really* don't like. I try to think about something else instead because he seems to be taking ages sorting out whatever he's going to do next. I want to think about something nice, but I can only come up with horrible stuff, like when our cat Parsley got hit by a motorbike and Holly's dad had to put him to sleep.

Now he's saying something about electrodes. He pulls up my t-shirt a bit and puts something cold on my ribs, then bends over me and puts something else in my eyes. It doesn't hurt, but it feels really strange. I want to blink, but I can't, because of the tongs.

He wheels this big white globe in front of me. There's a hole in it, with a place to rest your chin while you look inside, which I do. Nothing happens for a few seconds, then lights start flashing all over the place. I look at those for a bit, then he takes the globe away and puts a laptop in front of me. The screen has a chequered pattern, like a chessboard with too many squares. At first, nothing happens, and then the pattern reverses – so the black squares are white and the white ones are black – and we go back and forth like that for a bit.

Dr Brown doesn't say anything about whether the results are good or not. He just takes the things off my eyes and asks me to lie on the couch, which is a relief. Then he turns the lights down really low, explains that I have to stay there for twenty minutes before the next bit of the test, and leaves the room.

While Mum goes off to find the loo, I have another go at a nice memory, but now all I can think about is Parsley. He was big and orange and furry and lovely, and the motorbike broke his back and didn't even stop. After about five minutes I can feel tears coming. I haven't got a hanky and I don't think I'm meant to get up, plus I'm worried Dr Brown'll notice if I've cried all the drops out of my eyes.

It's funny he's called Dr Brown. I mean, being named after a thing that isn't a thing any more. People are called Brown, Green, Black, White and Grey, and there's a girl at my school called Emma Pink – although I think that's quite unusual. I've never heard of anyone whose surname is Red or Yellow or Purple. That's quite strange, when you think about it. Why some colours and not others? I'm wondering if it's different in other countries, hoping that will get me off the subject of what happened to Parsley. Rusty says he's going to murder the person who was riding that motorbike if he finds them, but I don't suppose he ever will – and even if he did, he'd probably just shout a lot.

When Dr Brown comes back into the room he doesn't switch on the main light again. Instead, he brings a really bright lamp and shines it in my eyes like when they interrogate captured soldiers in old war films. But he doesn't ask any questions, just does the whole thing with the tongs and the electrodes again and repeats the tests. Then he tells me not to rub my eyes and tells Mum to come with him so they can talk to Dr Gupta. I sit there hoping he isn't telling them that I've been making it up to get attention.

*

After what feels like an hour, all three of them come in, looking very blurry because of the atropine. Dr Gupta clears his throat, like he's about to make an important announcement. 'There's nothing for you to worry about, Grace. Dr Brown tells me that your results are interesting, and we think you ought to have a few more tests.'

I look at Mum, to see if there really *is* nothing for me to worry about, or if he's just saying that. It's a waste of time because I can't make out her expression. 'What sort of tests?'

'A brain scan, first. We'll see if they can fit you in this afternoon.'

My stomach's churning, like I'm about to be sick. 'What's going on?'

'That's what we need to find out,' says Dr Brown.

'You think I'm going blind.'

'Good heavens, no.' Dr Brown says this quickly, in a jolly voice like he's telling me not to be stupid, but in a nice way. 'We want to see if there's any activity in the area that processes colour information.'

'So you *do* believe I saw colours?'

There's a moment's total silence before Dr Gupta clears his throat. 'Actually, it's not impossible. If you're happy to go ahead, I'll make a phone call.'

Dr Brown drives us to the hospital himself, which makes me think that this must be a very big deal, and – despite all his reassurances – that really scares me.

The brain scan takes longer this time. I just about manage to keep it together and not press the emergency button for them to get me out, but by the time it's finished, my head hurts so much that I can hardly see. Mum and Dr Brown are talking as we leave the hospital, but I'm too busy concentrating on not being sick to take in what they're saying. The corridor in front of me is flickering at the edges. It looks like the walls are moving, and the double vision comes back so that the nurses and wheelchairs and trollies are smearing into each other. Suddenly, there's a boy, right in the middle of the corridor like he landed from space, standing out really distinctly from everything around him. His head's shaved, and I can see blood all down the side of it, coming at me like a jagged red scream. Then I'm dizzy and falling, and then there's nothing at all until I hear Mum asking if I'm all right.

I'm on the floor, with her and Dr Brown kneeling beside me. 'Blood,' I tell them. 'On that boy's face. Bright red.'

Mum's scared, but Dr Brown looks really excited, like it's the best day of his life.

Seventeen

'There'll be some more tests.' We're back at the surgery, in Dr Gupta's room, and he's printing off a bunch of pages from his computer while Dr Brown taps away on his laptop. 'Similar to the ones you've just had, except that you'll need to go and stay somewhere for a week or two.'

'You mean a hospital?' I'm not liking the sound of this. I don't want to go in one of those tube things again, and all I really know about hospitals – from experience, I mean – is that my dad died in one. I remember having to wait in a little room with Mum – orange carpet with marks on it and bad paintings of flowers – and a doctor coming in to tell us that they hadn't been able to save him.

Thinking about that, I miss the next bit of what Dr Gupta says, but now he's talking about something called a 'new facility'. That sounds more like an office than anything medical, so perhaps it won't be too bad. 'So you do believe me?' I ask him again. 'About seeing the colours.'

'Well . . .' He says this in the way adults do when it's something that they can't – or don't want to – talk about, so I know he isn't going to answer the question properly. 'There is definitely some activity in your visual cortex. I'm going to give you an eyepatch to wear. You'll need to remember to swap it from one eye to the other – morning for one eye, afternoon for the other. It's to help with the double vision. That's the current thinking, anyway. We're really' – he smiles apologetically – 'feeling our way at the moment.'

Mum looks worried. 'I don't want Grace to be a lab rat.'

'The study won't be invasive, Mrs Ballard – no drug testing or surgical procedures. It's simply monitoring the progress of people like your daughter in a controlled environment, and—'

'Do you mean there are others like me, who've seen colours?' I don't mean to interrupt, but I can't help it.

'Well . . .' It's the same kind of 'well' as before. 'It's extremely rare' – Dr Gupta talks to Mum like I'm not there – 'but there have been a few other reports of these indicators in adolescents, accompanied by similar migraine-type symptoms. It's an important study, Mrs Ballard. It could lead to a real breakthrough.'

'Would she have to go at once? Only, term's started.'

Things are starting to come back into focus now, and I can see that Dr Gupta's looking at Mum like she's refusing to give food to a starving baby. 'It needs to happen as soon as possible. After all, no one wants this state of affairs to continue. Because all the subjects are of school age, educational facilities will be provided.'

I don't like the word 'subject' much – that sounds *a lot* like a lab rat. Also . . . 'How come everyone's the same age? All adolescents, you said.'

'We did wonder if we might find some cases in the younger age group,' Dr Brown tells me, 'but there haven't been any so far. We're not sure why no children have presented – it's possible that what seems to be happening to you may be something that can only happen in a teenage brain ... There's an awful lot we still don't know, of course' – he gives me an apologetic smile – 'but we think it's to do with neural plasticity – the ability of the brain to change and repair itself. Yours is still maturing, so it's more ... well, more flexible, than an adult's.'

I'm thinking this seems pretty cool when Mum says, 'Where would she have to go?'

'A place called Aveney Park,' says Dr Gupta. 'It's in Norfolk, but the transport – all the expenses, in fact – would come out of the emergency fund. And of course the subjects will be paid for participating.'

Well, that definitely sounds all right, although he doesn't say how much. I immediately have this vision of everything being back to normal and being able to afford to go to festivals and see bands, and how great that would be. I have to force myself to concentrate on what Dr Gupta's saying about how important the study is, and how it could end the greyout and help stop the ecosystem being destroyed. Dr Brown's beside him, nodding away in agreement and looking like all his Christmases have come at once. Then Dr G starts on about medical breakthroughs in the past. He talks about anaesthetic and vaccinations and penicillin, and how millions of people's lives have been saved over the years because people were willing to do stuff like this.

After about thirty seconds I'm thinking that it'll be totally shit if I don't do it. Not because of the money, but because everyone who isn't horrible knows that you ought to help people if you can. And this isn't just one person – it's the whole world, so it's mega.

I'm wondering when somebody's going to get around to asking me what I think about it. I mean, it's *my* eyes and brain. Dr Gupta's still going on to Mum about how the public have a responsibility to science and helping to advance knowledge, especially in circumstances like this, and how the risks are much less than crossing the road. Dr Brown's still nodding like his head is on a spring. Mum's still looking like she's going to refuse, so I wait until Dr G pauses for breath and say, 'I want to do it.'

'We need to think about it, love.' Mum means we need to ask Prune and Rusty what they think about it.

'No, we don't. They'll need as many people as they can get for the study, won't they? And if there are only a very few of us who have the right … whatever it is, then it's really important to say yes.'

Part II

Part II

Eighteen

Motorways are the worst: endless anonymous miles into a grey nowhere. This car is huge and official-looking, and it's got air conditioning, which is great because it's still boiling hot even though it's the beginning of October. The driver looks official, too – dark suit and tie. Apart from when he arrived to pick me up, he hasn't said a word, and I'm sitting by myself in the back, like I'm a rich girl with a chauffeur. I try not to fiddle with my eyepatch. Holly says it's cool, but I think it makes me look like a bull terrier in a wig, and it's pretty uncomfortable, too.

We're going through one of those places that aren't really town but aren't country, either. I can see the edge of a golf course (the sign says it's closed), then a huge DIY store and a car re-spray place (both closed, because why bother). There are a lot of dead birds everywhere – more than London – sad lumps of feathers at the sides of the road.

Aveney Park sounds grand but it could be anything, really. Turns out it's probably going to be more like a couple of months than the couple of weeks that Dr Gupta said I'd be there. That means I'm going to miss quite a lot of school, but they're going to send lessons and stuff, and I can send things back for marking. It was hard enough to concentrate when I was *at* school, and I bet this'll be worse, because honestly, exams seem pretty meaningless right now.

I know I'll miss Mum. We've never been apart this long, and I'm worried about what might happen while I'm away. Prune and Rusty promised to look after her, which I hope means she'll be OK even if she's not – if that makes sense. I know she would say it's not my responsibility to worry about her, but I can't imagine how I can stop. And now, isn't it sort of my job – me and the others coming to Aveney Park – to worry about bad stuff on a massive scale? Aren't we being asked to help fix this whole thing?

We had to go back to Dr Gupta's surgery yesterday. One of the men who's in charge of the project was there, too, and he did something called a buccal swab, which sounds gross but is actually just scraping a few cells from inside your mouth for a DNA test. Then he said I had to sign something saying I agreed to be in the study, and the Official Secrets Act as well. That's to do with something called Emergency Powers. Mum had to sign, too, because I'm not eighteen yet. She did, but I could tell she was worried, even though the in-charge man kept saying it was just routine. It basically means that I can't be on social media while I'm taking part in the project, and I'm not allowed to talk about the tests and monitoring and things. As I'm not a scientist and it's not like I actually *know* anything, I can't see what the big deal is, but after I signed the paper at Dr G's surgery I checked my social media for the first time in ages. I'd assumed I'd just be locked out of it, but everything was actually gone, right up to the most recent photos I'd uploaded, of me and Holl and Jake at the bank holiday fun fair, like I was never there at all.

Rusty said he thought 'Emergency Powers' was probably like a Defence of the Realm Act, which is what we have in war time, apparently. Defence of the Realm sounds more like a bunch of knights in armour fighting off dragons than anything you'd actually need, but – according to Rusty – it means that the government can do whatever the hell they like and no one's allowed to criticise them. Put like that, it seems a bit worrying, but Prune said we were a democratic country and not a dictatorship and that Rusty should shut up, so he went off in a sulk to drink whisky and watch a cowboy film.

Rusty does exaggerate quite a lot, but I do think it's strange that Aveney Park doesn't seem to have a proper address. The one they gave Mum is just a bunch of letters and numbers. I don't think it can be in the Sat Nav, either, because the driver isn't using one – although that might just mean that he's been there loads of times and knows the way. Still, if anyone wants to write me a letter, they can, and I can write back, and the people in charge will 'organise postage'. Rusty thinks this means they'll censor the letters. I don't exactly love the thought of some complete stranger reading what I've written, but Rusty does tend to exaggerate quite a lot, so ... Plus, it's the only way for me to contact anyone because I can't have visitors and I'm not allowed to bring 'electronic devices of any sort'. So: major digital detox, on top of everything else.

I don't know if Holl will write to me. She went really quiet when I told her, then she said, 'Right, so you'll be cured, then,' and it sounded really bitter. I kept telling her no one had said anything about a cure, but it was like she didn't believe me. She said she liked the eyepatch, but kind of unwillingly, and then she said, 'Well, you'll be OK, won't you?' and that she had somewhere to be. She hasn't reached out since. I didn't expect her to apologise – I mean, it's not like I feel *betrayed*, because if it had been the other way round, I might not have believed her about seeing colours, either – but it was awkward because it's like she's angry with me. I'm lonely without her. Holl said she told Jake about Aveney Park, but he hasn't messaged me or anything. OK, so that's my pride, really . . . Like, did he really not give me another thought?

Anyway, whatever. I'm actually more worried about how it'll affect my relationship with Holly – assuming we get over the whole colour thing, that is. I mean, it's not like I dumped Jake or he dumped me – it just sort of disappeared in the greyout, and I really hope she understands that.

I really don't want to keep on thinking about it, so I try to turn my mind to something – anything – good. Or even, just about what it might be like when I get there. I'm nervous about all the tests and things, but it *is* an exciting feeling that you're going to be part of something that might be really, really important.

The fields are getting bigger, and they're all flat, right to the horizon. The sky is only a slightly different shade from the earth. Norfolk obviously isn't big on hills, and all the grey empty space makes it feel like the world is dissolving into nothing.

I try to imagine how the view would be in colour, but I can't. It makes me feel sad, because it's like we had this beautiful planet, and we ruined it.

Nineteen

It's getting dark now, and the few other cars on the road pass us like smudges. There are woods on either side and what looks like a chain-link fence, which turns into a row of very tall metal stakes placed close together. We turn onto a bumpy track and stop in front of a barrier. I can just make out a little square booth and a man in some sort of uniform coming out of it. The driver rolls down his window and hands over a piece of paper, and Uniform Guy raises the bar and lets us through. There are more trees, really dense, on either side of a gravel drive, which go on for about a mile until we get to a bend and then it's just fields – or I think it is, because I can't see that well in the dusk – and I can make out this great big shape in front of us.

Aveney Park: so colossal that it makes Mr Zhang's house look like a garden shed. The front part is lit up by floodlights. It looks seriously old and like a cross between a castle and a house, as if it might have been quite simple when it was first built, but people kept adding extra bits. I sit in the car, staring, while the driver gets my bag out of the boot. I'm imagining cobwebs, walls covered in sinister portraits, and a laboratory in a dungeon, so I practically jump out of my skin when Dr Brown taps on the window.

'It's not as scary as it looks, I promise,' he says, seeing my face as I scramble out of the car. 'You're just in time for the induction session.'

I follow him down a dark, tree-lined path round the side of the house, then through a little door in a wall that leads to a courtyard. The walls of the house are on the other three sides of the yard, and there are piles of logs and a big iron fire escape that goes right up to the roof. The curtains haven't been closed and, when I look in through the window, I see a bunch of people about my age walking down a corridor. Every single one of them is wearing an eye patch.

No one's going to hurt you, I tell myself. This is a good thing you're doing, and it's going to be fine.

Twenty

'My name's Kieran. I'm seventeen, from Devon. I had my first colour episode three weeks ago. I had this really bad headache and I was seeing double, and then my mum spilt a pan of boiling water – some of it went on my hand and I saw the burn come up red. It was only for a couple of seconds and I thought the shock made me imagine it, but then it happened again last week when my dad nearly hit a tractor on the road and that turned red. It was like the first time, with the headache – really quick, then back to grey again, and I felt really ill ...'

Kieran is super-freckly – the same mottled-stone look that my mum has – and I'm sure he'd have red hair if I could see him properly. His accent isn't full-on pirate like the bloke Rusty started imitating about a hundred times day after I got the eyepatch, who plays Long John Silver in that old film, but it is a bit farmy ... Or how country people sound in films and things, anyway. I don't really know because we've never had much money for holidays, so I've hardly been anywhere except London.

There's ten of us here: five boys and five girls. We're sitting on sofas and armchairs in a gloomy room that smells like when you change the dust bag on Prune's old-school hoover. I'm guessing that they had to make this place over in a hurry, because I noticed some carpentry stuff in the corridor, so maybe they haven't got around to cleaning yet (for all the difference that would make to how it looks).

Dr Brown's here, with a man called Dr Seagrove who's in charge of the whole thing. He's bald, with a concrete-coloured face that's so wrinkly it looks like there might be actual dust in some of the creases. He's got those old-fashioned bifocals that make the person's eyes look like they've been cut in half; quite odd when you think he's an eye specialist and could probably have the newest type of glasses just by snapping his fingers. The woman sitting next to him is Professor Petrossian. She's got frizzed-up dark hair with white lightning streaks down each side. It's a style that's straight out of the old *Bride of Frankenstein* film and crazy popular right now, although it doesn't really go with being plump and friendly-looking, which she is. She introduced us to the two nurses, Ms Anson (short, round and smiley) and Mr Virtanen (very pale with white hair and big eyes, like an alien), and a dark, smart-looking guy called Mr Okonjo, who's a teacher.

Dr Brown said we all had to introduce ourselves and tell everyone about seeing colours – he told us to call them 'episodes' – so that's what we're doing. So far, it's been Kieran and another boy called Kareem, who's from Bradford. He said his first episode happened when he was mugged: a guy pushed him down on the pavement and Kareem saw his red trainers. Now it's a girl called Alice. She's sixteen and from Manchester and looks a bit like Holly ... Or I think she does: it's hard to tell without colour, and perhaps I'm just seeing that because I'm already missing her. 'I'm in my school swimming team, and it was a competition. I'd been OK in the morning, but by the time we got to the place I was feeling ... you know, a bit like carsick only everything goes fuzzy and it's all ... *bleurgh* ...' She looks round when she says this and everyone's nodding like they know exactly what she means. 'I was watching the heats and there was this one girl who was massively ahead of everyone else, and the others on her team were cheering their heads off. You know that thing you get in indoor swimming pools where the noise echoes? Well, I could hear that, but *way* louder, like it was inside my head. Everything was crowding in on me and I knew I was going to ...'

She stops and looks a bit uncomfortable, and Kieran says, 'Be sick?'

Everyone's nodding again. It's a relief to know I'm not the only one who's had the whole puking thing.

Alice grins at him. 'Yeah ... The second I stood up to get to the loo, I saw the girl's swimming hat – bright red – this scarlet flash going down the pool. The coach was worried because I threw up. He kept asking questions, so in the end I had to tell him. He spoke to Mum and told her I needed to see the doctor, and ...' She shrugs. 'Here I am.'

'It happened to me when I fell off my horse,' pipes up a girl who sounds like the queen. 'I'm Sophie, by the way, and I'm sixteen, from Hampshire. I had the symptoms too, before it happened. I landed flat on my back and Maisie went cantering off and I saw her

red girth. It was such a shock that I thought she must have kicked
me in the head or something—'

'What the fuck is a girth?' The boy who asks this is sitting on a
chair slightly apart from everyone else and staring at Sophie in a
really aggressive way. Ms Anson gives a slight gasp, but everyone
else stays quiet. Sophie looks a bit astonished – either at the swearing or like, *how could you not know that?* I'm kind of glad he asked,
because I haven't a clue what a girth is, and, judging by the looks
on several other people's faces, neither do they.

'Goes under the horse's belly to hold the saddle in place.' The
boy who says this is a square-jawed, sporty-looking type who'd
reminded me a bit of Jake until he'd opened his mouth, because he
sounds as posh as Sophie. The boy who asked the question glares
at him, too. I stare down at the floor so I don't catch anyone's eye.
There are boys at my school like that – and one or two girls – who
always act like they want to challenge the world, and you soon
learn to be really careful around them.

'No big deal,' says the other boy. 'I'm Marcus, seventeen, from
Kent. My first colour episode happened when I touched an electric
fence by mistake . . . ' I look up and notice that everyone is leaning
towards Marcus, like they're trying to sort of separate themselves
from the rude boy. I glance over at him, and he's got this look on his
face – defiant, but like he doesn't know what to do or say next . . .
I guess we're all out of our depth, really.

A girl called Rosie goes next. She's from Southampton. She
doesn't sound as posh as Sophie or Marcus, but she seems a bit of
a princess: no colour makes it harder to tell if someone's rich, but

her eyepatch has silver rhinestones on it and she's got an expensive-looking film noir hairstyle, with pin curls. 'I was with a boy, you know . . .' She tosses her head. 'He kissed me, and it was like suddenly I was boiling hot and . . .' A couple of people giggle and she looks furious. 'It was *horrible*.'

I'm just thinking that actually things could have gone *way* worse with Jake when Alice says, 'Better than him turning you into a vampire.'

Marcus grins at her. 'Yeah, that's *so* over. The hot new super-power is making girls throw up.'

That makes everyone laugh – because it's funny, but also because it's a release of tension, although I notice that the aggressive boy is busy picking at something on his hoodie. He only raises his head when Treyshawn – who's from London, too, south of the river – starts telling us that his first episode was when he fell off his bike and cut his knee.

Then it's Cerys, who's Welsh. She's only fifteen, and really shy. She's been peering at everyone through this curtain of long dark hair – with the black patch, it looks like she's only got one eye, which is a bit freaky – and when the horse was mentioned she gasped, like she'd just heard Sophie say she was from outer space. She whispers that her colour episode was when she got stung by a bee and saw a red mark on her arm. That just leaves me and Mr Angry. I'm deciding I'd better not mention about where I live in case he gets the wrong idea (although I don't sound anything like Sophie or Marcus), when he starts talking.

'OK. I'm Ryan, I'm seventeen and I'm from London . . .' The

place he names isn't that far from where I live, although the kids from there go to a different school. It's one of those estates that was designed by an architect who hates people. Ryan seems to be talking directly to – or maybe *at* – Marcus, which gives me a chance to have a closer look at him: tall, with dark hair and high cheekbones. So not bad at all, but being around a person like that is so tiring that even if he was the fittest guy in the world, you'd still end up hating him.

'My dad lost it. He'd been going to Gamblers' Anonymous but it all fell apart when my mum left. We had a fight – his nose was bleeding where I hit him, and I saw the red blood. I'd got the head-ache and the rest of it, as well.'

I notice that nobody except Marcus is actually looking at him. Everyone else – including me, now I've had a glance round – has got their head down like they're trying to avoid a confrontation.

Ryan sounds quite matter-of-fact, like he doesn't want our sympathy. It's also interesting that he didn't just come straight out and say he'd hit his dad but told us the reason for it, so he must care a bit about what we think.

His mum left. I wonder if he misses her. When I sneak a second glance at him, he catches me looking, and – incredibly – he smiles. His mouth is actually beautiful, and the eye not covered by the patch is lovely and mischievous-looking, even without its real colour. I quickly look down at my lap, but it suddenly feels like there's no air in the room. Then, of course, I'm super-aware of him, even though I really, really, don't want to be.

Something that *is* good about greyout: no one can see you blush.

Twenty-One

I hear Dr Brown say my name, and when I look up everyone's staring at me. 'Oh, sorry. I'm Grace, and I'm sixteen. I'm from London as well. My first colour episode happened because my mum's a painter – well, she's an artist, but mostly it's doing walls in people's houses, to earn money – and what's happened affected her really badly, so she started pouring out all these cans of paint . . .' I know I'm gabbling but I can feel Ryan's eyes on me, and talking about Mum makes me feel like I'm going to cry, so I need to get this part over before it happens. I'm really wishing I hadn't started talking about Mum and just said some paint got spilt, but of course it's too late.

Cerys's visible eye goes really round when I say about Mr Kowalczyk shooting himself, although I just say 'a man who lives in our road' in case anyone has actually heard of him and thinks I'm showing off. When I finish, deliberately not looking in Ryan's direction, Alice catches my eye and gives me a really nice smile, so I know she must be OK. I'm thinking perhaps we can be friends, and what with that and the relief of having said my bit, I almost miss what Dr Brown says next.

' . . . so I want you all to look out for each other, and I'm giving you these.' He motions to Ms Anson, who holds up a bunch of wristbands, like people wear in hospital. 'Take the one with your name and pass them on.'

Everyone looks a bit surprised, but we put them on anyway. They're printed with our names, dates of birth, blood groups, allergies – I don't have any – and a barcode. That makes me feel like something in a shop: Grace Ballard on special offer, 99p. Marcus looks at his, then says, 'Really?' in a drawly voice.

'Just standard procedure,' Dr Brown says. Alice and I exchange glances. I wonder if she's thinking the same as me, which is that actually there isn't any standard procedure: this has never happened before, so they're making it up as they go along.

Now Ms Anson is passing round a bunch of things attached to lanyards. They're small white boxes, each with a big dark button on them that look like the things old people wear round their necks in case they fall over.

'You need to wear these alarms all the time, even in bed,' Dr Brown says. 'If you have a colour episode you must press the button immediately.'

Kieran looks up from fiddling with his wristband and says, 'What happens then?'

'Nothing drastic – just a few tests. There'll be blood tests every morning, too, after breakfast, with what's called Observations. We'll take your blood pressure, pulse and temperature. And there'll be eye tests, similar to some of the ones you've had already. You'll be called for those. The atropine drops will make things blurry for a while, so you might want to sit quietly for twenty minutes or so afterwards. Your rooms are upstairs, and you can do your schoolwork in the library – we'll show you round the house after dinner.' I'm expecting Dr Brown to hand over to Mr Okonjo for some sort of timetable but he just says, 'Remember to swap your eyepatches over at 2 p.m. so you're giving each side equal time, and that's basically it, I think . . . Dr Seagrove?'

Dr Seagrove stares at us through his cut-in-half eyes for a moment, then clears his throat. 'I'm sure I don't need to tell you how important this study is. If we succeed in finding a cure – and I say "we" to include you, because we're all in this together – then we'll have not only the moral, but also the emotional, satisfaction of knowing that we helped to restore the world, in all its beauty and glory, to billions of people.' He turns to Professor Petrossian. 'Anne, is there anything you'd like to add?'

Professor Petrossian opens her mouth like she's got something she wants to say, then closes it again, frowning. 'I think that's enough information for the time being. The important thing is that you know we're keeping an open mind about how this study will proceed. We' – she smiles at Dr Seagrove – 'may be scientists, but we're primarily here to learn from *you*.'

Some people are looking pleased at this idea, but I notice Ryan narrowing his eyes. I guess he's suspicious of anyone in authority. Then I look away quickly because I definitely do not want to be caught staring. I'm really annoyed at myself. What's going on? I can't like someone who makes everybody nervous, that's just wrong – and it's doubly wrong if they make *me* nervous, too.

Stop it, Grace. Just. Stop. It. As if there isn't enough to think about.

'OK.' Dr Brown rubs his hands together. 'Now, are there any questions?'

My mind immediately goes blank because Ryan is looking at me again, but Kareem says, 'Why are we here? I mean, why this place and not a hospital?'

'We don't need a hospital set-up for what we're doing, and – as I'm sure you know – every medical institution in the country is overstretched as it is. Aveney Park has been loaned to us by a benefactor. Given the circumstances, the government considered it to be the best option available.'

'Are there any other studies like this?' Sophie asks. 'I mean, we're from all over the place – Devon and Bradford are miles apart.'

Dr Brown looks at Dr Seagrove like he's not sure what the reply ought to be. Dr Seagrove looks at the floor for a long moment, and then says, 'There are other studies, but not here. Avian studies as well.'

'What's avian?' Ryan asks.

'It means birds.' Marcus sounds superior, and, out of the corner of my eye, I see Ryan glare at him. I'm glad he asked, though, because I didn't know what it meant, and I bet lots of the others didn't know, either. That's the second time he's asked what something meant when no one else did, and both times he took the risk that he'd look bad in comparison to Marcus with his posh person's vocabulary. Maybe he just doesn't care. Despite the fact I'm trying hard not to, it makes me like him more.

'The human samples in other countries are very small, too.' Dr

Seagrove stares at each of us in turn. 'People like you are extremely unusual, and that makes you exceedingly valuable.'

Exceedingly valuable: so, *not* on special offer. I look down at the barcode on my wrist and feel very weird indeed.

Twenty-Two

The minute the meeting's over, I notice that nearly everyone is looking round for their phone, like they've lost a limb and haven't realised it yet. I get that people are worried they're going to be bored or feel like their friends are going to forget about them ... I wish I could message Holly, or even Jake. Even if they just came back with something stupid, it'd be nice to have that connection.

As Mr Okonjo ushers us into the dining room, I grin at Alice and she grins back, which makes me feel a bit better. Then her eyes widen because the space is vast, and even gloomier than the room we were in before, with murky-looking windows that must be stained glass, because there's a pattern with flowers. The room has dark, wooden-panelled walls and long tables with benches.

Alice says, 'It's like a boarding school or something.'

Sophie's right behind us. 'They're not all like Hogwarts, you know.' Then she tells us the name of her school like we should have heard of it. I haven't, but it's probably one of those places that charge thousands of pounds a year, and you can bet they've never had a chunk of ceiling fall down in the middle of a lesson.

Alice is looking blank, too. Then she says, but in a nice way, 'Well, that's good, because I forgot to pack my magic wand.' I'm liking her more by the minute. Actually, I think Sophie might be OK, too. It's just that I've never talked to anyone like her before – there must be kids in my road who go to public school, but I've never met any of them – and she makes me a bit nervous. And even if this isn't like actual boarding, it is sort of the same as when you go to a new school, having to find out who everybody is and what they're like.

'Do they let you keep your horse at school, then?'

Sophie shakes her head, but she's smiling – pleased that I'm interested, I guess. 'I was at my mum's house. She took me to the GP and everything.' As she says it, she inches away from Ryan, who is standing in the middle of the room, gazing around, and – in spite of the greyout – looking properly hot. The fact that he's scowling just adds to it. I'd begun to wonder if attraction could exist without colour, but it obviously can. But, but, but . . .

Remember your first impression, Grace. He's trouble, and you've got enough of that at the moment.

I know exactly what Holl would say if I could tell her about this: Don't turn him into something else in your head. Plus, don't make up some elaborate fantasy because he looked at you like, once.

Or twice.

Or three times.

The food's quite strange – by which I mean *even* stranger than food generally is nowadays. It comes in plastic packets, all sealed, like it's been created in a laboratory, and you have to cut them open and tip the contents onto your plate. No label, just a barcode. The first course is a dark grey stew that looks like industrial waste, followed by what I think is banoffee pie – which looks sort of OK, although not enough to make you want to put it in your mouth – for afterwards.

Nobody says much at first, partly because Mr Okonjo is hanging around our table and partly because we're still sizing each other up. Rosie's moaning about the stew and everyone's giving her side-eye, like *WTF*, when Dr Brown puts his head round the door and asks Mr Okonjo to come and talk to him, so we're by ourselves for the first time.

There's silence for a moment. Then Kareem, who's sitting next to me, says, 'You know what's really strange? I looked this place up on the internet, and there's nothing there.'

Marcus and Kieran are nodding like they did the same, and I'm feeling stupid because although I googled to see if there was anything about the study (there wasn't), I never thought to look up Aveney Park itself. Too busy worrying about leaving Mum, I guess. Alice, who's sitting on my other side, obviously didn't google it either, because she says, 'Really nothing?'

Marcus shakes his head. 'When I couldn't find it, I asked my brother to have a go. He works in online reputation management – damage limitation when people have tweeted something stupid and found themselves in a shit-storm – and he can find *anything*. But he couldn't find Aveney Park. As far as the internet's concerned, this place doesn't exist.'

Treyshawn, who's sitting opposite him, just shrugs, but it sounds pretty weird to me. 'Didn't you think that was strange?'

'Not really. My brother reckoned they'd had it taken off for security reasons.'

'That's what my dad said.' Rosie pushes her half-eaten stew away. 'He told me I was making a fuss over nothing.'

Marcus looks surprised. 'Why didn't you just refuse to sign the form if you didn't want to come?'

'Oh, you know ...' Rosie shrugs, but I do know, and I bet everyone else knows too. You'd have to be pretty strange, as well as unbelievably selfish, to want to miss out on a chance to make history and help billions of people at the same time. Plus, don't tell me the idea of being special didn't appeal to her. 'Look,' she snaps at Cerys, who's been staring at her plate, 'just eat it, why don't you? I'm not going to.'

Rosie pretends not to hear when Ryan, who's sitting next to Treyshawn, mutters, 'Bitch,' but Cerys just whispers her thanks and takes the food. I wonder what her life at home is like. I mean, none of us are exactly plump, but she looks like she's never had a proper meal.

There's an uncomfortable silence, so I say – but not in Ryan's direction – 'I wondered about the Sat Nav. The driver didn't use it when we were coming here. Maybe he just knew the way, but ...'

'It wouldn't be on there,' Kieran says. 'It's not on Google Earth or any of the satellite maps. They blur things out if they think there's a security risk – like with military bases.'

'But this isn't a military base. It's some benefactor's house – Dr Brown said – so it's not as if it's a target for terrorists.'

'Yeah, but for all we know, the benefactor might have lent it out in the past for any number of things. Military stuff, or high-level summits or whatever.'

Several people start talking at once, but everyone shuts up immediately when Mr Okonjo comes back. Behind him are Dr Brown and a big guy in army uniform, iron grey and so stiff that he looks as if he folds himself away at night like a deckchair. 'This is Captain Franchot. He's in charge of security and he's going to explain some rules.'

Captain Franchot stands at the end of the table, eyeballing everyone and speaking very emphatically like he's talking in BIG CAPITAL LETTERS. The army being here explains the man in the booth outside, but it kind of makes me feel like I've done something wrong. Captain Franchot produces a big paper map and spreads it on the table. Aveney Park house is in the middle, with loads of land all round it. There's a large light grey bit marked 'DEER PARK', big blobs of dark grey for woodland, and the outlines of a farm and fields. Captain Franchot taps it with a leather-covered stick to show us where we can and can't go. The woods and the farm are out of bounds, and there will be soldiers on patrol. I'm wondering how much we'll actually want to be outside, because it's bound to look as grey and flat and boring as the map does. We're not allowed to leave the grounds 'for security reasons' and we must 'respect the boundaries' in the house – which basically means that if you see a door marked 'Private', don't open it.

Then he folds up the map and says, 'No electronic devices of any sort are allowed. We've checked your luggage and removed a couple of items from bags . . . ' Kieran looks like he's about to say something, but Captain Franchot holds up his hand to stop him and says, 'You'll get them back when you go home. And if anyone has phones on them, you need to hand them over now.'

Ryan shrugs, takes a mobile out of his pocket and puts it on the table.

'Thank you. Any more?'

Nobody moves or says anything, but Captain Franchot folds his arms and stands there staring at us. The silence gets longer and longer, and it's like junior school – 'We're all going to sit here until whoever did it owns up'. I'm just wondering if he's got special equipment for detecting phones, when Rosie says, 'I need to keep mine.'

Captain Franchot puts his hand out, palm up. 'There's a landline in the office for emergency calls.'

'It's just, I got this puppy for my birthday, and I need to make sure he's OK.' She turns these really big eyes on him, all appealing like he's her dad or something.

He looks like he's going to explode. 'Hand it over.'

She practically throws it at him. 'Well, can I use the landline, then?'

'I said, only for emergencies.'

Alice mutters, 'Hashtag entitled,' in my ear, so that I have to turn a laugh into a cough. Captain Franchot gives me an evil look, but it's OK because Mr Okonjo steps forward and says he's going to take us on a tour of the house.

Twenty-Three

The kitchen is industrial-looking, with big steel units that you could climb into, and huge fridges which are probably full of plastic packets of food. We stack our plates in a giant dishwasher and then Mr Okonjo takes us down a long corridor and shows us where the nurses' rooms and doctors' offices are. 'So many tests,' Rosie moans.

Treyshawn, who's next to her, says, 'All those needles . . .'

Kieran cackles. 'You'll be a human sieve.'

Treyshawn gives him a little shove. 'I hate them, man.'

'Who doesn't?'

I notice one big door halfway down the passage that's twice the size of the rest: metal, with a panel of buttons beside it. 'What do you think that is?' Alice mutters in my ear.

'Storeroom? Maybe it's temperature-controlled or something. Fridge or whatever.'

'Bet it's for samples,' says Rosie.

'It's for your blood.' Kieran says it in a horror film voice, and Treyshawn shoves him again. It's nice to joke around again, even over something like this, but I can hear someone – I'm guessing Sophie – making tutting noises.

We follow Mr Okonjo to the front part of the house, which is empty and echoey because the ceilings are massively high and they've removed all the curtains and carpets. No sinister portraits, either – in fact, there are larger squares of wall that are paler than the rest, where they've taken pictures away. It's a shame, because I was totally up for a bit of 'this is the sixth duke, who ran his wife through with a sword for winking at a peasant' or whatever. There's a coat of arms, though, in the enormous hall, and a glass chandelier that's practically the size of my bedroom at home.

Sophie and Marcus are all confident, up at the front, chatting to Mr Okonjo. The rest of us are strung along behind. Kieran and Treyshawn are acting as if they're in one of those old crazy-scientist-doing-experiments-on-people films that everyone's been watching, calling Dr Seagrove 'Dr X'. Ryan's slouching at the back, looking like he's determined not to be impressed. We traipse up the main stairs to see the library, which is where we're going to do our schoolwork. It's got a big table and empty bookshelves so high that you'd need a ladder to reach the things at the top, if there were any. I suppose they must be valuable, like the pictures, and that's why they removed them.

Then we cross a wide landing and go into a labyrinth of grey corridors with doors on either side marked 'Private', 'Private', 'Private' as far as you can see. There's a fire door every now and then, but I didn't notice any CCTV – unlike my school, where there's cameras everywhere. Apart from the big one on the ground floor, there are no doors that need swipe cards or codes, either, although I bet all the 'Private' ones are locked.

I'm starting to wonder why Mr Okonjo has brought us here when he says that the staff wing (wing!) is just round the corner, and that although there will always be at least two people on duty, we should know where to come in case there's an emergency and we can't find anybody.

After that, we explore as much of the rest of the house as we're allowed to see. The higher you go, the smaller the staircases are. The main one, which goes from the hall to the first floor, is massive, but the ones higher up are narrower, with no carpets or anything. The staircase to the third and fourth floors, which is where our rooms are – girls on the third and boys on the fourth – is still bigger than in a normal house, though. It's got stone steps, and a huge glass skylight way up in the roof.

We're going down another grey corridor, on the second floor, when Alice and I stop to look at a bunch of old photographs on the walls. They're the only pictures we've seen so far, of farmers ploughing fields with horses and bringing in the harvest. We're staring at a picture of a big, jolly-looking woman playing the accordion to a group of men outside a pub when a voice behind us says, 'She must have pleated tits.'

This is so unexpected that I start giggling, and, when I turn around to see who said it, there's Ryan. He grins at me when I catch his eye and, for a nanosecond, it's like a freeze-frame and we're the only two people there, and I've got butterflies fluttering in my stomach. Then Marcus, who's dropped back a bit, says, 'Oh, ha ha'.

He's not really having a go – you can tell from his tone – but Ryan instantly grabs him and slams him against the wall.

Mr Okonjo's already gone around the next corner with some of the others and doesn't see it, but Cerys looks terrified and so, for a second, does Marcus. Then he sort of relaxes, but like it's an effort, and says, 'Come on, mate.'

'Who are you calling mate?'

Before I've even thought about what I'm doing, I put my hand on Ryan's arm. The muscles are rock hard and I can feel a current of anger vibrating under his skin. 'He didn't mean anything.' My voice sounds squeaky and ridiculous.

Ryan looks down at my hand, and then at me. For a second, he looks so furious that I jump back, like I've been burnt. Then his face changes completely and I can't tell what he's thinking, but he takes his hands off Marcus. 'All right.'

Marcus steps away from the wall and looks at him for a moment. I don't know if he's expecting an apology, but he doesn't get one, so he lopes off to catch up with the others. Ryan glares after him like I'm not even there. I'm shaky, but trying not to show it, aware that Alice and Cerys are staring at me. We all stand there for a moment in silence, then Sophie calls out, 'Come on, you lot,' so we run to catch up, too, leaving Ryan by himself in the corridor.

Mr Okonjo takes us back to the ground floor and shows us the Games Room, where there are loads of chintzy-looking armchairs, and books and board games, as well as an old television, which is fixed so you can only watch DVDs. I can tell that Marcus is avoiding me – embarrassed, I suppose, about being rescued by a *girl* – although I notice he keeps looking in Alice's direction. Ryan's avoiding everyone's eye, which is probably just as well, but there's this feeling like no one really knows what to say. Word's obviously got round about what happened in the corridor, and it's a relief when Mr Okonjo says we should collect our stuff and get up to bed.

Twenty-Four

My room is at the front of the house, but I can't see a thing out of the window because outside is that total darkness you never get in cities because of the streetlights. I clean all the dead flies off the windowsill – they're everywhere now, but you notice it more against white paint – and listen hard in case there are a few owls left, but there are no sounds at all.

It's stupid, but I don't want to put the bedside light out because it's like the darkness could just swallow you up. I get into bed and stare at the ceiling for a bit, trying not to think about Ryan and Marcus.

I try thinking about Mum instead, wondering what she's doing, but that's no good because it makes me want to cry. Then I find myself remembering all those films where people go into the middle of nowhere and there's a bunch of crazy survivalists or an inbred cannibal family. I mean, this is the perfect set-up: a house you can't find on a map, and no one's got a phone . . .

When someone taps on the door, I practically pee myself.

*

'I didn't mean to scare you.' It's Alice, in her dressing gown and without her eyepatch. 'Is it OK if I come in?'

'Why not? I can't sleep either. I keep thinking about horror films.'

'I know, creepy. But at least it's not cold.'

'It's bigger than my room at home, too. Have you got a desk?'

'Yeah, under the window like yours. And there's a kitchen.'

'In your room?'

'Down the corridor. A little one. Bet Sophie's school is like this.' Alice grins at me and puts on a posh voice. '"It's not like Hogwarts, you know."'

'As long as it's not a mad scientist's laboratory, either.'

'Don't think so. Although . . .' She sits down on the bed, looking thoughtful. 'I was thinking about what Kareem said – Aveney Park not being on the internet. There aren't any maps, either. On the walls, I mean. You'd think a place like this would have some, showing all the land and the nearest villages, even if they were just really old ones.'

'Here be dragons, you mean?'

'Well, not quite, but . . . *you know*. And there were a lot of spaces where they'd obviously taken pictures and things down.'

'Probably because of insurance, if they're worth a lot. And Captain Franchot's got a map.'

'Only of *here*. It's like, we know we're in Norfolk, but we don't know *where*, or how far the nearest town is, or anything. Maybe it doesn't matter.' She shrugs. 'Didn't you think it was interesting that everyone seemed to have their episodes when they had a headache, and when people were having a row or there was something violent, like Sophie falling off her horse, or Ryan punching his dad . . . ? I thought you were really brave with Ryan, by the way.'

'Not really,' I say, carefully. 'I just didn't think what I was doing.'

'Do you think he *would* have hit Marcus?'

'I don't know.' I don't want to say Ryan's name out loud in case I somehow give myself away. 'Maybe.' Change the subject, Grace. 'Talking of Marcus, did you notice him looking at you?'

The way she lowers her eyes as she says, 'No,' makes me sure she *did* notice. 'He is quite hot, though.'

'If you like posh boys.'

'You sound like Ryan.'

I make a face at her. 'Interesting that nobody had an episode right then – the whole violence thing.'

'Because nobody had a headache?'

'I suppose. Do you think there are people out there who've had colour episodes but didn't tell anybody? Would you have? If your swimming coach hadn't been there?'

'I don't know. The way it happened, I sort of had to, but otherwise I'd have just thought that no one would believe me. My older sister, Ellie – who's supposed to be the *sensible* one – said I was making it up. When me and Mum came back from the doctor's and told her it was real and I was coming here, she was so angry.'

'Yeah,' I say, thinking of Holly. 'I got that, too, from my best friend.'

'After the Official Secrets person said they'd be monitoring Ellie's social media and she couldn't post anything about it, she wouldn't even speak to me.'

I hadn't really thought about them monitoring other people's social media – I'm the only person in my family who's on it – but I suppose they'd have to, although I still don't really get why there's quite so much secrecy. 'I wonder if they've been monitoring Holly's social media. She's the only one I told.' I decide not to mention Jake. 'I think she was jealous. I can sort of see why, but it's not like we can suddenly see in colour again. I suppose it's like we're in with a chance, though, and no one else is . . . Do you think it'll happen?'

'I don't know. I want it so much I can't even let myself hope, because it just feels like it's impossible.'

'I know what you mean.'

'But also . . .' Alice picks at a loose thread on her sleeve and doesn't look at me. 'I feel like, why me, you know? I mean, if we can see colour and nobody else can, it won't be fair.'

'We didn't earn it, you mean?'

Alice nods. 'Random. You know what, though? If the greyout does end – for everybody, I mean – we should get loads of different-coloured paint and make everything as bright as we can. Not just stuff that was colourful before, like shops, but *everything*, so everyone can look at it and feel happy.'

Twenty-Five

I try and get to sleep after Alice has gone, but I just lie there in the darkness thinking about what she said. I feel so weighed down by the greyout that it's like my whole body's full of wet sand.

Ten minutes later she's back, looking worried. 'I've just remembered about my necklace. It broke, and I thought I'd put it in my pocket but now I can't find it. I think I must have left it on one of the tables in the Games Room. It was my last present from my gran – a locket with a photo of her and my grandad, and it's really special. Will you come down with me and get it? I'm worried I might get lost.'

I can see it's really bothering her, so I get out of bed and put on my bathrobe. 'I suppose it'll be all right. They didn't say we weren't allowed to go downstairs at night, did they? Except ... We won't be able to see. We don't know where any of the light switches in the corridors are, and we haven't got our phones.'

'We can use this.' She holds up a key ring with a little torch on it.

The door to the landing is at the end of our corridor. This is *just* like one of those bits in a horror film where one or two people – who've obviously never seen a horror film in their lives – go off on

119

their own to investigate where the strange noise is coming from, and wind up dying horribly. Like Alice said, it's not cold, but I'm shivery inside from nerves.

When I turn the door handle, it doesn't open. I wiggle it a bit, but still nothing. Alice has a go, but she can't open it, either. 'That's odd. I mean, what if there was a fire? How would we get out?'

'Hang on . . .' I think for a moment. I'm sure you're not meant to lock fire doors, but I don't know if this actually is one or not. There's no keyhole, anyway. 'There must be another exit.'

We walk back past our rooms and around the corner – more corridor – and then another corner with even more corridor and what looks like an outside door at the end, with a sign saying: 'PUSH BAR TO OPEN'.

I do, and it does. There's a fire escape like the one I saw in the courtyard when I arrived. Alice wedges the door open with a sand bucket so we can get back in again, and we start going down the iron steps, hanging onto the handrail and each other, because it's pitch-dark and the keyring torch isn't a lot of help. Halfway down, the whole place floods with blinding light.

Alice clutches my hand really hard. 'Security lights,' I whisper, thinking of the ones in Mr Zhang's garden at home. 'Sensors.' It's definitely the same courtyard I walked through when I arrived: logs stacked up, the house on three sides, and the garden wall with the door in it on the fourth.

We stand quite still, but no one comes. 'There's doors into the house,' Alice whispers. 'We might be able to get in.'

*

Everything is locked. After a minute the security lights go off, but when we look through the windows we can make out the corridor that leads from the Games Room to the kitchen, and the kitchen itself, with its row of enormous fridges.

It makes sense. I mean, who doesn't lock up at night? And I can see why they might not want us wandering around the house when there's no one there to supervise. I'm about to tell Alice not to worry about her gran's necklace because they're bound to have a place for lost property, when a light comes on in the corridor and we both duck under the window.

'I thought we were on the same team!'

A woman's voice. I think it's Professor Petrossian, and she sounds really angry. Then a man says, 'Keep your voice down.' It's a hoarse half-whisper so I can't tell who it is and I don't dare stand up for a look.

The might-be Professor Petrossian mutters something, and then we hear two sets of footsteps, going in opposite directions, and the light goes out.

My heart is thumping like crazy, which is a bit stupid because we haven't actually done anything wrong – or not *bad* wrong, anyway. Before either of us can say or do anything, there's the sound of more footsteps, this time from the other side of the garden wall.

'Army patrols,' Alice whispers. 'Like Captain Franchot said.'

Her eyes are wide and scared, like mine must be. We stare at each other for a second, then sprint across the yard, up the fire escape and back inside. We walk back to our rooms fast, in silence, and stand in the corridor for a moment, listening. I can't hear anything, but it doesn't feel safe out here. Alice whispers, 'Talk in the morning,' before she goes into her room and closes the door.

Twenty-Six

I fall asleep eventually and dream about Dad, which is weird. He's just a shape, murky and underwater like a shipwreck, but I know it's him. When I wake up, way too early, the room is full of pearly grey light that makes the air look strange and foggy, and for a moment I can't remember where I am.

I lie there for a bit and try to get back to sleep, but I keep thinking about the dream and wondering where Dad actually *is*, now. I was thirteen when Parsley died, and I was sure he'd gone to heaven, but that was really because I couldn't bear to think of him not existing anywhere. I used to think it about Dad, too, that perhaps they were together somewhere, even though they never met in life and Mum once told me that Dad didn't like cats much. Really, I've got no idea. Your soul probably just floats about for a bit, like a bubble, and then it goes pop or something.

The idea of something going pop makes me start worrying about Mum and whether she's OK, and if Prune would actually tell me if she wasn't, and whether *I* would tell me if I was Prune. I realise I probably wouldn't, which makes me feel *really* anxious.

All these thoughts are going round in circles inside my head, and I have to stop stressing because there's nothing I can do about any of it. I need to think about something else . . .

Which means something else that isn't complicated and uncomfortable, like Holly or Jake.

Or Ryan. Definitely not him.

I focus on the row Alice and I overheard last night and how strange it all is, but I just wind up with lots of questions and no answers.

In the end, I creep down the corridor and try the door to the landing again. I still can't open it, so I decide to have a shower; way better than at home because there's loads of hot water and nobody hurrying you so they can use the loo. Then I get dressed and put on the eyepatch – which doesn't seem to feel any more comfortable – and stand by the window, watching the low mist on the dark fields. I will myself to see pale morning colours creeping over the landscape, like in a poem, but nothing happens.

Alice comes into my room at twenty past seven, and we watch three of Captain Franchot's men walk up the drive towards the entrance with an Alsatian on a lead.

Alice frowns. 'They've got guns.'

'Well, they would, wouldn't they? They're soldiers.'

'I suppose, but . . . oh, I don't know.'

I get what she means. 'Wonder how many there are.'

'Quite a few, if they have to do patrols. They *really* don't want us wandering around on our own, do they? Perhaps they're worried about spying.'

'That's when you don't want other countries to know your military secrets and stuff. Plus, it's not actual information – just research, like in a laboratory.'

'Yeah,' Alice says darkly, 'and they don't let people into laboratories because they don't want them to see the horrible things they do to animals.'

'No way. There's our parents, for a start – we couldn't all ... I don't know, *disappear*, without them asking questions.'

'Er, Official Secrets? They couldn't say anything without being prosecuted.'

'But no one's going to hurt us, are they? It's like Dr Seagrove said – we're precious, my Precious.' I try to do Gollum from *The Lord of the Rings*, but it doesn't come out right.

'Yeah, but he also called us "human samples", remember?'

'Still ... If it stops being OK, we can leave. It said so on the form we signed.'

Alice says, 'I guess,' but she looks a bit doubtful. 'That row, though.'

'That was Professor Petrossian, wasn't it?'

'I'm sure it was. It might just have been an argument about some science thing, but the way she said it, it was like she felt *betrayed*.'

I hadn't thought of it like that, but Alice is right.

'Did you get much sleep?'

'Not really. I kept thinking about not being able to open that door. I tried this morning, but it still wouldn't open.'

'They must have opened it now, otherwise we won't be able to get down to breakfast. Perhaps it's some automatic timer thing. We can check it out on the way – and we've only got five minutes, so come on.'

Like I noticed last night, there's no keyhole, and nothing that looks automatic, either. On the stairs side, there are two big bolts that we didn't notice before because the door was wide open and you couldn't see them. There's also a sign which says, 'FIRE DOOR' and, underneath that, 'KEEP SHUT'.

It seems the door is either wedged open with a big stone door-stop, or it's bolted. Both of those things must mean that the people who run this place don't have to bother about regulations.

I don't suppose it's that big a deal, but all the same I feel a prickle of unease.

Twenty-Seven

Alice does find her necklace in the Games Room, which is a small bit of relief after the events of the night before. We head into the dining room for more sealed packets, this time with squashed croissants and Danish pastries inside. Dr Brown's sitting at our end of the table, and Alice and I glance at each other before sitting down. We hadn't agreed not to tell the others about the bolts on the door, but now we definitely can't discuss it. Treyshawn and Ryan are sitting together, chatting quietly. Ryan looks more relaxed than I've seen him yet, though Marcus and Sophie look like they've made a point of sitting as far away from him as possible. Alice and I sit in the spaces they've left, next to the rest of the group.

Kieran and Kareem are chatting to Rosie, who's still moaning about not having her phone. Kieran, who told us he helps train the sheepdogs on his dad's farm, is trying to reassure her about the puppy. 'Your parents will look after it, won't they?'

'I don't know,' Rosie wails. 'They're getting divorced and it's like they don't have time for anything except hating each other.' She shakes her head. 'I've been awake most of the night, worrying.'

Kareem frowns. 'They'll feed it though, right?'

'Well, *yeah*.' Rosie rolls her eyes. 'But puppies need attention.'

Puppies aren't the only ones, and that explains a *lot*. Alice and I exchange glances again and I know she feels as sorry for Rosie as I do.

Sophie suddenly leans across the table and says to Rosie, 'I know it's hard if they're ignoring you, but honestly, it's better than my parents. They split up just before greyout, and they spend all their time scoring off each other and trying to weaponise me.'

I'm amazed that Sophie would say this in front of everyone, because she doesn't seem the type – more stiff upper lip than sharing private stuff – and I notice surprised looks on a quite a few faces. In fact, Sophie looks kind of surprised herself.

Lots of people say sympathetic things, and I find myself holding my breath in case Ryan comes out with something sarcastic, but he stays quiet.

While I'm trying to avoid looking in his direction, I notice Marcus keeps sneaking looks at Alice, which is interesting. When Dr Brown leaves the room, part of me wants to ask about the doors on the boys' floor, and whether they are the same as ours, but Mr Okonjo arrives to take us for the first tests.

We are taken to the corridor where the nurses' rooms are, and he lines us up in alphabetical order for the tests. Kareem (Ahmed) is first, and I'm between Kieran (Atkins) and Treyshawn (Cassell). Alice, whose surname is Dekker, is between Sophie (Cole) and Ryan (Lang). He's next to Rosie (Riordan), which is pretty unfortunate, but at least Kieran's diverting her attention from the loss of her phone by talking about dog training. Marcus (Ronson) and Cerys (Walker) are at the end.

I get Ms Anson. She's all smiley and friendly and how-are-you-settling-in, although she doesn't ask any questions beyond confirming my date of birth and the other basic stuff that's on my wristband. I thought she might want to know more, but then I remember what Alice said about animals in laboratories. You wouldn't ask a white mouse about its lifestyle, either.

Ms Anson's room looks the same as the nurse's room at Dr Gupta's surgery, even down to the Kerr + Bell calendar. There is one difference, though, which I don't spot immediately because of everything being grey. Normally, bits of medical equipment and boxes of stuff like tissues and surgical gloves have branding on them. Here, they're just plain cardboard with a label to say what's inside, so maybe they're special government issue or something.

I'm nervous, but it's all pretty straightforward, and the eye tests are way less complicated than the ones Dr Brown did. Afterwards, Ms Anson gives me a little paper cup with two pills in it, which I can't see properly because the atropine is making everything hazy, and tells me to take them.

'What are they?'

'Supplements, dear. Vitamins and minerals.'

This seems OK – I mean, you can buy those things at the super-market – so I swallow them.

I grope my way to an armchair in the Games Room. Kieran and Kareem are already there, and the place fills up as people come back from seeing the nurses. We talk about our favourite colours while we wait for the blurriness to wear off. I hadn't thought about having a favourite colour since I was a little kid, but I've had this conversation a lot since the greyout. It's sort of like when Prune and Rusty talk about stuff that happened years ago. That's normal for old people, but it's sad to talk about colours like they're part of your past.

Alice and Kieran both say their favourite was blue. Kareem's was green, Treyshawn's was purple, and Sophie says chestnut, but like her horse, so it's *orangey* brown, not *brown* brown. Rosie says pink and Cerys, red – which surprises me because I feel like it's a noisy colour, and she's exactly the opposite.

'In China,' Kieran says, 'red's a lucky colour.' Cerys smiles at him and nods, though she seems too shy to keep on talking.

'Does that mean everyone in China's going to be unlucky now?' asks Alice.

I can see what she means, but it can't actually work like that – surely a thing is still lucky, even if you can't see it? Anyway, it feels like everyone in the world is unlucky now.

When Alice asks me for my favourite colour I say, 'It used to be yellow – sunflowers and summer – but now it's all of them. If I could see *any* colour now, that would immediately be the best one because it wouldn't be grey. It's like being so hungry that any food would do.'

'True,' says Treyshawn. 'It's like you're starving. What was yours, Marcus?'

'Blue.'

'Typical,' Ryan mutters. I guess he means because it's colour of the Conservative party. I want to tell him not to be a dick. I mean, what's the point? For all he knows, Marcus just likes blue, like Alice and Kieran do.

Marcus is obviously thinking the same, because he says, 'I just like it, OK? And more *turquoise* than bright blue. What's yours, anyway?'

'Red.'

'That's the colour of the Republican party in America,' says Marcus, 'and they're right wing as well, so . . . '

Ryan scowls even more.

'It's Labour, too,' Kieran says. 'And Communism.'

'Left wing and right wing and luck . . . ' Alice says. 'Weird how it means different things to different people.'

Now she says this, it's obvious, but I've never thought that much about it before . . . Like, it's not what things actually *are*, it's how we perceive them. Colours make the world beautiful, but they make divisions, too – pink for girls and blue for boys, even. It's the labels that some people put on them, and they stuck. Although, even if they hadn't, it seems like there are a million other reasons people can find for division – to be sexist or racist or hate anyone with a different religion or—

'Shit!' Marcus leans forward and, for a second, I think he's going to jump out of his chair and land one on Ryan. Then I realise he's staring straight at Alice. It's like she's hypnotised him.

Sophie jumps up. 'Are you OK?'

Marcus shakes his head and claps his hand over his mouth. His face has gone from grey to almost white. 'Episode,' he croaks. 'Red.' Then he crumples forward and falls on the floor, right at Alice's feet.

Twenty-Eight

We all jump up then, but Sophie elbows her way past everyone and presses Marcus's alarm. The next second, Dr Brown and Mr Virtanen are bending over him, and Mr Okonjo's herding the rest of us out of the door and into the dining room.

Mr Okonjo keeps telling us that Marcus is going to be fine and there's nothing to be concerned about, but he sounds worried. The minute he leaves, everyone starts talking at once.

I take Alice to one side. 'It looked like you triggered him. Are you wearing anything that used to be red?'

'Yeah, my top. He was looking at it.'

'He wasn't looking at your *top*, Alice. That was just ... in the way.'

'Well, he also looked like he was going to puke, so it's hardly Romeo and Juliet. Seriously though, that happened *really* fast. He didn't say anything about having a headache, did he?'

Sophie, who must have overheard us and is looking a bit pissed off, says, 'I was talking to him all through breakfast, and he didn't mention it.'

'Maybe he told the nurse.'

As Alice says this, I think of the pills in the little paper cup. 'Perhaps what they gave us was meant to speed things up or something.'

'How?' Sophie looks scornful. 'They're just vitamins.'

Alice looks thoughtful. 'That's what they *said*.'

'Don't be paranoid. It's a coincidence, that's all.'

'Maybe,' Alice says, 'but nothing was *happening*, was it? We were just talking.'

'Ryan was being foul to him.'

'Not as much as yesterday, when Mr Okonjo was taking us round the house. You didn't see, but Ryan would have hit Marcus if Grace hadn't stopped him. Why didn't it happen then?'

'Yeah, blame me.' Ryan's suddenly in her face.

'I wasn't blaming you.' Alice looks flustered. 'I was just pointing it out.'

'Just pointing it out,' Ryan mimics. 'Anyway, he's a twat.'

His face tenses up and everyone backs away, staring at him through their single uncovered eyes. There's dead silence. Ryan stares at everyone in turn and, one by one, they duck their heads or look away. He looks at me last, and I stare right back. I don't really know why – mostly because he's being a dick again, just when it felt like we were all coming together a little. I'm pissed off with him, and with myself for liking him, and I have no idea what I'll do if he starts having a go at me. I don't get the chance to find out, though, because at that moment Mr Okonjo comes back and says Marcus is having some tests, and that he's going to take the rest of us outside and show us where we can play football and stuff. Everybody starts asking questions, but Mr Okonjo holds up his hand and says we're to ask Dr Brown at lunchtime, so that's that.

'Why does he have to be so angry all the time?' Alice still looks upset. 'I wasn't accusing him of anything.'

'Maybe . . .' I stare at Ryan, who's slouching along some way ahead of us. 'Maybe it's because he can't fight this – the greyout, I mean – so he's going to be even more fighty about everything else because it's the only way he knows how to relate to anything.' I'm surprised – and quite pleased – at how neutrally this comes out. Plus, I managed to avoid saying his name, so I could sort of pretend I was talking about someone else. 'Like it makes him feel like he's in control.'

'And makes everyone else feel terrible.'

'There are boys like him at my school.'

'Are there?'

'Some, yeah. Why, do you go to a school full of boys like Marcus?'

'There aren't really boys like either of them. It's a girls' school with a mixed sixth form. Not a posh boarding school like Sophie's, but it is a private one. My gran left money for it, otherwise I couldn't go, because my dad lost his job.'

I feel bad, as if I've interrogated her, but Alice seems happy to talk. I hadn't realised until now how much I'd been feeling Holly's absence, even before I left for Aveney Park. The feeling of maybe having a close friend again makes me feel better, despite how worried we both were just a few hours ago. A few minutes, if you count Marcus's episode.

We've followed Mr Okonjo through the courtyard and around the house. It's so hot it's like the air's been microwaved. The plants in the flowerbeds by the back wall have ragged holes in their leaves. They must have been watered this morning, because the earth is covered in fat, glistening blobs. They're all sliding along in the same direction: a slug army. *Gross.* Plus, there are flies everywhere. It's bad enough inside, where every windowsill is covered with dead ones, but out here ... Everyone's flicking them away, but it doesn't do any good.

We walk across a big, sloping lawn dotted with trees. There's a post-and-rail fence running along the bottom and Mr Okonjo takes us through the gate to the deer park. There are a few big trees here, too, but mostly it's grass – scrubby, because it's only rained once in three months – with woods and a few buildings in the distance, like we saw on Captain Franchot's map. We're right at the back, and when we turn to look at the house I can see it's even more colossal and jumbly than I thought. With no colour, it looks like something out of an old horror film. There are loads of different bits of roof, sloping this way and that, with chimneys dotted about. At the far side of the main part there's a long brick wall and an arch with two huge wooden doors that looks as if it might be the entrance to a stable yard.

I'm squinting, trying to imagine how it must have been in the past, with colour – women in long dresses with parasols parading around, maybe, and guys on prancing horses – when Alice says, like she's been thinking about it for a while, 'Actually, there are horrible boys at my school, too. Maybe they don't show it all the time, but when stuff happens, like if anyone has sex, the boy tells everybody and the girl gets called a slut.' The way she says it, I know she's talking about herself. I want to hug her, only I can't because then she'll know I guessed.

Instead I say, 'That happens at my school, as well. One girl left, in the end.'

'It's not fair. When it was like ...' she gestures towards the house, 'the Victorian times, or whenever, at least it was just a few people – neighbours or the vicar or somebody – doing the shaming, but now stuff can go viral so it's a bunch of people who don't even know you, calling you names. I'm not saying Ryan would do that, just ... what's wrong with them, you know?'

'I don't think he's that bad. I mean, he did call Rosie a bitch for being mean to Cerys. I think he's just angry with the world.' That comes out a bit weird and breathless, and Alice gives me a funny look. 'I think we ought to catch up,' I add, quickly. Fortunately Sophie, who's at the back of the group ahead, spins round and yells for us to come on.

Even after we've caught up, I can feel the conversation we've just had hanging in the air between us. I can't think of anything to say, and we all trudge along in silence for what seems like ages, until Cerys, who's walking beside Sophie, suddenly says, 'What do you think blind people see?'

'Eh?' Alice gawps at her. I don't think it's so much the abrupt question as the fact that we've never heard Cerys speak unless someone spoke to her first.

'They don't see anything,' Sophie says, but kindly. 'Just darkness.'

I think I get what Cerys means. I'm also not sure Sophie knows what she's talking about. 'But darkness is a thing, isn't it? It's because there's no light, so it's ...' I have to think for a minute. 'Absence.' Greyness: I suddenly remember how it felt the last time Jake kissed me. 'That's a *thing*. What colour is nothing?'

'Transparent?' Alice offers. 'If that's the opposite of seeing.'

'It hasn't really got an opposite, though. I mean, silence is the opposite of noise, but silence is a thing. We know what it is. We don't actually know what not seeing *is*, do we? Sorry, I'm not explaining this very well. It's like ... well, if someone's in a coma, where are they? How can you be nowhere?'

Alice frowns. 'Like you can't imagine not existing, you mean.'

'So what colour is death, then?' asks Sophie. 'Black? White?'

'I bet it's like this.' Alice sounds gloomy. 'A load of grey empty space.' It reminds me of what I was thinking in the car on the way here, and how Mum said it was like the world had died. Cerys looks really worried – probably wishing she'd never said anything in the first place.

'I know what you mean, but it must be the same as the blindness thing – nothing doesn't have a colour, because it's just ... *not*.' As I say this, it occurs to me that, one way or another, I've been thinking about death quite a lot, recently. Instead of thinking about the future, which is what you're meant to do when you're young, although right now there doesn't seem much point. Except ...

How would it feel to kiss Ryan?

It would definitely have a colour. Excitable red, warm yellow, maybe even panicky orange. Or maybe all three.

A lot better than grey.

We're walking towards a bunch of outbuildings now: corrugated roofs and that rough concrete that looks like porridge, in a yard surrounded by what looks like a wire-mesh fence. Off in the distance I can just spot another fence, made of metal stakes like the ones I saw on the way here. I'm wondering if they go right round the whole estate when Alice says, 'I thought this bit was supposed to be a deer park, but I can't see any. I hope they haven't killed them all.'

Sophie, who's obviously a country girl – Hampshire and the horse – says something about culling, and the two of them start arguing. I look over at the digger standing by the buildings and imagine it scooping up dead fawns with pretty spots and huge, sad eyes. I don't know if it's that or the greyout or worrying about Mum or all of it at once, but it's like that little flicker of hope – the thought of kissing Ryan – is extinguished in a huge wave of despair. Suddenly I'm crying and can't stop. It's a good job that Alice and Sophie are into this big head-to-head about whether or not you should kill deer. It's not so obvious when people are crying if you can't see that their eyes are red, but all the same I hang back.

I duck behind a tree and take off my eyepatch, which is even more uncomfortable than usual because of being wet. I wipe my eyes and take deep breaths . . . And then I nearly jump out of my skin when someone puts a hand on my arm.

Cerys, looking more worried than ever. 'Are you OK?'

'Yeah.' I try for a smile, and it works, almost. 'Just . . . you know.'

'Are you worried about stuff at home?'

'A bit. I mean, it's OK here, but . . . yeah. My mum.'

'Me too.' Cerys stares into the grey distance for a moment, then says, in an even quieter voice than usual, 'My mum's not even *at* home. She sort of . . . lost it after my little brother was born – there's three of us – and now she's in hospital all the time. I'm the eldest so I help Dad with the boys and everything. He said I should come here, but he lost his job – it was a clothes factory – so we've hardly got any money. What I get from doing this will help, but I'm worried about how he'll cope, because I do most of the cooking and stuff.'

'That must be hard. How old are your brothers?'

'Eight and five. Too young to understand. It was bad enough before, but this . . . '

Her one-eyed stare is so forlorn. I can't think of a single thing to say that'll make her feel better, so I give her a hug. 'We'd better catch up before they get too far away.'

'Yes . . . And . . . ' Cerys taps her cheek. 'Eyepatch.'

'Right.' I put it on again.

'I hate mine. It's really—'

Whatever she was going to say is severed by a terrible scream, and we both start to run.

Twenty-Nine

The scream goes on and on, and it's coming from the outbuildings. I spot a bunch of people bending over someone on the grass. As we get closer, I can hear Mr Okonjo shouting to everyone to stand back, and when they do I see that it's Alice, curled up in a ball on the ground.

Rosie's got her hands over her ears, and everyone else is standing there looking really shaken and like they don't know what to do.

'Why isn't anyone helping her?' I run towards Alice, but Mr Okonjo grabs my arm and pulls me back. 'Do something!' I yell at him, but he just hangs on to me and won't let me get near. After what seems like ten minutes but is probably about thirty seconds, Alice stops howling, but she's shaking and gasping for breath like someone's just held her head under water. Even then, Mr Okonjo won't let me go to her, just keeps saying we have to wait for the medical staff.

I wrench myself away from him and spot Sophie, standing with her hand over her mouth, her visible eye huge with shock. 'What happened?'

'Electric fence.' She points to the strand of wire running along the top of the mesh. 'Marcus said he had an episode when he touched one, remember?'

'Yeah, an *episode*. But it's a fence, not two trillion volts, so it wouldn't be strong enough for . . . ' I look at poor Alice, who is still shaking. 'Nobody's *doing* anything.'

'Don't, Grace.' Sophie puts a hand on my arm. 'They'll sort it out. And Mr Okonjo pressed her button, so he obviously thinks it *is* an episode.'

'Drama queen.'

I look round: Ryan. Now he's *really* being a dick. And I just thought about kissing him. What's wrong with me? Disgusted with myself as much as him, I snap, 'Why don't you just shut up?' and turn my back on him before he can say anything. I'm half expecting him to get in my face, but it doesn't happen. Instead, there's an engine noise and a quad bike comes racing across the grass. When the rider stops and takes off his helmet, I can see Mr Virtanen's pale face. He kneels beside Alice and checks her pulse. I can't see what else he does, but she stops shaking.

I wish they'd tell us what's happening. I mean, it looked more like a fit than a normal colour episode. I think about the pills the nurses gave us, and how Sophie said Alice and I were being paranoid.

Rosie's crying, and several people have got that twitchy look and they're patting their pockets like they really want their phones so they can take pictures. They're as scared as I am, though, that's obvious. Only Ryan's staring down at the grass, hands in his pockets, like he doesn't care.

*

After about five minutes, Mr Virtanen looks up and says, 'She's going to be fine. Nothing to worry about.' Mr Okonjo herds everyone away and tells us that the ambulance is coming to take Alice back to the house. When I ask if I can just wait with her, he tells me to stop interfering, and his voice is tight. Then he says he's going to take us to where they've marked out a football pitch, and marches off with everyone trailing behind him.

I'm at the back by myself, trying to process what's just happened and feeling useless. I can't get rid of the image in my head of poor Alice, shaking and screaming. I should have done something. She must have been in so much pain. What if she isn't OK?

Don't even think that. Nobody's died from having an episode, and she will be OK. I push away the thought that I don't actually *know* that nobody's died, and mentally replay what Mr Okonjo just told us. The fact he said 'the' ambulance, not 'an' ambulance, must mean that they've actually got one here, which isn't exactly comforting. Unless it's for safety regulations – although, judging by the bolts on the fire door, they couldn't care less about those.

I was right about the ambulance; in a couple of minutes there's one bumping over the grass. It stops next to Alice, who is still lying on the ground by the fence. I can see Dr Seagrove and Dr Brown getting out, and in no time at all they've got her on a stretcher and are loading her in through the doors at the back. We're quite a long way away – I'm rubbish at distances, but it's got to be a hundred metres, at least – so it's hard to make out anyone's expression, but I catch sight of Dr Seagrove's face and I could swear he's smiling.

Thirty

I'm careful to keep out of Ryan's way as we go and look at the
football pitch, but everyone's on edge and nobody says much at
all. Marcus doesn't reappear at lunch (white fish that nobody wants
because it's covered in gluey grey sauce), and Dr Brown tells everyone he's resting. I suppose that's fair enough because you do feel
terrible afterwards, we all know that. But there's no explanation of
why Alice had such a bad reaction to touching the electric fence – if
that's what happened – and nothing about how she is doing.

I'm thinking that she must be in her room by now, so I go
upstairs as soon as we've finished eating, but she's not there. I
wonder if I ought to go back downstairs and ask Dr Brown if I can
see her, but I bet I wouldn't be allowed. Also, I don't feel like I want
to talk to anyone at the moment, so I just sit on Alice's bed. After
a bit, I pick up her special necklace and open the locket to look at
the photo. Her grandma's got flowers in her hair and her grandpa's
wearing a suit, so it must be from their wedding, years ago, when
no one even dreamt that anything like this could happen . . .

Seeing Alice's grandpa's big 1970s lapels makes me think of

Prune's wedding album. It fascinated me when I was eight or nine, although by that time she and grandpa had split up. I suddenly have this really sharp memory of him buying me an ice cream on a sunny day when I was very little, and how happy I was.

Somehow, that's the last straw. Everything's overwhelming, and I feel like I'm falling apart.

I sit on Alice's bed for ages, but no one comes to find me. You'd think they'd be checking up to make sure we're getting our schoolwork done, but apparently not. Then I remember how the fire escape goes right to the top of the tower and decide to investigate. That's right away from everybody, and, even though the weather is still super-hot, it has to be cooler up there than in a small, stuffy room.

The top of the tower is a big flat square, surrounded by battlements. It's quiet and there are no flies, which is great – but, whichever way I look, all I can see is a grey, flat expanse of land, which you can barely tell apart from the sky. There are a few combine harvesters and things dotted about the fields, but they don't seem to be moving. It's like staring into infinity: dull, empty space for ever and ever. When I lean over the battlements, it's a long, long way down, and for a moment I imagine myself falling and think of Sophie asking what colour death is.

Please let Alice be all right. I think about the two of us talking before breakfast, me saying, 'If it stops being OK, we can leave.' Given how incredibly important this research is and that they probably won't get it all right first time round, will I actually *know* if it stops being OK? Sometimes it's hard to know what 'not OK' even is. When Mum had her bad time I sort of got used to her being depressed and me worrying about her. The knot in my stomach never went away, and stuff like lying to Ms Kovacs about why Mum couldn't come to parents' evening started to seem normal. After Mum tried to kill herself, I had to go and see a counsellor, and he said it was like boiling a frog. Meaning, if you put a frog into boiling water – not that anyone would, unless they were totally horrible, but *if* you did – it would hop straight out again, but if you put it in cold water and heated it up slowly, the poor thing wouldn't realise the danger until it was too late. That was like me, because things with Mum didn't get weird all at once, but slowly. It's the same with plastic, because nobody realised for ages how much damage it could do. Which, when you think about it, makes the entire human race as stupid as that frog. Or actually more stupid, because we're supposed to know stuff like that, and frogs aren't.

Alice, though, and those tablets . . .

A soft grey mass in the corner catches my eye. It's a dead owl, slumped on the ground like it crash-landed. Beautiful, ash-coloured wings. I've never seen an owl up close before, and it seems so sad that it's dead – even worse than the other birds, somehow.

'Shouldn't you be doing your homework?'

As I whirl round, I get this weird plunging sensation in my chest, like the tower is a lift shaft and the cable just broke. Ryan is standing in the middle of the square, grinning, sure of himself. I wonder how long he's been there. 'Shouldn't *you*?' I snap.

He shrugs. 'Given up on school. What's that?'

'An owl.'

Determined not to show I'm rattled, I stand in front of it, ready to stop him if he tries to touch it, but he just looks and says, quietly, 'That's a shame. You upset about your friend?'

'My friend the *drama queen*, you mean?'

'Yeah ...' He doesn't look at me. 'Sorry. Don't know why I said that.'

It sounds genuine. 'It's OK.' I say it automatically, not knowing if it is or not.

He lifts his head, and suddenly I'm so self-conscious it's like I have to remind myself how to breathe.

'I saw you.' He's grinning again. His teeth are ever-so-slightly wonky, which is almost unbearably cute.

'Uh ... *Saw* me? When?'

'Both of you, last night. I was up here when the light came on. You were running back up the fire escape.'

'What were you doing?'

'Exploring. You?'

'Alice left something in the Games Room. We wanted to use the stairs, but the door was bolted on the outside. We went down the fire escape, only all the doors in the courtyard were locked.'

'They would be. There are bolts on our inside door, too.'

'Why?'

'They don't want us wandering around. Won't stop *me*, though.'

Now he's showing off, which makes me relax a bit. 'How come?'

'Ways and means.' He taps the side of his nose.

'But even if those doors weren't bolted, all the doors with

146

"Private" on them must be locked, and the soldiers probably patrol inside the house, too.'

'More than you know.'

'What do you mean?'

'Soldiers. You've only seen a few, right? But there's a couple of hundred, barely older than us.'

'Where?' I look over the battlements. 'I can't see anyone.'

'That big yard, next to the house. Converted stables.'

'How do you know?'

'I can climb, can't I? You can get all over the roof.'

'When?'

'Last night.'

'Didn't anyone see you?'

'Uh-uh.'

'But . . . why so many? If it's just to guard the place . . . '

'No idea. Look . . . ' He's beside me now, leaning over the battlements. I can feel the heat of his body, and have a sudden, tingly memory of how his arm felt when I touched it last night in the corridor. 'There's a car.'

He's right, there is: a big black one, smart-looking, like the car that brought me here, coming up the drive. It stops outside the front door and a man gets out. He's smart, too, wearing a suit. He stands there for a moment, looking around, and then someone with a bald head comes down the huge front steps to meet him.

'That's Dr Seagrove.'

'Yeah,' mutters Ryan. 'And look who's with him.'

It's Ms Anson, her arm around a girl's shoulders. As the girl gets into the car, she looks up, just for a second.

Sophie, without her eyepatch.

Ms Anson puts Sophie's bag into the back of the car. Dr Seagrove shakes hands with the man, who gets back into the car, and drives off.

I look at Ryan. 'What do you make of that?'

'What do you expect? Someone's trying to protect their precious daughter.'

'Protect her from what, though? And how did she get in touch with him?'

Ryan shrugs. 'No idea. But if you have a colour episode, you might want to keep quiet about it, that's all I'm saying.'

'Have you had one?'

He shakes his head in a way that could either mean he hasn't, or he has and he's not going to tell me. I'm about to ask him which when his fingers graze my arm – a tiny electric shock – and he says, 'See you later,' and disappears off down the fire escape.

Thirty-One

I stay put for a bit. If there was a colour for this feeling, it would be bright yellow – a sunburst inside my chest. And it's definitely not self-hypnosis, like it was with Jake, when I was flattered that someone so popular had chosen me. If anything, this is the opposite of that.

The glow of happiness doesn't stop me wondering why Ryan said to keep quiet if I have a colour episode. We've got no reason to think that Marcus isn't OK, and although Alice looked terrible, they got the ambulance to her really quickly.

Ryan didn't *seem* that bothered – not like he was upset, anyway. Perhaps that was just a pose, or him thinking that anyone in authority must have it in for him.

Maybe I am just being paranoid, like Sophie said.

Sophie, who didn't seem worried, but who's just climbed into a big shiny car with someone Ryan thought was her dad and been driven away. Why?

However I look at it, something just isn't right. Now, the prickling unease I felt before is jagged anxiety.

I've *got* to find Alice. I climb down the fire escape and try to find somebody who can tell me what's happened to her, but there's no one around. Eventually, I run into Ms Anson but, when I ask, she says that Alice is resting and Dr Brown's going to speak to us all later. When I mention Sophie leaving, she looks alarmed, then cross, and shoos me off to the library.

Nobody's working. Kareem's teaching Kieran to play chess, Rosie's reading a magazine, Cerys is staring into space and Treyshawn's sprawled in an armchair, dozing. Marcus isn't there – which is hardly surprising – and neither is Ryan.

'Sophie's gone.'

'What do you mean?' Kieran looks up from the board. 'Gone where?'

'I don't know. A car came and got her.'

'What car?' Rosie tosses the magazine aside.

'I'm guessing the guy I saw was her dad.'

The mix of yearning and envy on Rosie's face confirms what I thought at breakfast, but all she says is, 'How come?'

'I don't know. Ms Anson wouldn't tell me.'

Treyshawn opens his eyes. 'Weird.'

'What about Alice?' Cerys asks. 'Is she OK?'

'Ms Anson said Dr Brown would tell us later. Doesn't necessarily mean it's bad, but . . .'

We all look at each other like no one knows what to say. Kieran and Kareem lean over the chessboard, muttering to each other. Everyone looks confused, but not as panicked as I feel. I wonder if I'm overreacting, that what happened to Alice might have looked a lot worse than it was. I decide not to tell them about the conversation with Ryan because I don't want it to seem like it's me who's being a drama queen, and go back upstairs to fetch my school stuff.

In my room, I open the wardrobe and gaze at myself in the small mirror on the back of the door, seeing what Ryan saw. I don't know what I'm expecting, but I haven't changed since the last time I looked: the rat-coloured skin that's supposed to be olive, the patch and the one visible black eye that is supposed to be dark brown. The only thing that's the same as before – although messier, because I didn't bother getting a haircut – are the black corkscrew curls. But Ryan has never seen me any other way ...

Perhaps that's the thing. I think I look bad because I know what I'm supposed to look like.

Or I think I do. It's getting harder to remember. Just like Jake said, the new memories are covering up the old ones, like if you had a brightly coloured room and painted it over in grey.

We *have* to fix this.

What was it Alice said? *I want it so much I can't even let myself hope.*

I put my head round the door of her room, just on the off-chance, and it's empty. I mean, *really* empty. All her stuff – backpack, books, the necklace, everything – has gone. Like Alice was never there.

Panic rises in my throat as I shut the door and run back towards the library to tell the others. We *have* to find out what's going on.

I'm flying down the stairs that lead from our rooms to the second floor when the whole place goes dark. A nanosecond after that, there's a massive crash. Something big smashes through the skylight two floors up and plummets straight down on top of me in a hail of glass. I jump back just before it crashes onto the landing floor, missing me by a millimetre. A body.

It's like the world suddenly stopped, and me with it, and I can't move or do anything except stare.

A soldier, barely older than me. His eyes are wide open, but his shape is all wrong. He's tangled, like a puppet with the strings cut. Although I can barely believe what I'm seeing, I know, from the angle of his neck, that he must be dead.

When I look up I see, just for an instant, the silhouette of some-one leaning over the jagged hole in the skylight, black against grey. Then there's a single drop of blood – bright, glistening red – sus-pended in the air before it splashes down onto my face.

My head is agony, like someone poured acid into my brain. As I curl up to try and block out the pain, I can hear shouting and footsteps, more and more, until it's a solid wedge of noise coming straight towards me. I see a grey blur of faces with open mouths, yelling, and I'm yelling too, in pain or panic or fear or all three, and then—

Thirty-Two

I open my eyes. *What's happened?* All I can see is white. *Am I blind?*

I blink. No, not blind. White ceiling, quite low. Something stuck on it. Round, plastic. Smoke alarm?

Turning my head feels like a huge effort, but I manage it. I'm lying on a high, narrow couch. It's in a small space, with nothing but rows of grey cardboard boxes and a desk and a chair. In my hazy memory, it looks like Ms Anson's room but – I struggle into a sitting position – no Ms Anson. Just me.

Think back. Soldier's body, twisted on the narrow landing. A figure leaning over the skylight. Single drop of bright red blood. Falling down, down, down . . .

I had a colour episode.

Do they know?

Ryan's voice in my mind: *You might want to keep quiet about it.*

I can't hear any noise from outside, but the door is ajar so it's probably not a good idea to get up and start poking around. Plus, I don't feel exactly great and if Ms Anson finds me collapsed on the floor, she's never going to believe I didn't have a colour episode. I haven't decided if I'm going to take Ryan's advice yet. Just because you like someone doesn't mean they're right about everything. Although, given that we haven't had a chance to talk to either Marcus or Alice after their episodes, and Sophie's been taken away, keeping quiet seems like the best option.

That single red drop . . .

Mr Kowalczyk suddenly pops into my head – the terror in his eyes, the gun, the blood streaming down his chin and neck, bright and vivid – and I feel like I'm going to faint.

'How are you feeling?'

I must have fallen asleep, because the next thing I know Ms Anson is staring down at me. She's not looking so smiley and friendly now. Her eyes are hard, like dirty marbles.

'OK.'

'No, don't get up yet. Why didn't you press your button?'

I stare at her with what I hope is a puzzled expression.

'You had a colour episode, didn't you?'

'No.'

'You fainted.'

'It was the shock – the man falling. What happened to him?'

'An accident, that's all.' She says it like it's no big deal. Surely she's not going to tell me he got up and walked away?

'He's dead, isn't he?'

'That doesn't concern you.'

'Er . . . yes, it does. I *saw* him. It was horrible.'

Her eyes are boring into me like she's trying to see inside my head. 'It's important that you tell me what happened to *you*. You know that, don't you? You need to be honest. Have you had a colour episode?'

'No.'

'Are you absolutely sure?'

I'm starting to feel squirmy inside, like being six years old. 'I didn't.'

'You need to tell me. If you don't, we haven't any hope of finding a cure for this.' She takes my hand. 'It's important, Grace. I won't be angry. We're all in this together, aren't we? I'm just trying' – her eyes are soft now, I'm-your-best-friend stuff – 'to help you, so that you can help everyone else. Help the planet, before it's too late.'

That would have totally done it for me before, in spite of her being so cold about the poor soldier, but since this morning – plus what Ryan said on the tower – I'm not so sure. 'What's happened to Alice?'

'Is that why you're not telling me? Because you're worried about her?'

'Obviously, but I didn't have an episode.'

She stares at me. 'You must have done.'

'Why won't you tell me how she is?'

Ms Anson sighs, like I'm causing trouble and she's being really patient. 'She's going home.'

'When? Can I see her?'

'I'm afraid that won't be possible.'

'Can I phone her? I know it's not an emergency, but—'

'We're not allowed to give out phone numbers. The Data Protection Act—'

'You don't need to *give* me the number. You could dial it for me, and—'

'I'm sorry, but no.'

'But . . . ' I give up. 'Is she OK?'

'She's fine.' She squeezes my hand. 'You don't need to worry – but we will need to talk about your colour episode again tomorrow.'

'But I didn't—'

She holds up her hand to stop me, and says, briskly, 'I'll get you some dinner, and then you'd better go straight to bed.'

The alarm clock says half-past eight. After I'd eaten a few mouthfuls of the rice-and-sludge thing on the tray, Ms Anson marched me upstairs and waited while I undressed and told me not to leave my room until tomorrow. I noticed there's a board over the skylight, and the door on our landing was open, although I bet she bolted it on the way back down.

She said everybody had been sent to bed early. 'Enough excitement for one day' – like she was trying to make a joke of it – and it is dead quiet up here, so perhaps they're all asleep.

I lie awake for ages, wondering what to make of it all and whether I did the right thing not saying anything about the colour episode. I wish they'd explain stuff a bit more. Just because Alice is going home doesn't mean she's all right, whatever Ms Anson said. I didn't even get to say goodbye. I bet *they* can get around the Data Protection Act if they want to – they'd just say 'Emergency Powers', and it would be like *Expecto Patronum*.

What was the soldier doing on the roof, anyway? And I wish I knew if Mum is OK. It's all such a mess in my head . . .

I dream about the soldier, his body falling through the skylight in a slow-motion explosion of glass, and hundreds of drops of blood hanging in the air, shiny like crystals on a chandelier. The staircase becomes this rickety, Alice-in-Wonderland thing, turning round and round, a spiral in the middle of nothing, and there's a pattering, clattering noise, louder and louder—

It's not a dream. There's someone banging on the window.

Thirty-Three

That's not possible. I'm three floors up in a stately home and they probably don't even make ladders that long. But when I turn on the light and pull back the curtain, I see Ryan hanging on to something beside the window.

I can't believe my eyes, but I can't exactly leave him there, either, so I undo the latch and help him inside. 'How did you do that?'

'Drainpipe.' I step back as he jumps off the desk. He isn't wearing his eyepatch. *Stop staring, Grace.* 'My room's above yours.'

I want to ask him how he knows this, but I don't. 'You're soaked.' What a stupid thing to say. It's raining. Of course it is, I can *hear* it.

'No shit, Sherlock. Have you got a towel?'

I hand it to him, and he starts drying his hair. My hair always looks like an explosion when I've been asleep, so I comb it through with my fingers while he isn't looking.

Then he sits down on my bed, staring at me like he's expecting something. Two beautiful, wicked eyes. I suddenly realise that my t-shirt barely covers my knickers, and grab my bathrobe.

'Why are you here, exactly?'

'Treyshawn told me what happened to you on the stairs and I wanted to see if you were all right. I had to come that way' – he jerks his head at the window – 'because you can't open the fire escape door from the outside.'

I suddenly remember what Alice said – the shaming thing – and have this image of him telling the others he spent the night in my room. 'Right. Thanks. I'm fine, but you need to leave.'

'OK.' He puts his hands up, like surrendering. 'In a minute. I've got something to tell you.'

I glance at the clock. 'At half-past three in the morning?'

He shrugs. 'Couldn't sleep.' He ducks his head for a moment and I can see that, underneath the showing off, he's actually nervous, which is sort of cute. Plus, he was worried about me.

'OK.' I perch on the desk to keep a bit of space between us and – let's be honest – so I can carry on looking at him, wet t-shirt and all. 'Go on.'

'That soldier – he was blind.'

'Er . . . I don't know much about the army, but I'm pretty sure—'

'No, he *went* blind. On the roof.'

'How do you even know that?'

'I was there. I got out of a window, upstairs – like I told you, it's easy to climb up if you know what you're doing.'

'OK, but why was *he* there?'

He shrugs again. 'Exploring, same as me. A couple of them, messing about. They said they'd all volunteered – two hundred of them – because they get extra money. They're not Captain Franchot's guys, they're part of the greyout project, like us. Young squaddies.'

'You mean they have colour episodes?'

Ryan shakes his head. 'Two-legged rats, they called it.'

'So . . . what are they testing on them?'

'They don't know, but they got injections this morning. One of them reckoned it was something called . . . ' Ryan screws up his face, trying to remember. 'Omniscient, maybe? Something like that. Anyway, we're up there and this guy suddenly shouts out that he can't see. We thought he was joking, but he wasn't. He was staggering about, and then he lost his footing and . . . Well, you saw what happened.'

'Was it you, leaning over? I saw somebody else up there.'

'Yeah. I cut my arm.' He pushes up his sleeve to show me a large cut with a piece of loo paper stuck over it.

'I saw your blood. In colour.'

'Did you tell them?'

'No.'

'Good.'

'I don't think Ms Anson believed me, though. Did anyone see you up there?'

'Uh-uh.'

'Spider-Man. You're sure?'

'I told you.' Ryan grins. 'I'm good at this stuff.'

'What about the other soldier, though? You said there were two.'

'He's not going to dob me in and land himself in trouble, is he?'

'I guess. Did Dr Brown say anything about what happened to the soldier who fell through the skylight?'

'Said it was an accident – nothing about injections or tests.'

'Did you tell anyone else about him being blind?'

'Thought I'd keep quiet – for now, anyway. Better if *they* don't know we know. Anyway, then Dr Brown said Sophie wasn't suitable for the study' – Ryan sounds as if he doesn't believe this – 'and Marcus will be back with us tomorrow, but Alice has gone home. Oh, and Cerys had a colour episode when we were eating – red stained glass in the dining-room window – and they took her away, so I bet we don't see her for a bit, either.'

I think of Cerys asking me if I was OK and telling me about her family. 'Was she all right?'

'I think so. It was a normal one, anyway. Not like Alice.'

'Did anyone see Alice before she left?'

Ryan shakes his head. 'She'd gone by the time they told us.'

'Do you think she's going to be all right?'

Ryan looks past me, into the dark outside the window. 'I don't know.'

'Maybe she asked to go home.' I don't really believe this, but I want to see what Ryan thinks . . . Also, even if she *had* asked, surely she'd have wanted to say goodbye?

'Nah . . . Even if she had, I reckon they'd have talked her out of it.'

I remember Ms Anson guilt-tripping me about saving the planet. 'You're probably right. So maybe that means that she's not suitable for the study, like Sophie.' Ryan rolls his eyes. 'OK, *if* that's true about Sophie. Or, if it's not that, then . . . ' I think of Alice, shaking and gasping on the ground, and hear the echo of Dr Seagrove's voice in my head: *People like you are extremely unusual, and that makes you exceedingly valuable* . . .

So why let one of us – or maybe two of us – go?

Ryan's sigh is deep, like the sound is weighed down with stones. 'Look, I shouldn't have woken you.' He gets off the bed and leans across the desk beside me to open the window, so close that I can feel damp warmth from his clothes and skin.

'What was his name?'

'Whose name?'

'The one who fell.' I'm not sure why, but I need to know.

Ryan looks surprised. 'Lee. He was all right.' I shuffle out of the way as he climbs on the desk and puts one leg over the sill. Then he turns and says, 'You look nice with two eyes, by the way.' For a second, I don't understand, but then I realise I'm not wearing my patch, either. For a weird, awkward moment it feels like we're both naked, and I don't know where to look.

Then he climbs out of the window and disappears back the way he came.

As I turn off the light and get into bed, I feel dazed, dizzy almost, and it's a few minutes before I'm clear-headed enough for proper thinking.

Unless it's the world's biggest coincidence, whatever was in those injections must have blinded Lee. Ryan thought the soldiers said it was called something like Omniscient. Bet I could find it if I googled.

So frustrating.

I think about Alice and Sophie and Lee, round and round in circles, and don't come to any conclusions, and then I fall asleep, thinking about Ryan.

Thirty-Four

'I don't know what happened. Somebody said something about a blood test, and there was a needle, and then they gave me a pill and I can't remember anything after that.' Everyone's crowding round Marcus at breakfast, asking him what happened. I'm keeping my head down in case Ms Anson appears, but, so far, we've only seen Mr Okonjo, who's looking really stressed. Ryan's keeping quiet about yesterday, and he's apparently too busy talking to Treyshawn about bikes to even look at me. It almost feels like I might have dreamt him coming into my room, even though I know I didn't because I wiped his footprints off the sill this morning.

'Nothing at all?' Kieran asks.

Marcus shakes his head. 'I must have been asleep for hours.'

'That's normal,' Rosie says. 'What happened when you woke up?'

'Nothing. Ms Anson told me to go up to bed.'

'Where were you?' I ask.

'Ground floor. Somewhere near the nurses' rooms, because we went down that corridor and up the stairs . . . I'm not sure. I felt really out of it.'

We didn't see where they took Marcus because Mr Okonjo made us all go into the dining room, but I woke up in Ms Anson's room after I'd had an episode, so perhaps they put him in there, too. The injection sounds like it was to knock him out, so they could have done something while he was unconscious ... But wouldn't he *know* if he'd had some sort of operation? He'd feel sore, and there'd be stitches or whatever. 'How about now? Are you OK?'

'Yeah.' Marcus rubs his eyes. 'I think so. I've got this on my arm where the needle went in' – he rolls up his sleeve and shows us a dressing – 'but it doesn't hurt.'

'God, I hate this place,' Rosie says. 'I wish I could go home. It's not fair – Sophie and Alice did. They won't even let *me* make a phone call.'

Marcus asks her what she means about Sophie and Alice going home and everyone apart from me and Ryan starts talking over each other, explaining about that and about the soldier falling through the skylight. I'm still looking around for Ms Anson when Mr Okonjo returns and tells us that the Observations have been put back until mid-afternoon and we're free to go, so I decide to get out of there before she finds me.

I take my schoolwork up to my room and end up spending a totally useless morning worrying and unable to concentrate – but on the plus side I avoid Ms Anson, and she's not around when I go back down for lunch, either.

More revolting grey food. Ryan's chatting with Treyshawn again and doesn't even look in my direction. I finish as quickly as

I can and then, as I haven't walked round the outside of the whole house yet, that's what I decide to do.

Grey, grey, grey, even though the rain's stopped and it's stifling hot again. As I step into the courtyard, I spot a weird semi-circular shape in the sky and it takes me a moment to realise I'm looking at a rainbow: thin lines, like they've been drawn with a pencil, but sort of luminous. Rainbows usually make you feel happy, but this is more like some aliens have put a barrier up there to stop anyone flying away. As if the whole planet is one big, colourless prison.

I go through the garden door and walk along the path. It's overgrown on both sides and you can't see the lower part of the house wall, but there's enough light to spot that the ground is covered with huge, prehistoric-looking slugs. Some of them are eating each other.

I'm trying not to tread on them – difficult when you're trying not to look at them, either – when I hear footsteps and dive behind a clump of bushes in case it's Ms Anson.

I'm crouching down next to a dead wood pigeon, trying to ignore the mass of maggots squirming inside its breast, as the boots – several pairs, so probably soldiers – go by, when I spot the entrance to a cellar, almost covered by the undergrowth. When I'm sure whoever they were have gone, I creep towards it, but with all the trees it's too dark to see much. In spite of the heat, the stone steps are dank and slippery, and I bet, if I could see them properly, they'd be green, and the brick walls, too. I grope my way down, trying not to think about slugs and rats and whatever else. At the bottom, there's a mound of frilly white fungus that smells like decay and a wooden door with a sign saying 'KEEP OUT' in huge letters. The big iron hinges look old, but the padlock is much newer and looks flimsy, like you could undo it with a hairpin. I did that once with the lock on one of the sheds at home when Rusty lost his keys, but I haven't got a hairpin now. I'm also not sure what I'd find if I did manage to undo it, because it feels like no one's been down here for ages.

I scramble back up to the path. If Ms Anson is out looking for me, I'm betting she'll go towards the back of the house, so I do the opposite. She may not be trying to find me, of course. Perhaps she's busy with whatever's made them put off the Observations – we haven't seen Mr Virtanen or either of the doctors this morning, either.

I stand in front of the house, in the middle of the empty gravel drive, and look up at my window with the drainpipe alongside it, that Ryan must have climbed down.

So high up . . .

I'm suddenly ambushed by this feeling of missing Holly so much that it's all I can do not to cry. I wish I could talk to her and explain that this isn't some big, glamorous adventure, but confusing and scary and lonely and just plain *strange*. And tell her about Ryan being hot, of course – except I couldn't, because Jake.

Why is it all so *complicated*?

I suddenly remember what Alice said about the shaming thing and wonder if that's what Ryan was saying to Treyshawn at breakfast, because they couldn't have been talking about bikes for all that time, could they? He might have been saying he'd been in my room, making something up about what happened.

He wouldn't, would he?

But he'd obviously gone to the bother of finding out which room was mine, so . . .

I should have hugged Alice when she told me about that.

I really hope she's OK.

I feel so *alone*. I sit down on the steps leading to the front door. There's an ants' nest at the bottom, like a miniature volcano, so I stare at that for a bit and concentrate on trying to keep it together.

If Ms Anson wants to talk to me, she can come and find me. She'd seemed certain that Alice *was* OK, so she must either have seen that for herself, or Dr Seagrove told her. She'd been certain about me having a colour episode, too. I think about the way she stared at me. *You must have done.* But she couldn't actually *know* that, could she? Perhaps she just thought that if she insisted enough, I'd agree with her – though surely it would mess up the results of the study if she bullied me into saying I had one when I didn't?

I try to tell myself I'm making a fuss about nothing, that something this huge and important is bound to be complicated, but talking to myself like that doesn't work any more. Whatever happened to Alice might not be too bad, and Marcus is definitely OK now. But that soldier, Lee, is *dead*. And Ms Anson talked about it as if it were nothing. I remember the argument we heard, Professor Petrossian saying to someone she thought they were on the same team, but that was before anything happened to Alice or Lee, so . . .

What, exactly? Don't we all need to be on the same team for something like this? But I think about Ms Anson's eyes drilling into me, and Lee's body dropping through the skylight, and Sophie being driven away in that huge car, and it doesn't feel like we are.

Then I stare at the grey landscape and the trees with no birds and think about the slugs and the flies and the chemicals being pumped into the soil.

Help the planet. Help everyone. Before it's too late.

This is a good thing we're doing, isn't it?

It has to be.

Thirty-Five

'Want to go for a walk?' I must have dozed off for a moment because Ryan's standing in front of me and my heart thuds, stupidly, against my chest. He's wearing a hoodie in spite of the heat and looking pleased with himself. That better not be because he's been telling lies to Treyshawn, but it's not like I can ask. 'Something to show you. Come on.'

The eyes, the cheekbones, the teeth . . . He *is* gorgeous. And he's been kind. And, as far as I know, he's honest – and there doesn't seem to be so much of that about at the moment. I decide to give him the benefit of the doubt, at least for the time being.

A high chain-link fence topped with barbed wire runs along the edge of the wood. I know we're not supposed to be here, but right now I don't care.

There's a road on the other side of the fence, and fields beyond that, with pigs. 'Nice, aren't they?' Ryan says. 'Peaceful.'

I look at him, surprised. The pigs do look peaceful, wandering about and snuffling at the ground, but he doesn't seem like the kind of person who'd notice that. We watch them for a couple of minutes, and then he says, not looking at me, 'You OK?'

'I don't know.' I don't mean to say that, it's just what comes out of my mouth. 'I mean, I'm missing home, but it's not just that. It's ... everything, really.' *Including you*, I think.

'I'd miss home if my mum was still there, but ... ' Ryan turns to me, shrugging. 'You know.'

'When did she leave?'

'Last year. I don't blame her. She put up with my dad for long enough.'

I'm *really* surprised, because (a) he just said, out loud, that he was missing his mum and (b) he's being mature about it and not making her the bad guy. Now I'm thinking I was definitely being paranoid about him talking to Treyshawn about me. I remember the induction session. 'The gambling?'

Ryan rolls his eyes. 'And the rest. Do your parents get on?'

'Well, my dad's dead, so ... '

'Shit. Sorry.'

'I was six, so it was a while ago. I've always thought he and Mum would have been happy together if he was still alive, and everything would have been all right, but perhaps that's just wishful thinking.' Actually, I don't think that so much since Mum and I had that conversation, but I don't say so. I suppose it *was* good to get it out there, but I sort of wish she hadn't taken away my idea that their marriage was rock solid.

'Why did he die?'

'There was something wrong with his heart, but no one knew.'

I stare down at my feet hoping he's not going to ask anything else, because it feels too difficult to talk about.

'Poor you.' Ryan raises his hand as though he's going to touch my cheek, and for a horrible moment I think I might be going to cry. He's so close to me that I can feel his breath on my face, and now my heart is thumping so loudly I'm sure he can actually hear it. I frown and blink, determined not to let any tears out, as his fingers hover, the tips just touching my hair by my ear, very gently . . .

And then he hesitates and lowers his hand.

'Come on.' He jerks his head towards the trees. 'Let's walk a bit more.'

We keep going, but in silence. I'm thinking about what just happened and feeling pleased with myself for not crying, but wishing he'd kissed me. It was something and nothing at the same time, like one of those shades Mum used to paint rich people's houses, colours that couldn't make up their minds whether they were mauve or grey or beige or a bit of all three at once.

I'm starting to wonder if we're even allowed to be in this bit of the grounds when Ryan stops behind a massive oak. 'I found this.' He pulls up his hoodie and untucks something from the waistband of his jeans. It's a small radio, with wired headphones.

'*Found* it?'

'You know.' He grins and hands me an earbud, then puts the other one in his own ear. 'Thought you'd want to know what's going on.'

'. . . *The government's continuing refusal to put a cap on food prices has led to a second night of rioting in towns and cities across the UK, with more chaotic scenes as shops and supermarkets were looted and set alight. Thousands of troops have been deployed in an attempt to keep the peace, but the damage to property is extensive as, in many places, firefighters were not able to get to blazes in time to prevent them spreading. It is estimated that as many as thirty thousand people may have been left homeless after the first night of full-scale rioting, and there have been reports of attempts to take over empty properties in affluent areas. Two hundred and seventy people are known to have died, and over five thousand are reported as having been injured. In the nine weeks since the Monochrome Effect was first observed, the cost of basic foodstuffs has risen by almost two hundred per cent. Leading supermarkets have confirmed that they have been stockpiling dry and tinned goods for the last two months, and a government spokesperson conceded this morning that although talks about rationing are progressing, there is still considerable opposition from multinational food companies. The situation is set to worsen as the threat of total ecological breakdown continues – scientists estimate that one-third of all bird species have now become extinct – and similar riots have taken place across the world. Martial law has been declared in the following countries—*'

I can't listen to any more.

Masked figures throwing petrol bombs. Smashed windows. Desperation. Flames. Chaos.

And what about Mum and Prune and Rusty? Mr Zhang's house isn't in good enough shape for anyone to do more than camp in it, but still . . . I bet Rusty would do something stupidly heroic, trying to stop the intruders, and then—

'Worse out there than in here.' Ryan sounds like he doesn't care.

'What about your family?'

'My dad'll be OK. He'd join in. And my brother, wherever *he* is.'

'Don't you know?'

'He left home just after Mum went. His girlfriend was pregnant – she'll have had the baby by now.'

I look around me and imagine being born into a world without green grass or blue sky, and never having any sense of wonder at how beautiful a sunset or a rainbow can be. 'Not sure I'd want to bring a baby into this.'

'Me neither. Especially not with my brother for a dad.'

I take a deep breath and go for it. 'What about you?'

'Me?' Ryan looks baffled.

'Do you have a girlfriend?'

'Oh, right. I did, but we broke up.' He says it matter-of-factly, then laughs. 'Well, she dumped me. You?'

'The same . . . Actually, I think we sort of dumped each other.' It's weird, because that stuff is normally a big deal, even though people pretend it's not, but it honestly feels like it's totally unimportant and I don't know why I even bothered saying it. Ryan looks sceptical, so I decide to keep it simple. 'It was the greyout – like our feelings got lost in the fog or something.'

OK, so it's not the whole truth, but he nods like he knows what I mean. 'Yeah, that . . . You worried your mum's going to lose it again?'

I stare at him for a second, wondering how he knows, then remember I told everyone when we introduced ourselves. 'Yes, I am. And if they'll all be safe – what they said about empty houses in affluent areas.'

Ryan narrows his eyes. 'So?'

'No, not *that*. We're not rich or anything.' When I explain about where we live and why, Ryan nods like he gets it. Then, because I can't bear to think about what might be happening right now at home when there's nothing I can do, I change the subject. 'You know when you saw me and Alice go down the fire escape? We heard this argument when we were in the yard, Professor Petrossian and someone else – a man – and she said something about how they were meant to be on the same team. She sounded really upset . . . None of it makes any sense.'

Ryan looks thoughtful. 'Did you see Petrossian yesterday? I didn't – or this morning.'

'She's probably doing research.'

He raises an eyebrow. 'You think?'

I feel a flash of anger. 'I don't *think* anything. It's just all so *weird*. Like how nobody seems to care if we're doing school stuff or not.' It sounds lame but I can't quite say what I mean, how messed up everything feels now. 'I don't *know*, OK?'

Ryan takes a step back, hands held up like, *OK, chill.* 'Let's walk a bit.'

It seems as good an idea as anything, so I follow him. I'm glad he doesn't say anything else, because it all feels like too much at the moment, and my head's all over the place. We go back towards the fence and past a couple more fields with pigs wandering about, and then one where people have dumped stuff. There are tyre tracks in the gateway, puddles from last night's rain, and a heap of rubble: smashed-in televisions, old fridges and an office chair ... It's all grey and you can't tell what half of it is, except for being stuff that no one wants any more.

Maybe it's because I'm upset, but as I'm staring at it I start to get a warm, prickly feeling – not a headache, but actually quite nice.

'It's just junk,' Ryan says. 'Come on.'

'Wait.'

He gives me an intense look. 'Episode?'

'Maybe. Different, though – not hurting. I need to concentrate.'

I do, and then, like a miracle, colours start to appear before my eyes. Not just red, but all of them, pale at first, then brighter and stronger, like someone's turned up a dial inside my head: a yellow car door, a blue plastic milk crate, a red knob on a cooker, petrol rainbows shining in the puddles ...

It's so wonderful that I can't speak. Everything's bright and glowing, with the blue sky above and the leaves, red and gold, in drifts on the ground.

Out of the corner of my eye, I catch a quick movement in the trees. 'Look! A fox.'

It runs towards the fence, a ripple of russet fur. Then it must realise we're there, because it stops and looks up, one front foot slightly raised like it's asking a question. Its golden eyes are the loveliest thing I've ever seen.

Then Ryan gasps, and I know that he can see the colours, too. 'Magic.'

It's like we're the first two people who ever existed, and it's all been put there just for us.

Thirty-Six

I turn to look at Ryan: dark brown hair, tanned skin from the months of hot weather, and – my heart skips a beat – his uncovered eye is an astonishing electric blue. He's glowing, too, like he's lit up from the inside, like an angel or something.

'Take your patch off,' he whispers. I do, and he removes his at exactly the same time, so it's like looking into a mirror. 'You're amazing.'

'So are you.' I can't stop smiling.

We stare at each other for the longest time and I feel the colours sort of tingling all over me, like they're part of a spell. Out of the corner of my eye, I can see that the fox is watching us, not moving a muscle.

Then it turns and slinks away like it's remembered it's got somewhere to be. The colours start to fade, as if it's taking them away with it.

'No,' I whisper. 'Please don't go.' I feel so desolate and empty that I can't bear it. I'd forgotten how beautiful the world could be. The thought that none of us might see anything like that again, ever, is like all the sadness in the universe. My eyes prickle, and I turn away from Ryan and pretend I'm having trouble putting my patch back on. When I turn back, he's staring at the heap of rubbish, screwing up his eyes like he's willing the colours to come back.

'That was incredible – and it didn't hurt.'

'True.' He frowns. 'Maybe that only happens if you're stressing about something, or there's an accident or whatever.'

'We didn't press our buttons.'

'No.' The word cracks out like a whip, as definite as if he's slammed down a barrier between us. 'And we're not going to.'

'We have to. I know what you said before, and I get it, but if it means other people can see what we just saw – I know it's all been a bit crazy, but we've got . . . I don't know, a duty, if we can help them—'

'Do you want to end up like Alice?'

'We don't know how Alice ended up, Ryan. That's the point.'

'We know what happened to Lee. He *died*, remember?'

'That was an accident. Not going blind, but he shouldn't have even been on the roof. None of you should. And you heard what they said on the radio, about the food prices, and the birds – and what about your brother's poor baby, who'll never—'

'It's too risky. We don't know what's going on.'

'Ryan, we have to!'

'No!' Before I can stop him, he grabs my lanyard, yanks it up and over my head so hard that I nearly lose my balance, and hurls it over the fence.

'You idiot!' I stumble away from him, but he catches up almost immediately and gets hold of my arm. 'Get *off*!'

'You can't tell them.' We're staring at each other again, only now he looks dangerous, eyes like steel, like he's capable of anything. I suddenly realise I've only got his word for what happened on the roof: for all I know, Lee wasn't blind at all, and they got into a fight and Ryan pushed him through the skylight. He nicked the radio, too, and he's probably taken other things as well, and – no matter how nice and sympathetic he seems to be towards me – I'd be an idiot to trust him about anything.

'Leave me alone.' I glare at him. 'I'm going to tell them whether you like it or not.'

'You can't!'

I don't wait to hear what he's got to say next. I'm running, fast as I can, back to the house.

There's no one in the nurses' or doctors' rooms, so I take the stairs two at a time and pelt around the endless grey corridors, trying to find the staff wing. By the time I get there, my lungs feel like they're about to burst.

The big wooden door is ajar. I knock, but no one answers, so I give it a little push, thinking I'll go inside and wait. I don't think Ryan's followed me up here, but I shut the door behind me anyway. This is so much more important than him – I've got to do what's *right*.

The first door off the hallway is a sitting room. It's big, with a high ceiling, a grand piano and a huge bookcase with shelves behind glass and a cupboard underneath. I stand in the middle, trying to catch my breath and feeling like I don't want to touch anything in case I break it. I don't want to sit on any of the chairs, either, because they've got a stately home sort of look, like they should have ropes across to stop people putting their common modern bums on them. In fact, the only thing that makes the room look different from a stately home is a bunch of X-ray-type things laid out on the glass-topped coffee table. They look like giant grey walnuts, so they must be brain scans – ours, I guess.

There's a row of silver-framed photos on the mantelpiece: men in suits, looking pleased with themselves. I suppose they must belong to the benefactor Dr Brown told us about, who lent this house. I guess he or she didn't bother removing them because they aren't valuable, unlike the paintings and books.

I spot a guy who looks a lot like Mr Kowalczyk in one of them, and go over for a closer look. It is him, standing with a bunch of other men in suits in front of a board with different company names on it. I recognise Kerr + Bell's cross-inside-a-bell logo, too. Mr Kowalczyk was a businessman, so maybe he ran it, or one of the other companies.

Right across the top of the board, over all of the other names, is the word 'Omnisant'. Which is somehow familiar.

Why, though?

Then I remember what Ryan said the soldier said.

Not Omniscient but *Omnisant*. Not a substance, but the name of the company that owns it.

Just as I pick up the photo for a closer look, a noise from somewhere outside makes me jump, and the frame slips out of my hand and crashes onto the hearth.

I freeze. No one comes in, so it must have been somebody passing the outside door. That means I'm safe for the time being, but the glass on the photo is broken into three pieces. I shuffle the other photos along so there won't be a gap, and look round for a bin.

There isn't one. I can't just leave with the pieces because my pockets aren't big enough and someone might see. The only place I might be able to hide them is the cupboard underneath the bookshelves.

There's a little key in the lock, and when I turn it, both doors come open. One side's got empty shelves, so I push the evidence right to the back of the bottom one, where it's too dark for it to be spotted. There are no shelves on the other side, and most of the space is taken up with something big and cement-coloured, made of leather: a backpack. It looks familiar, and, when I open the pocket on the side, I can see a silver necklace at the bottom, with a locket.

Wherever Alice has gone, she hasn't taken her things.

Thirty-Seven

Ryan was right.

I shouldn't tell anyone, and I need to get out of here, *now*.

My hands are shaking as I zip the pocket up again and shut the cupboard door on the backpack. I feel unsteady as I scramble to my feet, like I'm on a boat. The walls are moving, in-out-in-out, like the room is breathing, and suddenly the carpet – dark grey before – is a red wave that rears straight up into my face and knocks me backwards.

The brain scans on the coffee table are neon – red, blue, yellow, green – pulsing with light. All the colours in the room are bright and violent, like they're shouting into my face.

Next thing I know I'm curled up on the carpet and there are feet in dark shoes coming towards me. When I look up I can see a whole person, but the colours of the flesh and clothes are melting into each other so they're like a moving smear of paint . . .

I can't breathe, let alone speak. Is this what happened to Alice? Will they take me away, too?

Eyes are coming towards me now, closer and closer. They must be attached to a face, but I can't see it, only two gigantic dark holes, so near that they merge into one, swallowing me so that the whole world goes black like someone turned it off.

White again. Ceiling?

Sounds. Not me, someone else.

Head feels like a rock on top of my neck. Need to turn it and look.

The colours are gone.

I'm not on an examination couch this time, but a bed. Rails at the sides. Hospital?

Trolley. Drip stand. But no nurses or machines with dials. No sheet or bedcover. I'm still dressed in my t-shirt and jeans, but my eyepatch has gone.

Think back. The red carpet, like a giant wave, the colours flashing and pulsing, the melting figure, the enormous dark eyes . . .

Episode. But I didn't press my button.

I had an episode before. The rubbish dump. Ryan. The fox. The *colours*.

Wait.

Don't have a button. Ryan threw it over the fence, and I ran back to the house.

In the staff wing . . . Backpack. Necklace. Alice.

I should have listened to him.

Marcus came back OK.

Marcus came back OK.

Marcus came back OK.

I have to keep telling myself that.

A white coat appears in my eye-line, and then, as its wearer bends down, a face: Ms Anson. Which must mean I'm still at Aveney Park.

'What's happening?' The words come out as a croak.

'You had a colour episode.' Her voice is brisk and efficient. 'No, don't bother denying it. How are you feeling?'

'Not great. Can I sit up a bit?'

'If you like.' She presses a button at the side of the bed to make the top part more upright.

'Thanks.'

No window. That, and the fact that the ceiling's quite low, must mean that I'm below ground level.

Marcus said he was somewhere on the ground floor when he woke up, but that doesn't mean he wasn't somewhere else before that.

'We took a blood sample,' Ms A says. 'We need to do it straight after an episode.'

When I look down, I spot a small round plaster on my arm. 'How long have I been here?'

'Only a few minutes. You were brought here as soon as Dr Brown found you.'

So that's who it was.

'What were you doing in the staff wing? It's out of bounds.'

'I was trying . . .' Think, Grace. 'I wanted to tell someone I'd lost my button.'

184

'We noticed. How did you manage that?'

'I'm not sure. We were messing around outside, doing hand-stands, and it must have fallen off and got lost in the long grass.'

She narrows her eyes. 'We'll get you a new one. Try and look after it this time. How did you get into the staff wing?'

'The door was open.'

'Really?'

That typical grown-up logic of swallowing a lie and not believing the truth. '*Yes*. How else could I have got in? It's two floors up.'

Ms Anson ignores this and checks my pulse with cold fingers. 'Did you do anything else?'

She raises her head, eyes beady. 'How do you mean?'

'While I was . . . out.'

'As I said, it's only been a few minutes. We kept you under observation.'

'Is that all?'

'What else would there be?'

'I don't know.'

That fits with what Marcus said. Which means that the next bit must be the sleeping pill. Perhaps it's one that makes you forget stuff. That's definitely a thing because Mr Grice told us in a science lesson, when someone asked a question about anaesthetics.

'I'll be back in a moment.'

Maybe I should just swallow the pill. If they *are* going to do some sort of operation, I'll be in agony, so there's no way I'll be able to just lie here . . .

But if I'm unconscious, I'll never find out what's going on.

I remember me and Jake sitting on our bench on the heath, and me saying that we had to trust the scientists because we had to trust *someone* – although I'm not sure why we ever imagined that adults would take care of stuff, given the way they've messed up the planet.

But those beautiful colours. The memory of them is so fresh now. Anything that brings them back again has to be good, doesn't it?

The problem is, I don't trust anyone here.

Footsteps. Ms Anson's coming back.

'Right. I need you to make a fist.'

A needle and a syringe. I think Marcus mentioned a needle, but not what they did with it – whether it was an injection, or . . . *Ow.*

Sharp scratch, near my elbow.

Ms Anson hands me a glass of water and a doll-size paper cup with a white pill inside.

The syringe looks empty, so she's obviously not going to fill it with whatever it is until I'm out.

Marcus came back OK.

The endless, deadening greyness. The dead owl by the battlements.

The fox's golden eyes. Ryan's, electric blue, unbelievably gorgeous. So much beauty.

Yes or no?

It's not like I trust Ryan one hundred per cent, but . . .

But he was right. We don't know what's happened to Alice, but it can't be good, otherwise she'd need her things. She wouldn't leave that necklace, given the choice.

'Hurry up.' Barked; a command.

That does it. Here goes nothing, as Mum would say.

I put the pill in my mouth, work it under my tongue and take a gulp of water so she'll think I've swallowed it.

I lie there, hoping the thing won't dissolve before I get the chance to spit it out, and trying to look relaxed and dopey. I've no idea how quickly it's supposed to work, but I don't want to make her suspicious. I count to one hundred in my head, then close my eyes.

I can hear Ms Anson moving round the room, and then the sound of something being wheeled towards me. Apparatus – but for what? I can feel Ms Anson's breath as she bends over me, checking, but I will myself to stay quite still.

Then she steps back. She's fiddling with something, and there's a slight tugging feeling so I think she must be attaching something to the syringe. It's a bit uncomfortable, but not much; a small, dull ache. Would I be able to *feel* if something was going into my vein? If I'd ever had an operation I'd know this stuff, but I haven't.

Ms Anson walks off again, and this time the sound of her footsteps changes, which means she must have gone outside the room – and then she closes the door behind her.

I count to one hundred again, then open my eyes and spit the pill down the neck of my t-shirt.

*

JAMIE COSTELLO

The syringe is attached to a long dark tube, which is threaded along the rail at the side of the bed and goes down to somewhere I can't see without moving.

Goes *down* . . . Nothing flows uphill. That means whatever's in there isn't going *into* me, but coming *out*. Of course. And it's not the tube itself that's dark, it's what's inside it.

Blood.

Thirty-Eight

Blood. I open my eyes wider, then shut them again, a little queasy. That's OK, isn't it? Lots of people give blood. Half a litre at a time, I know from Prune. It looks scary, travelling away from me like that, but it's nothing to worry about. *Nothing. To. Worry. About. Just stay calm and don't move.*

I feel clammy and sweaty, but not dizzy or anything – although perhaps I would be if I stood up. I wonder how much blood Ms Anson's going to take. I can't tell how long I've been lying here – time seems to be speeding up and dragging, all at once. It doesn't seem to take long when Prune goes to donate. But Marcus didn't come back for a whole day, so perhaps there's something else, as well.

Maybe that's the thing that hurts.

No. Stop. Think about something else.

Police with riot shields and batons. Soldiers. Trashed supermarkets. World on fire.

Mum. Prune. Rusty. What if they get hurt? I think of how Mum

189

looked after she tried to kill herself, lying on a bed in A&E, frail, like she was made of paper. She promised me she wouldn't do it again, but . . .

I should have swallowed that pill.

But, but, but.

Alice. What Ryan said. All of the secrecy. And Lee going blind and dying and Sophie leaving. And Mr Kowalczyk, the fear in his eyes . . . But I don't even know if that's connected.

Ms Anson's back.

There's a scraping noise – chair legs – quite close to me, and a soft bump as she sits down. Rustling, like pages, so perhaps she's reading.

How much blood can one person lose?

Marcus came back OK.

Marcus came back OK.

Marcus came back OK.

After a long time – half an hour? Forty-five minutes? – I hear Ms Anson get up and start fiddling with something on the other side of the room. I turn my head ever so slightly in the direction of the noise, and risk opening my eyes. I'm feeling faint now, and the room looks hazy, but I can see she's got her back to me, bending over something on the trolley.

Then something near the bed starts beeping and I close my eyes again just as she's turning around to look. She's coming back towards me – closer, closer . . .

Relax. You're supposed to be unconscious.

I can feel her breath on my arm. She's touching the tube, and I feel pulling on my skin and she's going to take the needle out and it's going to hurt and I've got to keep still and relaxed and not tense up so she doesn't realise I'm awake and—

No. She's not taking the needle out. It feels like she's fiddling with the tube that's attached to the syringe.

She steps away from me. The noise is coming from somewhere behind my head, so she must be doing something to whatever the blood was going into.

Now she's fussing with my arm again, attaching something else to the syringe. Is this what's going to hurt?

Don't look. Don't move. Don't pass out.

Another sound, further away. The door opens, and then I hear Dr Seagrove's voice. 'Are you ready?'

Ms Anson bumps against the bed as she turns – and then I hear her walking across the room towards him ... And the door closes.

One, two, three, four ... No pain so far. Keep it together, Grace. Five, six, seven, eight ...

When I get to twenty, I open my eyes. Still no pain. There's another tube – also dark – attached to the syringe, but this time it's going upwards. Which means that whatever's in it is coming downwards, so it must be *going into me*. I crane my neck round to see a bag hanging from a drip stand, with something dark inside. There's a label with a barcode and some writing that's too small to read, except for one big letter: O.

*

That can't be my blood, packaged and labelled like that, so it must be from a blood bank. That means I'm having a transfusion.

No sound coming from outside, so perhaps I can risk lifting my head to have a proper look around.

Bad idea. I'm so weak I might as well be made of cooked spaghetti. Leave it for a minute or two.

Think. Blood out, blood in. I reckon that my blood, and Marcus's – and Cerys's as well, because she's probably down here somewhere – is interesting enough for them to want enough of it to have to give us some back. That must mean our bodies are changing our blood in some way. How, though? I really, *really* should have paid more attention in biology lessons.

OK, save that one for later.

Bit more counting, and then I'll have another go at lifting my head.

O ... K. OK. Better this time. I can do this.

Concentrate. Drip stand, chair and trolley beside the bed. Looks like there are several bags of blood hanging off the side of the trolley, so they must be having to replace quite a lot.

What else is on there? If I can move my head round jee-ust a bit more ...

Plain cardboard boxes. Those are probably medical supplies of some sort. A few paper towels, and ... a *newspaper*.

Must be Ms Anson's. Guessing the staff aren't allowed electronic devices, either. I manage to make out the headline: **SCIENTIST**

DEAD IN CAR ACCIDENT. Next to the article is a large photo of someone's face. I can only see the top half, but the eyes and the frizzed-up dark hair with the zigzag lightning streaks are familiar enough: Professor Petrossian.

Thirty-Nine

A senior professor of ophthalmology has been found dead after apparently losing control of her car, which veered off the road and struck a tree on Hampstead Lane, north London. Professor Anne Petrossian, 55, had worked as a consultant to global pharmaceutical giant Omnisant but resigned yesterday, in confidential circumstances. The accident is assumed to be the result of the Monochrome Effect, and no other vehicles appear to have been involved.

That, and today's date and another headline – **TOXIC CROPS: Public health warning over increased pesticide use** – are all I can see, and leaning forward and twisting my head round to read even that much makes me feel dizzier than ever. I'm sure there's not a chance Ms Anson would have left it on the trolley if she thought there was any risk of my being awake enough to spot it.

Omnisant again.

OK, so Professor Petrossian could have been driving in north London for a million reasons, but given that people still aren't supposed to drive unless it's for something important, she must have thought it was essential.

I imagine her crushed against the steering wheel, Bride-of-Frankenstein hair in a wild halo around her head and eyes wide open in terror. Hampstead Lane is really near where I live and – way more important – where Mr Kowalczyk lived. Maybe she didn't know he was dead because it wasn't reported, and she was on her way to see him. Even if they weren't friends, she must have known who he was because she worked for Omnisant. I'm sure that photo upstairs was Mr K, and that Omnisant are supplying stuff for this study – maybe even this big, no-online-presence house – to Dr Seagrove and co? And if that's true, why are they keeping it secret?

When big companies sponsor things and do charity stuff, they want everyone to know. If they're trying to save the planet, why aren't they yelling about it as loudly as they can?

OK, so the research itself is confidential, but this is a REALLY BIG THING.

Professor Petrossian had an argument with someone, and she resigned.

Now, she's dead.

I'm certain there won't be an investigation into the car crash, because there are hundreds of accidents like that since the greyout and not enough people to look into them. I close my eyes in case Ms Anson comes in suddenly and think back to Professor Petrossian in that meeting the night we arrived, when Dr Seagrove asked her if there was anything she wanted to say. For a minute, it had seemed like she was going to tell us something . . . Or perhaps I just think that now because of everything that's happened since. Or maybe because I know I won't be able to ask her anything again. But she definitely did say something about how they were keeping an open mind and learning from us.

Maybe that's what the argument was about: Dr Seagrove and Dr Brown had already made up their minds about how people could get their colour vision back. Or maybe Professor Petrossian didn't like the idea of using the soldiers for testing, or—

Wait a minute.

Testing.

Lee and his mate told Ryan they were getting injections of something they thought was called Omniscient – or Omnisant. What if it was our blood, or something *made* with our blood? Would that make sense? Dr Gupta told Mum and me that I was getting colour episodes because my brain has more . . . urgh, *something* . . . Anyway, because it's more able to change and recover than an older, stiffened-up brain. And if what's causing the trouble in everyone's brains are the pathogens or toxins or whatever they're called, then that must mean my brain is starting to try and repair itself because of something in my blood, which must mean . . .

Urgh. Come on, brain. Biology lessons, remember?

Right. White blood cells. There are several types . . . *and one of them produces antibodies, which attack invading bacteria, viruses, and toxins.*

Maybe that's it? It *would* make sense. And if you gave some of our antibodies to other people, then *their* brains might be able to repair themselves, too.

Which is great, but what if Professor Petrossian didn't have a car crash? And even if *that* was an accident, why tell us Alice went home when her bag is still here? And why don't they want us to know that they're taking our antibodies?

It's boiling a frog again. The ends justifying the means, and the fact that none of those things might be important by themselves. There could be a good explanation for any single one of them, but when you add them all up . . .

Footsteps.

Forty

I manage to look floppy and unconscious as Ms Anson hooks up the second bag of blood, and I repeat the same trick when she comes back to do the third one, and the fourth. I reckon that makes about two litres, which must be the same amount as they took out.

I haven't reached any conclusions about what's going on, either. It's like a huge maze in my head. Every time I think I'm getting somewhere, I hit a dead end.

Finally, and not a moment too soon because I'm starting to want to pee, it's finished. I nearly give myself away when whoever it is – I'm guessing Ms Anson – takes out the needle, but I cover it up with a moany noise, like I'm still out of it.

Whoever it is puts a dressing on the needle mark and then wheels my bed out of the room. I don't dare open my eyes but I'm guessing we're in a corridor – bumpy, like it's flagstones – and we stop and go into somewhere that must be small, because I can feel that somebody is squeezed up close to the bed . . .

We go up.

Then down another corridor – smoother floor – and a slight bump as we go through a door.

More footsteps. Voices, getting closer.

'Thank you, Sarah. Give us five minutes, will you?'

Dr Seagrove's voice. He must be talking to Ms Anson. Sounds like there's someone else in here, too . . .

Say something.

Faint pattering and clicking noises, like someone typing.

'Another fifty million or so.' That's definitely Dr Brown. What's he talking about?

'Nick, *please* . . .' Dr Seagrove sounds tired, like it's the end of a really long argument.

'I'm really not happy about this.'

'They signed a *contract*, Nick.'

'Yes, without knowing *what* they were signing. Cole's lawyers—'

'That contract should never have been shown to them! Sophie and her mother signed the same non-disclosure agreement as everyone else. It's just unfortunate that they did it without informing Mr Cole.'

What are they talking about? Sophie's surname is Cole, so it must be her dad. *They spend all their time scoring off each other and trying to weaponise me . . .* So they're in the middle of a messy divorce and Sophie told me she was at her mum's when she fell off her horse and had the colour episode. Which means . . . that neither Sophie nor her mum told her dad that she'd signed up to come to Aveney Park – but Sophie obviously thought it best to phone *him* when she wanted out. Guessing that's because Mr Cole, who seems to be pretty rich, would have gone ballistic and started pulling strings left, right and centre – and whoever let her make the phone call must have known there'd be trouble if he discovered where Sophie was and found out she'd been prevented from contacting him. And of course, once he knew what was happening, he'd have insisted on seeing the contract.

'We should have vetted the subjects more carefully.'

'For God's sake, Nick! These kids are as rare as hen's teeth.'

'There were at least six younger ones we identified.'

'Who would have had to be accompanied by an adult! It just wasn't practical.' Dr Seagrove is sounding really agitated now, and it's getting difficult to keep dead still with my eyes closed so near to this amount of tension.

Someone – I'm guessing Dr Brown – lets out a long sigh. 'Remember when we made the breakthrough? I thought . . . Well, never mind what I thought – but I certainly never thought that three years later we'd be *doing* this.'

Three years? That was way before the greyout. What did he mean? And it sounded like Dr Seagrove hadn't wanted the younger subjects – the ones Dr Brown told me at Dr Gupta's surgery didn't even *exist* – because the adults with them might have started asking awkward questions . . . And Dr Brown had said something about fifty million – what was that?

Silence now – just more keyboard action. After a couple of minutes, there's the sound of a chair scraping back.

'Looks fine.' Dr Seagrove again. 'We can talk about this later.'

Dr Brown must be hanging back, because Dr Seagrove says, 'Come on,' and then they leave.

'Grace? Can you hear me?'

Ms Anson's in the room again. Better not answer too quickly, in case she gets suspicious.

'Grace?'

'Mmm ... ?'

More footsteps: two people moving around.

'Should be wearing off now.' Mr Virtanen's voice.

I flutter my eyelids and do this whole groggy act, which obviously works because they're looking at me like it's all normal.

'Let's get you upstairs. There'll be some dinner in your room.'

I don't recognise the place, but when they let me get up, which takes a bit of time because my head feels light as a balloon and everything's spinning, and we go out of the door, I can see we're in the ground-floor corridor where the doctors' and nurses' rooms are. Which means that the big door that I thought was a storeroom must be the lift.

Ms Anson gives me a new button – 'Don't lose it this time' – and then she and Mr Virtanen walk me up the stairs, one on either side like I'm an invalid, and stand right outside the door while I use the loo. It's quarter to eleven, according to the alarm clock in my room, and pitch-dark outside. After I eat the food (more rice-and-sludge, plus an oozy block of grey ice cream which could be almost any flavour), they tell me to get some sleep.

After they've gone, I wait a bit then stick my head out of the door to check there's no one still around.

All clear, so I tiptoe shakily down the corridor to the kitchen. Perhaps there's a broom in one of the cupboards with a handle long enough for me to reach out of my window and bang on the one above.

I need to talk to Ryan.

Forty-One

'... and I *know* this is an experiment, so there are bound to be problems, and *of course* I want it to work, but there's a big difference between *some* stuff going a *bit* wrong and a *lot* of stuff going *massively* wrong, and I'm sorry I called you an idiot—'

'It's OK, Grace. Slow down.' Ryan's sitting on my desk. I was so relieved when he climbed down the drainpipe after I bashed the broom on his window that I've been gabbling at him for five solid minutes, about finding Alice's backpack and the blood transfusion and Professor Petrossian and Omnisant and everything. 'Come here.'

I step into his arms. He slides off the desk and hugs me. I hug him back, not thinking about what I'm doing, just doing it. We don't speak or move and it feels warm and comforting and perfect, and I wish it could go on forever, but now isn't the time so I gently disengage myself. 'The thing is, we're all meant to be in this together, right?' I realise this sounds lame the moment it comes out of my mouth, but I'm so confused. 'That's what Dr Seagrove said.'

'Yeah, right.' Ryan hops back on the desk again, rolling his eyes.

'All in it together, like always. Cerys hasn't come back, in case you were wondering. She's probably gone the same way as Alice.'

'What do you mean? Do you really think Alice is . . . ?' I can't bring myself to say it.

'Sorry, I shouldn't have said it like that. But we don't know yet so there's no point going there. I've been thinking about us having the colour episode at the rubbish dump, both at the same time. Weird, right? I reckon you were right about those "vitamins" not being vitamins. You know, when Sophie said you were being paranoid. I think it *is* something to speed up the colour episodes, and people got given different amounts – but we got the same, which is why we reacted at the same time.' He grimaces. 'I know, so much for magical moments, but that makes more sense. Also, what you just said Dr Seagrove said about the contract . . . Have you got a copy?'

'In here. And it *was* totally magical.' I say this while I'm bending down to search in my bag, so he can't see my face. 'But Dr Brown said none of us knew what we were signing, so I don't suppose we'll be able to understand it properly.'

I put it on the desk and we stare at it, but all I can see is a bunch of legal phrases and I don't have a clue what they mean. Then I spot something that seems to make sense. 'Wait, what about this – "Retention of material with your consent for medical research or other use at their discretion absolutely . . ."'

'So they can do whatever they want with it.'

'"To be preserved for three months or such other time as the party of the first part—"'

'Who's that?'

'I think it's what it says at the top . . . There. "The government and affiliated bodies or agencies." Bet that means Omnisant. Anyway, "such other time as the party of the first part may determine." And it's the same about the length of the study, look – "six weeks or for such other time . . ." blah, blah, blah.'

Ryan blinks. '*Such other time*. That could mean any amount of time – like, forever.'

'Yeah . . . You'd think they'd have put "a reasonable amount of time" or something like that. I know absolutely zero about law, but—'

'Hang on. Does that mean they *own* our blood?'

'Sounds like it. They can do whatever they want with it for as long as they want, and they can continue the study for as long as they want. And they can't have our blood without *us*, so . . .'

'So, they own us.' Ryan shakes his head in disbelief. 'Is that even legal?'

'They've paid us, haven't they?'

'That was for taking part in the research programme.'

'Bet they'd say it was the same thing. And as for "legal", even if it isn't – and I'm guessing that either Sophie's dad's lawyers found a loophole or he's rich and powerful enough for it not to matter – they can always say it's under Emergency Powers, can't they? That can mean *anything*.'

'I bet Sophie's dad's got shares in Omnisant. Either that or they'll give him a shedload of money to keep quiet about what's been happening here.' Ryan slumps down on the bed and stares at the floor.

I stare at him.

What Dr Brown said: *Another fifty million.*

Of course.

Money. Why hadn't I thought of it before?

People like you are extremely unusual, and that makes you exceedingly valuable.

Makes us . . .

Worth millions. Literally.

The realisation is like being drenched in iced water, and I must have shown it, because Ryan says, 'You OK?'

'I think I know what's going on.'

'Well, *yeah.*' He gives me a sarcastic grin. 'What's going on is we're screwed. We've been tricked into selling ourselves to Omnisant for peanuts, and they're going to turn our blood into a national resource.'

'That's the whole point. They're not.'

'But you just said—'

'No, *listen.* I've just realised why Dr Brown was arguing with Dr Seagrove, and what Professor Petrossian meant about not being on the same team. They're not going to use our antibodies to *give* colour vision back to people, Ryan. They're going to *sell* it.'

Forty-Two

'*What?*' Ryan's eyes are like saucers.

'It's obvious. Omnisant is a massive company, right? Like, global. If I'm right, and they are the only ones who've got the antibodies in the right mixture – you know, so it works – they can charge whatever they like, can't they? They've got the government's backing, right?' It's like there's an earthquake in my head with loads of thoughts erupting at once so I can't speak fast enough to get them out. 'The Omnisant people must have just gone to the government – all the governments, at least in the rich countries – and said, hey, we can fix this. And everyone – prime ministers, presidents or whoever – wanted to believe that the problem could be solved in like, you know—' I snap my fingers. 'It's like if you're drowning and someone throws you a rope. You don't ask questions, you grab it. Omnisant might not even have told them they were going to sell colour vision … But actually, even if they *did* tell them, people in power are rich, aren't they? They'll be able to afford it – and I bet half of them have got shares in Omnisant anyway, so they'll be all right. And I know it's not like birds have any money, but I bet they'll say the money they're paying will go into the avian research programme so that'll all be fixed and there won't be environmental meltdown, which means there'll be enough food to go around. Then the people at the top will say they're doing everyone a massive favour and they ought to shut up and be grateful, even if they'll never be able to afford to see in colour. Because that'll become the same as wanting some big luxury thing like ... oh, I don't know ... a gigantic yacht.' I'm actually panting now, trying to catch my breath, and Ryan's looking at me like I've gone completely mad. 'When all this started, I thought, it's shit but at least it's fair shit, you know? Because it was happening to everyone. But it's already not fair, and it *really* won't be in the future, so—'

'Hold on. If what you're saying is right – and I'm not saying it isn't – then there won't be just riots, there'll be all-out—'

'But there *won't*! If everyone's too worried about feeding themselves and their families to even think about how their whole world is grey and ugly, they'll just accept it as being yet more crap they've got to put up with, and after a while it'll become normal, and—'

'Grace, stop.' Ryan's off the desk again, standing in front of me. 'I get what you're saying.'

'It's *so* messed up.'

'Yeah, it is. And we need to do something.'

'Should we tell the others?'

'Marcus wouldn't believe it – he's the kind of twat who thinks anyone in charge must know best – and all Rosie seems to care about is her mobile, so ... ' Ryan shakes his head.

'What about Kieran and Kareem?' I say, remembering them whispering over the chessboard. 'I think they might be starting to worry, too.'

'No. Or not yet, anyway.'

'But—'

'We need to find out exactly what's going on in the basement first. Right now, it's too much guesswork – what we need is *evidence*.'

'How?'

'Well, we need to get in there, but we can't go downstairs because of the doors being bolted . . . ' Ryan runs his hands through his hair like he's trying to pull a solution out of his head.

'I think there might be an outside entrance, if we could get to it.'

'Oh?'

When I explain what I saw in the shrubbery – the steps down, and the door – Ryan says, 'You're *good*.'

'It says "Keep Out", though, so perhaps it's dangerous.'

Ryan shrugs. 'It's not like it's going to be full of landmines, is it? And it doesn't sound like there's an alarm. What sort of lock?'

'Padlock. Quite new, I think. Not too big, like you could maybe do it with a hairpin, only I haven't got one.'

He grins. 'I've got something better.'

'How come?'

'Let's just say I inherited it from a very dodgy uncle and I'm good at hiding things. I reckon we can get out on the fire escape and over the wall.'

'Seriously?'

'Don't look so worried. I'll help you.'

'OK . . . But how will we get back?'

'There's trees by the wall, right? We can climb, and we'll prop the fire door open so we can get back in.'

'What about the patrols?'

'Every hour on the hour – I've been watching. So . . . You up for this, or not?'

Moment of truth. I suddenly feel like I'm made of spaghetti again, and flop down on the bed. 'What if they catch us?'

'They won't.'

'You can't say that for sure.'

'What difference does it make? If what you're saying is right, then think about it this way. Sophie's dad took her away, yeah? And Marcus was OK after he had his episode. I'm guessing you're up here now because they read your fancy address and didn't think to ask any more questions.'

Remembering what Dr Seagrove said about us being like hen's teeth, I say, 'You don't look a gift horse in the mouth.'

Ryan must be right that they didn't check. And when I told Dr Brown about the episodes at Dr Gupta's surgery, I didn't mention Mr Kowalczyk's name, so they don't know that I have any connection with him at all – also, I can't imagine that Dr Brown would have Mr Kowalczyk's private address by heart, so the name of my road wouldn't have rung any bells, and Dr Gupta had probably never even heard of him.

'Alice and Cerys, though.' Ryan shakes his head. 'And Treyshawn had an episode too, just after lunch.'

I think of what Cerys told me about her dad losing his job. Alice's dad lost his, too. I don't know about Treyshawn's family, but can it really be true that all of us that aren't minted are going to be treated completely differently?

'The only reason' – Ryan sounds grim – 'that I'm not down there is that I haven't pressed my button.'

'I knew you'd had an episode before. That's how come you saw the colours at the dump, like I did.'

Ryan shrugs. 'I lied. But the thing is, when they find out that your family aren't rich or important – which they will – they'll—'

'OK.' I cut him off, feeling queasy. 'I get what you're saying, but we don't actually *know* that Alice, Cerys and Treyshawn are down there, do we?'

'Where else would they be?'

'I don't know, do I?'

'We need to find out. So . . .' Ryan takes off his button and mic drops it onto the bed. 'You in?'

I take a deep breath. Whatever I know or don't know, it *definitely* feels like the right thing to do, so . . . 'Yes.'

Ryan taps his eyepatch. 'Come on, together – one, two, three . . .' And we both pull our eyepatches over our heads and fling them on the bed. 'Right. Let's go.'

Forty-Three

Ryan squeezes my hand as two pairs of boots crunch across the gravel. As they get nearer to where we're hiding, I hear a panting noise. One of the Alsatians. I picture it sniffing in our direction, a growl building up in the back of its throat. I close my eyes and hold my breath, imagining the eruption of snarling and barking as it crashes through the bushes.

After what feels like an hour but is only a few minutes, we hear the soldiers walk past us, towards the back of the house. My legs are still shaking from scrambling across from the fire escape to the wall and climbing down through the tree branches. I've got a massive scratch down my arm, but otherwise – apart from being terrified – I'm OK.

'Come on.' Ryan's breath tickles my ear. I straighten up slowly and sidle along the wall behind him, pushing twigs away from my face, until we get to the concealed steps. When Ryan flashes the torch – we found one in the girls' kitchen, not very good but better than nothing – I can see the big door.

'Hold it for me, will you?'

I try to keep the torch steady so it shines on the padlock while Ryan gets to work with his lock pickers – the inheritance from the dodgy uncle who was, I'm guessing, a burglar – but my palms are clammy with fear. Ryan keeps muttering, 'It's all right, it's all right,' but his hands are trembling too, and it's like he's trying to convince himself as much as me.

'Got it. Come on.'

The door creaks open and it's so loud that I freeze, thinking Captain Franchot is going to appear any minute. When Ryan grabs my hand, I almost drop the torch.

'Let me.'

He shines the beam down a narrow passageway with a flagstone floor that dissolves into darkness at the end. I don't know what I was expecting, but it wasn't this; the ceiling's really low, and there's dust and cobwebs everywhere. When Ryan closes the door it's like being in a tomb, with a smell like the air's been trapped so long that it's died.

'Storerooms.' Ryan flashes the torch around. There are rooms on either side with iron grilles instead of doors, like a prison: racks of dusty wine bottles and stacks of boxes with the names of drinks written on the side. 'Must belong to whoever owns this place. They wouldn't miss a few.'

'That's not why we're here.'

'Not like they can't afford it.'

'Please let's get on.' I feel like I've got a cobweb stuck in my throat. What if one of the patrols notices the steps and they lock the door again? We'd be down here forever. 'You can always come back another time, and we need to see what's at the end.'

The other storerooms are full of furniture: tables, upended chairs and an old-fashioned bath with claw feet that's filled with rolls of wallpaper. Everything's covered in spiders' webs as thick as shawls. The darkness all around us seems to magnify sound, so I can hear our breathing. And a scuffling noise: something scurrying away into its hole.

Rats. Scaly tails, gnawing teeth and beady eyes. I try not to imagine them, or the scuttling things with too many legs that are bound to be lurking in the corners, or mammoth prehistoric slugs like the ones I saw on the path. I don't dare touch anything, and I almost don't dare walk forward in case something crunches or squishes under my foot or – worse – bites me.

When we get to the end, past more storerooms with a bunch of jerry cans and a huge grey metal box that looks a lot like the back-up generator at Mr Zhang's house, there's another door. It doesn't look as heavy as the first one, but there are three bolts, each with a padlock, and another 'KEEP OUT' sign.

'Shit.' Ryan hands the torch back to me. He's whispering now, examining the locks.

'Can you do them?' I'm almost hoping he'll say no, and then we can go back the way we came and tell ourselves that at least we tried. It suddenly feels like there's not enough oxygen, and I'm dreading what's behind that door even more than I'm hating standing here in the dark.

Click.

The first padlock. Now Ryan's onto the second. Soon it'll be the third, and then he'll open the door and we'll see . . . What? I don't know, but I'm so frightened I feel like I'm about to wet myself.

Click.

Now there's just one padlock left. I tell myself that it all looked pretty normal when I was down here with Ms Anson, so perhaps it *is* just treatment rooms. But what if there's someone there, one of the staff or a dog patrol or—

Click.

Third padlock. He's done it.

'Ready?'

My throat's gone completely dry, so I just nod.

'We need to stay together, OK?'

I nod again and hold my breath as Ryan slides the bolts back – one, two, three – then takes the torch from me and switches it off.

'Right.' Before I can even take a breath, he leans forward and brushes his lips on mine for an electric second that I wish would last forever.

Then he pushes the door open.

Forty-Four

The first thing we see is a thick plastic curtain. We stand behind it for a moment, listening, but – apart from our breathing – there's silence. When Ryan pushes the curtain aside, I can see a corridor, dimly lit by little bulbs spaced out along the walls.

Ryan nudges me. 'You waiting for Scooby-Doo?' he whispers. 'Shut the door after you.'

The air is warmer here and the ceiling's higher, but the place has a sealed-off feeling, so I can sense the whole weight of the house above my head, like we're in a submarine. There's a row of white doors on either side, all the way along until the corridor – more flagstones – ends in a brick wall.

There's no sound at all.

Ryan steps away from me, towards the first door. I'm guessing it's locked, but when he turns the handle there's a small sucking sound from the rubber seal, and it opens.

A hospital-type room, like the one where I was. In the dim light from the corridor, I can make out a lino floor, a chair, a trolley, and, in the far corner, a bed.

Not just a bed. A bed *with someone in it*. The realisation of the shape under the bedclothes and the head on the pillow, silent and still, is a physical jolt. I can see dark hair, but the face beneath is a pale, featureless smudge.

Ryan switches on the torch.

In the bed is a man. Young, I think, although I can't be sure because there's a bandage covering most of his face. He doesn't move or turn his head; in fact, it's hard to tell if he's even breathing.

'Reckon he's been drugged.' Ryan pushes me back and closes the door.

'Do you think he's blind?'

'Yeah. Must be one of the volunteers. What Lee said before he fell.' Ryan's face is bleak. 'Two-legged rats.'

Some of the rooms at this end of the corridor have empty beds, but we find two more soldiers the same as the first, still and silent, with bandaged eyes. It's the Rule of Three again: not just a one-off, but a pattern.

I feel sick. Three now, but this is just the start. How many more will there be? Whole hospitals full of young soldiers, blinded and doped? I reckon Ryan's thinking the same, because he's standing in the corridor, shaking his head.

'We need to hurry. Someone's bound to come down and check on them.'

The next two rooms are empty, and then there's the lift, which seems to be the only way – unless you come in like we did – to get in or out. If someone comes down now, we'll be trapped. I'm trying not to think about that – or worse, that someone might be down here already, on duty – but my heart's hammering and my hands are shaking as I open the next door along.

A storeroom.

'Forget it, let's carry on.'

'Omnisant, remember?' I hold out my hand for the torch. 'I want to try and find out what they're up to.'

The beam picks out a big white pedal bin with used surgical gloves sticking out from under the lid like ghost fingers trying to crawl out. Beside it are drip stands, fire extinguishers and rows of small oxygen cylinders, and metal storage racks piled with cardboard boxes fill the middle of the room. I spot the Kerr + Bell logo on the sides of some of them. About half of those have white labels, reading either Flumatoxin or Bemethiazide. There's nothing labelled rhenium – the word I thought Mr Kowalczyk might have been saying – but maybe that stuff's kept in a fridge or something.

Flumatoxin. Bemethiazide. I stare at the unfamiliar words, trying to sear them into my brain, then flash the torch round the room again. 'Can you see a pen anywhere?'

'What?'

'I want to write these down.'

'What for? They're probably painkillers or something.'

'*Seriously?*' I hiss. ' "Toxin" means it's *poisonous*, you dick.'

'No need to have a fit.' Ryan disappears around the corner of the rack and comes back again a few seconds later with a black marker pen. It writes thick, so I push up my sleeve and print the words on the inside of my arm.

'Happy now?' He says it like I'm messing about. I want to point out that at least I'm trying to find stuff out, which is more use than stealing alcohol, but I don't.

I switch off the torch and follow him out of the room to the next door along. He opens it and stops so abruptly that I bump into his back. He turns, frowning, and for a moment I think he's going to be sarcastic, but he just says, 'Grace . . . I'm sorry.'

Forty-Five

This can't be happening.

I stand next to Alice's bed, willing her to move, or speak, or even open her eyes, but she doesn't. Two thick straps over the blanket look like they're holding her down, and there are tubes everywhere: one up her nose, held in place with what looks like medical tape; another going into her neck, and more coming out from under the bedclothes. Her hair is scraped up under a sort of shower cap and her face is ashen. There's a machine beside her, a point of light moving across its grey screen in a series of jerks, making a faint blipping noise, and a drip stand with three transparent bags hanging on it. One of them, judging by the dark colour and the markings on the label, is blood. The other is full of a light grey pasty-looking stuff – some sort of food, perhaps? The line that's going into her neck has an odd-looking syringe attached to it and it's coming from a bag of clear liquid. There's a fourth bag, larger, hanging on the end of the bed, containing what I guess is urine.

Everything except breathing is being done for her.

I stroke her cheek with the backs of my fingers.

Wake up, Alice. Please wake up.

'She can't be ...' I falter. Can't be what? 'She's my friend.'

Under the lids, her eyes move. Is she dreaming? Thinking?

Is she even in there? Being able to breathe by yourself doesn't mean you're fully alive, I don't think. At least, not in the same way we're alive. Perhaps the combination of the electric fence and the 'vitamins' blew a fuse in her brain. I think of how she looked, lying on the ground, and of the conversation we had about death, just before it happened. Where is she? Has she become part of the grey, empty space?

'No,' I moan. 'No, no, *no* ...'

Ryan takes my hand. 'There's nothing we can do.'

I feel like I'm choking. I can't speak, so I concentrate on looking round the room – anywhere but at Alice.

There's something on the floor on the other side of the bed. A large, shiny white box. Plastic, with raised capital letters, also white, on the side. I can just make them out: AMARANTH. I don't know what it means, but I'm sure I've seen the word before, quite recently, only I can't think where.

I inch forward for a closer look, trying to avoid seeing Alice's face. There's a tube running down into the top of the box, with dark liquid running into it from somewhere inside Alice. Is that blood as well? I can't think what else it could be.

There's something else, too, beside the box. It's smaller, a bit like an old-school radio, but with winking lights on the top as well as dials. Does that tell them when the bags need changing? They look OK now – over half full – but we need to be out of here before someone comes to do it.

Think, Grace. Blood in, blood out.

Antibodies.

Alice's body jerks suddenly, making me jump back.

'Alice!'

Ryan squeezes my hand, hard. 'Sssh, Grace.'

'It's unbearable.' I can barely get the words out. 'Look what they've done to her.'

Alice's eyes are closed and she's not making any sound, but for about thirty seconds her back arches, straining against the straps, and her body shakes like the juddering monster strapped to the laboratory table in the old Frankenstein films I've watched with Rusty.

I look again at the dials and lights on the little machine. Maybe it isn't to tell the staff when the bags need changing. Maybe it's something to shock Alice's brain into having colour episodes.

What Ryan just said in the storeroom: *No need to have a fit.* I look at my arm. Could that be what Flumatoxin is? Something that gives you a fit and stimulates your brain so that you see colours?

'This is really messed up,' Ryan says – quietly, almost talking to himself.

I can't look any more.

Forty-Six

'Come on.' Ryan tugs my hand. 'We need to get out of here.'

We check the next two rooms: Cerys is in one, Treyshawn in the other, two statues, in pale and dark grey wax. Straps, tubes, dials and lights, all the same.

'Cerys and Treyshawn had normal colour episodes, didn't they? That means they must be doing something to keep them unconscious.'

'Bastards.' Ryan mutters the word through clenched teeth. 'Total bastards.'

I think about how Treyshawn was the only one of the boys Ryan properly got on with, and about Cerys, quiet and kind, worrying about her dad and brothers, and I have to squeeze my eyes shut to stop the tears coming. 'I reckon they've turned them into antibody machines,' says Ryan bitterly. 'But you can bet it's not going to happen to anyone they think matters.'

'But their families—'

'What are they going to do about it?'

We stare at each other.

'Last room?' There's one more door.

I shake my head. 'There might be someone down here on duty.'

'Doubt it. They'd have come out already, wouldn't they? And it's not like any of these' – he gestures at the other doors – 'are going to run away.'

'I guess ... OK, then. And then we're out of here.'

I don't know what I'm expecting to see but when I push the door open, I freeze. It's an office – desk, computer, files. The lights are on, bright and harsh, and there's a man sitting in the middle of the room with his back to us. White coat, white hair, pale neck: Mr Virtanen.

We stand quite still. I'm holding my breath, thinking he'll turn around at any moment, but he doesn't. It's like he hasn't heard us.

I take a step back, really cautious, and I'm about to close the door again when Ryan stops me, mouthing something. When I look again, I can see there's a black band around his head with something big and round on each side.

Earphones.

Ryan moves his hand over his eyes and mouths something else. I lean forward, watching his lips. *The ... Ahh ...?* He says it again. T ...? No. V ... VR.

Virtual Reality.

I inch forward, craning my neck so I can see the black box strapped to Mr Virtanen's head, and, when I look past that, I spot a syringe on the desk, beside the keyboard. What's he been doing?

The syringe looks like it's empty, and he's got all the access he wants to Alice, Cerys and Treyshawn . . .

He must have . . . No, surely not. But he has, hasn't he? Injected himself with the antibodies, and now he's in a private paradise of colour – sunrises, sunsets, flowers, birds . . . Of course he doesn't know we're here.

Ryan tugs my arm and we tiptoe backwards into the corridor, closing the door slowly behind us. 'Let's get out of here, before—' He freezes. 'What was that?'

'What?'

'Listen.'

A faint whirring noise, coming from the direction of the lift shaft, followed by a loud clunk. I start running for the cellar, but Ryan hisses, 'No time,' and yanks me towards the storeroom.

We can hear the lift door open as we feel our way around the metal racks of boxes and huddle down where we can't be seen from the door. I'm shaking, more scared than I've ever been in my life – more even than when I found Mum passed out on her bed.

Footsteps in the corridor. Heavy. Boots?

Soldiers. Two.

That means two guns.

Sounds like they're checking the rooms.

'Virtanen! Where are you?' Dr Seagrove's voice, coming from somewhere near the lift. 'Try the other entrance. The boy said he saw them go over the wall.'

Boy? Somebody must have seen us and told him. How, though?

Puzzled, I look at Ryan, who moves his hand up to his chest and taps. Of course. Whoever it was must have pressed his button; that would bring someone upstairs immediately.

The footsteps are getting further away. An echoey clang indicates something banging against the iron grilles in the passage, and one of the soldiers calls out, 'Clear!'

There's a scuffing noise like slippers on tiles, and a muttered conversation, too low for me to make out all the words. I hear, 'Door's not bolted.'

They know.

They're coming back.

Keep walking ... Please keep walking ... Just get in the lift and go.

They've stopped.

Right outside this door.

I feel dizzy, like I'm going to faint. It's like my brain is tingling inside my head, and there's a core of heat at the back of my skull. The near-darkness is pulsing all round me, like the air is throbbing, and for a moment I actually think I can *hear* it, but then—

The door opens.

Forty-Seven

I hold my breath.

There's a click, and I blink as the strip lights flicker into life.

The colours are immediate this time: brown cardboard boxes, the little blue Kerr + Bell logos, 'OMNISANT' in red letters, and green labels on the row of small oxygen cylinders beside me, all glowing.

And, in the gap under the shelving, a pair of brown army boots.

One of the soldiers is walking down the far side of the room. When he gets to the end of the rack, he'll only have to go forward a couple of metres and he'll see us.

Ryan motions me to follow and scrambles away on all fours. I start to move, keeping as low as I can, but the other soldier must still be in the corridor, so even if we manage to get out of the room—

'Stay where you are!'

I turn my head. I'm staring into a black hole – the end of a gun – but in the next second, Ryan's on his feet and pulling me upright.

'Stop!'

As we tear past the end of the first shelving unit, Ryan gives it an almighty shove, sending it over, right on top of the soldier. At the same moment there's a huge bang and a violent hissing noise all around us. Then bright white light with – amazingly – a burst of orange sparks. Someone's screaming, but it's muffled, like my ears have stopped working properly. There's a blur of khaki as we dive past the soldier in the corridor. Then we dart through the door and down the passage, past the iron grilles and back out into the night.

I'm practically on all fours as I scramble up the steps behind Ryan. My head is full of fireworks, like the explosion's happening inside me and not the cellar. I can barely think.

We get to the top and I'm trying to get upright, but I'm dizzy. I can't see properly and I'm stumbling all over the place, with Ryan grabbing on to me like we're both drunk. I trip on something and now we're both on our knees, and then it's like my ears pop and there's noise, deafening and close, shouting and clomping boots, and someone's shining a torch . . .

More soldiers.

Three guns, pointing straight at our faces.

'Don't move.' Captain Franchot's voice.

Ryan's shouting something about oxygen when there's a yell from behind us and someone lands on my back. I'm face down on the ground and I'm being crushed – there's a ton weight on top of me and hands around my neck, squeezing. I can hear shouting – shrill and crazed – 'What have you done? What have you done?'

All I can see is a spectrum of colour, solid lines of it like a vertical rainbow, and it feels like my head is about to explode.

Then it stops and I struggle into a kneeling position, gulping air and coughing so much it's like my lungs are being ripped apart. Ryan's talking to me, but I can't hear what he's saying because everyone's shouting. Captain Franchot is bellowing orders right next to my head and all I can see is boots. There are soldiers everywhere, crashing through the bushes and almost trampling us as they rush down the steps. Somewhere to my right there's a blur of khaki and a paisley pattern—

Paisley?

Pink and red teardrop shapes on a blue background, squirming like amoebas as the colours fade in and out . . .

Pyjama legs. Dark blue dressing gown. I look up and there in front of me is Dr Seagrove, eyes bulging out of his head, screaming as two soldiers drag him away from me.

I try to stand, but my chest is agony and I can't stop coughing. Ryan puts his arm round my waist and tries to pull me up, but it's like my legs haven't got the message. We only just make it behind the nearest tree when Ryan suddenly pulls my head down to his chest and wraps his arms round me and then—

The world explodes in a roar of sound and light.

Forty-Eight

I'm choking again, on air that's solid with dust, and my ears are ringing. Ryan's in front of me, saying something I can't hear. He's pulling on my arm, but it's like I'm paralysed.

'Come on,' he says, between coughs. 'We have to get out of here.' He tugs at me. *'Move!'*

I hear screaming in the background as I stumble through the trees, but it's like I'm outside myself, and my body's a meat puppet. I follow Ryan down the path and across the lawn and collapse behind some bushes, coughing. We can't be seen from the house, which is just as well because right now I can't get any further. I'm doubled over, heaving so much that my eyes are watering, and it feels like my lungs are trying to force their way up into my throat. It's a couple of minutes before I can even speak.

'Are you OK?'

'Not – sure.' My voice comes out raspy and I'm shaking all over, even though it's warm. Through tears, I stare at my fingers, which seem to be bleeding. As I watch, the colour fades to grey and then blooms again, bright and shocking. Then I look up and see flashes of Ryan's face in colour – the bright blue eyes, bloodshot from the dust; the golden tan on the sexy cheekbones; the tousled dark hair, the trickle of red by his ear. 'You're bleeding, too. Your face.'

'Just a scratch.' Ryan swipes away the blood with the back of his hand. 'Are you seeing colour?'

'Comes and goes. You?'

'Properly, but you're in shock.' He smooths my cheek with his thumb. 'We need to get out of here. That old bastard could have killed you.'

'Just ... give me a minute.' His touch is lovely, but my throat feels constricted, like Dr Seagrove's still got his hands round it. 'What just happened? The house ... ' I peer through the bushes. 'It looks ... I mean, it's all still there. That explosion – I thought ... '

'Oxygen cylinder. The soldier must have hit it when he shot at us. That's what I was trying to tell them when we got outside.'

'Oh ... Right. But the second explosion?'

'The other cylinders. They weren't that big, but it's not a big space. I don't think it's spread inside yet – depends what else they've got down there that's flammable—'

'Alcohol. And there was a thing that looked like a generator, and jerry cans, so maybe petrol or diesel.'

'There's no wind, but everything round here is dry as tinder. That rain we had wasn't nearly enough.' Ryan stands up. 'No one's coming yet. Anyone who was near the cellar would be ... ' He shakes his head. 'But there's plenty more. Come on.'

'Alice ... '

Ryan's face creases, and I know it's the effort of trying to push away his thoughts. 'Don't, Grace. She wouldn't have known anything about it. None of them would. You saw them.'

'Those soldiers. You thought they were sedated, but ... And they're blind, aren't they?'

'Were blind.' Ryan's voice is grim. 'Really, don't go there.'

I shake my head, trying to get rid of the images crowding my mind: heaps of mangled and melted equipment, charred bodies covered in dust and plaster—

The lights in the house go off abruptly. For a moment, there's only moonlight, and then—

'Ryan, look!'

A red glow, coming from the ground-floor windows nearest the cellar entrance. As I watch, the colour comes and goes. Red and orange to grey and black and back again, like there's a switch in my head: on, off, on, off.

'That's the kitchen – come on!' Ryan pulls me to my feet and starts to tug me along the deer park fence.

'Where are we going?'

'Away from here. Woods.'

'Wait!' I grab his arm. 'What about the others? The nearest fire station must be miles away.'

'There's a fire escape, remember? They can get into the courtyard. Even if the doors into the house and garden are locked, they can smash a window with one of those logs and come out through the back. Or they can climb down through the tree branches, like we did.' Ryan's already over the fence, pulling at me to follow. There's a huge tree about a hundred metres away, but it feels like ten times that as I stumble towards it with my throat and chest feeling like they're on fire as well.

Once we're safely behind it, I lean against the bark. 'Have – to – stop – a – bit. If you – want to . . . ' I flap a hand in the direction of the woods.

'I'm not—'

The rest of his words are swallowed by a dull boom from the far end of the house. Ryan peers round the trunk. 'That came from the stable yard.'

I look, too. 'The soldier volunteers! They'll be trapped. Should we—' I start coughing again.

'No. Watch – they're doing it themselves.'

Another boom, and the massive wooden doors shudder and groan. There's the sound of glass shattering somewhere over to the left – the kitchen windows – and smoke pours out over the windowsills. Thick tongues of flame – red, grey, red, grey – start to lick their way up the outside wall.

'What if the fire gets to them before—'

'It won't.'

As the huge doors give way with a splintering crash, I can see the front of a green army truck forcing them apart. There are soldiers standing up in the back, shouting, and more stream out behind the vehicle as it ploughs straight through the wooden fence and over the long grass at the edge of the lawn.

'Told you.'

The rooms on the first floor are burning now, and I can feel the heat. The fire must be roaring through the maze of corridors, and

I can picture the blackened wood and blazing carpet as it demolishes everything in its path. What if the others didn't manage to get down to the courtyard in time? Too late for us to help them now – we should have gone in before, not run away like cowards.

Ryan's staring at the soldiers. The truck is driving away, with a bunch of them chasing it. No one seems to be in charge – or if they are, the running soldiers aren't paying attention. Neither are the few who are left on the lawn, staring up at the burning house. In the bright, flickering light, their uniforms change from khaki to grey and back again. My head feels hot and cold by turns – fire, ice, fire, ice — until everything blurs and all I can see is a meaningless pattern of splotches against a black background.

'Grace!' Ryan's shaking me hard enough to make my teeth rattle.

I shove him away, then slide down to the ground and lean back against the trunk. His face looks blurry and incomplete, like a drawing by someone who keeps rubbing bits out. 'My head's gone fuzzy . . .'

'All right, but don't go weird on me, OK?'

'I'm not doing it on purpose.'

'I know. I'm sorry.' My skin tingles as Ryan drops a kiss on my forehead. 'Just sit there a minute while I see what's happening.'

'Those soldiers look like they've been hypnotised,' I say to Ryan's back. 'They must be in shock. Move over.'

I crawl next to him so I can peer round the tree at the house. I don't know if it was Ryan shaking me or just the effect of keeping still for a few seconds, or the fact that he's just put his arm around me, but the splotches and flickering have stopped, and everything is pretty much back to normal.

Real, full-colour normal.

'Wow. That's . . . ' I can't think of a word that even begins to cover it. Ryan's face, so close beside mine, is lit up and golden, so startlingly handsome that I feel a jolt in my chest, as if my heart has skipped a beat. Behind him, the fire, now that I can see it properly, is dazzling. Brilliant flames are shooting straight up into the night sky, and there's a golden glow, like Aveney Park has a gigantic halo.

I suddenly wonder about the soldiers standing on the lawn. Shock or no shock, it seems weird they haven't run away . . . Could they be volunteers who've had the antibody mixture? If they can see the fire like I can, it's not surprising they're rooted to the spot, because I could look at it – and Ryan – forever.

'I know, amazing. But if just one spark gets onto those trees, they'll go up like . . . Hang on. Over there – window next to the stable yard, ground floor.'

Someone's clambering out of it. White coat, bare legs: must be Ms Anson. She falls awkwardly, landing on all fours in the flower bed, and crawls towards the gravel path. More people appear behind her. I spot a pink t-shirt and long chestnut hair, which must be Rosie, and then one . . . two . . . three . . .

Five more people, all male. As they stagger across the path and onto the grass, I see that the first three have black eyepatches – Marcus, Kieran and Kareem – and the two behind are in suits: Mr Okonjo and Dr Brown.

'At least they're safe.' I stand up to call out to them, but Ryan pulls me back down.

'Grace! We're meant to be *hiding*.'

'Yes, but—'

'No, but. Look!'

'Where?'

'There.' A man is moving across the lawn, silhouetted against a sheet of bright flame. Dressing gown. Pyjamas. Slow, awkward movements, dragging one leg and carrying something large and heavy-looking. 'He's still alive.'

It's Dr Seagrove, and he's got a gun.

Forty-Nine

'Rifle,' Ryan mutters. 'Must have got it off one of the soldiers.'

For a moment, it's like nobody on the lawn has noticed him. Everything seems to have gone into such slow motion that it's almost like looking at a photograph. The soldier volunteers that are left are still staring up at the house, and everyone who came out of the window is huddled together on the grass, like they're trying to decide what to do next. Dr Seagrove stops about fifty metres away from them and bends over the gun. 'Better hope he can't figure out how to use it,' Ryan mutters.

I think of Dr Seagrove's face, screaming into mine, with crazy, bulging eyes. 'He doesn't know what he's doing. We've got to stop him, say we're sorry for going into the basement. I mean, it's not like we caused the explosion, or—'

'*Say sorry?*' Ryan looks at me like I'm an idiot. 'Yeah, that's really going to work.'

'We've got to warn the others, then.' Before I've thought about what I'm doing I'm on my feet, yelling. I see Dr Seagrove swivel round in our direction, and Ryan is shouting my name and tugging at my arm, and then . . .

One of the figures with eyepatches breaks away from the group and charges straight towards us, shouting something we can't hear. I can see his hair, blazing red, as, to the left of him, Dr Seagrove straightens up and . . .

There's a colossal bang and Kieran falls back, clutching his chest.

It all happens so fast I feel like I've been punched in the stomach. 'He just . . . he just . . . '

Ryan stares back at me, his mouth moving but no sound coming out.

Kieran is lying on the grass and Kareem is bending over him now, with the others running across the grass towards them, and . . .

Ryan pulls me back down just in time. Gunfire thuds into the tree and, with a splintering groan, a thick branch detaches itself and falls on top of us. We're tangled together, and with my head buried in Ryan's armpit, I can feel our hearts pounding in unison.

There's more gunfire, and screams. As we huddle out of sight, I imagine everybody stampeding for the cover of the trees on the far side of the lawn, falling as the bullets hit them. At the same time I'm thinking, *thank God he's not shooting at us* and hating myself for thinking it, and . . .

A single shot.

A beat of dense silence, then only the sound of our ragged breathing.

We wriggle apart and peer around the tree.

Captain Franchot is standing in the middle of the lawn, a gun in his hand. It's smaller than Dr Seagrove's weapon, which is a couple of metres away from where he's lying, face down.

He'd managed to hit several people before Franchot shot him. Kareem is lying on the grass next to Kieran. Ms Anson's a couple of metres away with Mr Okonjo bending over her, and one of the soldier volunteers, who nearly made it behind a tree, is a few metres further on. Rosie, head down, is crawling past him. She'll be OK now. The ambulance will come soon, and the firefighters, and then . . .

Another shot.

Mr Okonjo half turns, like someone's called his name, then falls on top of Ms Anson.

'What's he doing?'

Captain Franchot moves, leisurely like he's out for a walk in the park, towards Rosie.

'Ryan, what's he *doing*?'

Rosie turns to look at Franchot, and even from here I can see disbelief and panic pulling her face out of shape. I start forward, stupidly, and Ryan yanks me back as she tries to get up but falls, clutching her leg, and scrabbles frantically at the earth to pull herself forward, crying out like a wounded animal as Captain Franchot gets closer and closer . . .

Then he lifts his gun.

Fifty

'Oh, God, no . . .'

Ryan and I cling to each other in silence as Captain Franchot turns away from Rosie. He goes up to the people on the ground, one by one, and shoots them again, like he's making sure. No hurry: he could be turning off the lights before he goes up to bed. Then he walks away, into the trees.

I can't think of anything, except: Rosie never got to see her puppy again.

We stay still for the longest time, fused together and breathing like one person. 'No witnesses, I guess,' Ryan mutters eventually. It comes out ragged, like it's an effort to speak.

'I don't understand.'

'Me neither.'

'Do you think they even called the fire brigade?'

'Doubt it.'

'Someone's bound to see it.'

'Not so easy without colour.'

'Smoke, though. The smell.'

'Even if someone does, they can still make sure it doesn't get on the news – Emergency Powers or National Security or whatever. Come on, before he spots us.'

'Where, though? And what about his men?'

'I don't know. We'll just have to risk it.' Ryan picks up the big branch Dr Seagrove shot off the tree.

'That's not going to stop a gun.'

'Better than nothing.'

I glance around. In the light from the fire I can see that there's no cover at all for about fifty metres. There's no one moving on the lawn, and I can't see anyone in the trees beside it, either.

'Where we saw the dump,' Ryan says, 'there's a chain-link fence, right? Only a couple of strands of barbed wire across the top. We can climb over.'

'What if it's electrified? Alice, remember?'

'All the lights in the house were off before we saw the ground floor was on fire, which I'm guessing means no electrics. That thing in the cellar you said was a back-up generator, it's not going to be working now, is it?'

'OK ... No, wait. What if there's another one in a shed somewhere?'

'Like I said, we'll have to risk it.' Ryan looks exasperated. 'Have you got a better idea?'

'Just ...' I give up. 'No, I haven't.'

'Right.' Ryan grabs my hand with his free one, and we start running towards the wood. I'm thinking Captain Franchot might shoot us at any moment, that a bullet in my back will explode my lungs and I'll never see Mum or Prune or Rusty again. I force myself to keep stumbling forward over the tussocky grass. The blood is pounding in my ears and I can taste iron in my mouth, but somehow, we're both still running and both still alive.

By the time we reach the wood I'm gasping. Ryan virtually tows me along for the last bit, ducking under branches and lurching through gaps in the brambles. We stop, and I double over by the fence, coughing and heaving, feeling like I'll never be able to breathe normally again.

We can't hear the fire any more, and there's no traffic. The torch is long gone, dropped in the storeroom, probably, but there's just enough moonlight to make out the heap of junk on the other side of the road. The fence is higher than I remember – three metres, maybe more. Even if it isn't electrified, I'm wondering if I'll actually be able to get over it.

'That better?' Ryan stops rubbing my back and jabs the metal links with the branch. 'It's safe.'

'The top, though – there's barbed wire. Can you electrify that?'

'Dunno. Never heard of it, though. OK.' He drops the branch and takes hold of the fence. 'Finger and toe-holds, right?'

'Right.'

'I'll go first. Just follow me and do what I—'

'Stop!' A man's voice, harsh and loud. A second later, we're blinded by dazzling white light.

Fifty-One

I freeze. For a minute, I can't tell where the sound has come from. Like the light, it seems to be all around us. Then I realise there's someone in the bushes over to my left. Ryan picks up the branch again.

'Wait! Please . . .'

Please? That doesn't sound like Captain Franchot.

Ryan clearly doesn't think so, either. 'Keep away from us!' He shoves me behind him and raises the branch, brandishing it like a club.

'Don't . . .' Dr Brown steps forward unsteadily, a torch in his hand. He looks exhausted, a scarecrow in a suit, smears of dirt across his white shirt front. Behind him are Marcus, limping, and one of the soldier volunteers. They're both just as filthy as Dr Brown, their arms covered in scratches from the brambles. It's strange, seeing them in colour, almost unreal: Marcus's pale green t-shirt and floppy blond hair, and the volunteer's caramel-coloured skin and camouflage trousers. He's blinking and rubbing his eyes. I'm guessing that he had colour vision and can't believe what he's seeing.

Ryan bangs the end of the branch against the flat of his hand. 'That's close enough. What do you want?'

'Help us.'

'*Help* you?'

Dr Brown just looks at Ryan. It's like he's run out of words, and he's shaking like a leaf. Marcus is staring at us, his face slack with shock, and it's the volunteer who speaks. 'I'm all right, mate – it's these two. Give us a hand getting them over the fence, and we might be able to find the others.'

'What others?'

'In the truck.'

'No chance, mate.' Ryan sounds . . . not friendly, but like he's OK with the guy. 'They'll be long gone. Grace?'

'We need to stop talking and get out of here.'

'So can we come with you?' Dr Brown sounds pathetic, like we're the big kids and he's asking to play.

Ryan and I look at each other.

No choice.

I nod, and Ryan holds out his hand for Dr Brown to give him the torch.

'I'm sorry,' he says. 'Ryan, Grace . . . It wasn't meant to be like this.'

Fifty-Two

It wasn't meant to be like this. Dr Brown's words echo in my head as we help him and Marcus up the swaying fence, pushing, pulling, shoving, disentangling ourselves from the barbed wire on the top – no electricity, thank God – and scrambling down the other side. None of it was *meant*, I think, as we cross the road to the dump, but it still *happened*.

We get out of sight, huddling behind an overturned sofa and a mound of bulging black plastic bags, surrounded by the ripe smell of rubbish. Marcus is groaning, Ryan's got a gash on his hand from the barbed wire, and one of my sleeves is ripped. There's silence for a minute or two, then the volunteer says, 'I'm Kyle, by the way.'

I almost laugh. 'Grace, and this is Ryan.'

Kyle looks at him. 'You were on the roof with Lee when it happened.'

'Yeah.' Ryan looks awkward. 'That was me.'

'Connor told me. My mate – that's who was up there with you.' No funny looks or accusations, which means what I'd imagined about them having a fight up there must be rubbish, or Connor would have told him about it. 'He wouldn't leave here without me.'

'Looks like he has, though.'

Kyle's face darkens. 'You don't know that.'

The last thing we need right now is an argument, so I get in before Ryan can answer.

'Do you know where we are, Kyle?'

'Middle of bloody nowhere. Norfolk, was all they told us.'

Dr Brown clears his throat. 'There's a town about ten miles away.'

'Oh, great,' says Ryan sarcastically. 'Any ideas about how to get there?'

I think of the pigs we saw in the next couple of fields. 'There must be a farm somewhere near.'

'Yeah, but which direction? We're probably better off trying to hitch a lift.'

'There's a curfew,' Dr Brown says. 'There have been riots in a lot of places, and—'

'Yeah.' Ryan cuts him off. 'We know.'

Dr Brown stares at Ryan. 'How . . . ?'

'We're not stupid, OK?'

'The army won't be under curfew,' says Kyle.

Ryan's laughter is like a bark. 'Captain Franchot's guys? Are you insane?'

'Not them, the volunteers. I know you said they'd gone, but that truck took a real beating, and—'

'Then it won't be any good, will it?' Ryan snaps.

'No, but—'

'My foot ...' We all turn to look at Marcus, who's white-faced and slumped against a sagging mattress which someone's propped against the rusty skeleton of old farm machinery.

Ryan shines the torch on him. He's got his trainer off and his toes are a red, pulpy mass. Getting over the fence must have been agony. 'Not going to be much good walking, is he?'

No one says anything. When I look back in the direction of Aveney Park, I can see the red glow of the fire over the treetops and sparks flying up into the night sky.

'Did you see the fire?' I ask Kyle. 'I mean, properly?'

He grins. 'Incredible. Like the world was alive again. But then ...' His shoulders droop.

'Back to greyout?'

'Yeah, just now – after we crossed the road. The colours just dissolved.'

'Did it hurt? When it started, I mean.'

'No. It was weird, like pinpricks on the back of my head, and it felt warm ...' His face lights up. 'It was *brilliant*. I know the house was on fire and everything – and what happened after – but, best thing I ever saw, and ...' He stops, frowning. 'You don't think something bad'll happen to me? I mean, the others ...'

'Do you know if they actually saw colour?'

'Don't think so. Just weird stuff. Do you think we'll—'

'Look.' It's not just the red light of the fire, but something else: two rays of white light, sweeping into view. Headlights on full beam, coming this way.

Kyle says, 'Stay here.' Before anyone can stop him, he runs back towards the road.

Ryan is tugging my arm, muttering something, but trying to get away is pointless. Even if we burrow into the dump they'll find us easily, and Marcus can barely walk, never mind run. Kyle thinks he's being helpful, but Captain Franchot would kill us without a second thought, and he'll have told his men to do the same. I can't die here, surrounded by stinking rubbish, with Mum never knowing what happened to me . . .

At least I've been able to see colour one last time.

I look at Dr Brown, who's sitting on a car seat, his head in his hands, utterly defeated. *It wasn't meant to be like this.*

No shit, Sherlock.

Kyle's running back towards us.

Fifty-Three

'It's them!'

'You mean . . .' I stare at him, open-mouthed, relief pinwheeling inside my chest.

'Yes! They managed to swap the damaged truck.' Kyle turns to Ryan. 'That's what I was trying to tell you. We knew there was another one parked outside, and one of the guys took the keys. Connor's driving – I told you he wouldn't leave without me.'

'What about the rest of us?'

'It's fine. They didn't want' – Kyle lowers his voice and jerks his head towards Dr Brown – 'him, but I told them about Captain Franchot.'

The truck looks the same as the other one, but the whole of the back is covered in khaki-coloured canvas. The volunteer standing next to it – sandy hair, green eyes and a red handkerchief tied round his neck – must be Connor, because he obviously knows Ryan. 'You want a ride, right?'

'Yeah. Thanks, mate.'

'You lost your eyepatch.' He sounds suspicious. For a second, I wonder how he knows about the patch, but then I remember about him being on the roof with Ryan. 'She hasn't got one either.'

'Left them behind,' Ryan tells him. 'The fire.' I look round at Dr Brown, who's hanging back, but he doesn't seem to have heard. In fact, I don't think he's even noticed we're not wearing the patches. Marcus, who's being supported by Kyle, is wearing his, and that seems to reassure Connor, because he lets Ryan take him aside.

I guess Ryan must have told him at least part of what we found in the basement, because when they come back Connor moves the canvas for us to climb inside the truck. Every inch of the sweaty, stifling space is taken up by the soldier volunteers, who are crammed onto the long bench seats down the sides and on the floor between them. They're obviously pissed off, because there's quite a bit of muttering, but they shuffle up enough for Marcus to lie down on the floor and the rest of us to squash in beside him. Marcus groans when the truck starts moving, and I can see he's biting his lip trying not to cry. As I take his hand and give it a squeeze, Ryan, who's opposite, gives me side-eye. 'Anyone know where we're going?' he asks.

'No idea,' says one of the soldiers. 'Long as we get out of here, I don't care.'

There's a lot of nodding and someone else mutters, 'Too right, mate. Bunch of psychos.' This is obviously aimed at Dr Brown, but he doesn't reply. With the canvas flap blocking out the moon, it's nearly dark in here, but I can see that he's still looking dazed. I look round and catch the black glint of several pairs of sunglasses.

I'm guessing some of the volunteers had their vision messed up by the injections, but not badly enough for them to end up in the basement.

Ryan says, 'Sounds about right. Anyone got any water?'

'Sweet FA, mate.'

At least they don't seem to have guns.

It's like no one really knows what to say after that. There's just too much to explain and you can't find the words – or that's how I feel, anyway. Plus, you can tell when people are in shock. I probably am, too, because I'm shivering, and clammy with sweat. In any case, I reckon the volunteers have all the information they can handle right now.

I can hear branches scraping along the sides of the truck, and there are lots of bumps, so we must be going along back roads. I'm beyond grateful to be getting away from whatever's left of Aveney Park, but I'm exhausted and thirsty and I just want to go home. I want to see Mum so much – and Prune and Rusty – and hug them all forever.

I blink furiously. There's no way I'm crying in front of this lot.

I wonder, dully, how long Ryan and I will be able to see in colour. It occurs to me that nobody knows that we can except the two of us. Unless we're already back in greyout, of course, because right now it's too dark to tell.

Maybe Ryan and I need those 'vitamins' in order to make it work, just like Kyle needed whatever it was they injected him with ... Did all the stuff perish in the fire, or is there more somewhere? And – if we're so valuable and they need us so much – why did Captain Franchot kill Rosie? He made sure that Kareem and Kieran were dead, too. No witnesses, that's what Ryan said. Like keeping the whole thing a secret was more important than anything else.

I don't even know what this is about any more.

I close my eyes.

Fifty-Four

After about an hour, the truck jolts to a halt and Connor's face appears round the edge of the canvas. 'Checkpoint up ahead, for the motorway. We should be OK, but . . .'

'What about *them*?' It's the same guy who made the remark about psychos.

'They can get out and walk,' another volunteer says.

'He can't.' Someone else points at Marcus. 'Look at him.'

'He can crawl, can't he?'

'Hold on,' says Ryan. 'None of us knew what we were getting into.'

'*He* did.' The volunteer nearest Dr Brown jabs him with a finger. 'And none of you lot *died*.'

'Or went blind,' adds the guy next to him, who's wearing sunglasses.

Connor looks at me. 'Haven't you told them?'

Not sure why he thinks it's *my* job to explain things. 'Not yet.'

'In that case,' Connor turns to the volunteer, who's looking like he's ready to do Dr Brown some serious damage, 'you haven't heard the half of it, mate.'

'Told us what?'

'Later, Liam. Back off, OK?'

Silence. Then Liam says, 'All right. But what if they want to look in here?'

'Is there a groundsheet?'

'Reckon I'm sitting on something,' says someone up near the cab. 'Hang on.'

A minute later, Ryan, Dr Brown and I are lying on the floor of the truck alongside Marcus, covered in thick, dark plastic. I keep my eyes shut to stop dirt getting into them – the groundsheet's obviously been used recently – as the engine starts up again.

Ryan takes my hand. 'Are you OK?'

'Just about,' I whisper back, although I'm feeling anything but OK. 'The checkpoint's the army, right?'

'Must be.'

'What if they search the truck?'

'This lot don't want that to happen any more than we do. Don't think about it.'

Don't think about it. Yeah, right.

The plastic sheet is gritty against my face, and I'm trying not to think about suffocating. Ryan's hand is dry and warm, which is comforting, but lying here on our backs in the dark reminds me of the figures on those tombs you see in old churches – two dead people, side by side.

Apart from the engine and the blood thudding in my ears, there's no sound at all.

Please let us get through this.

The truck slows and stops, and Connor turns off the engine. I can hear boots on the tarmac, then voices and the crackle of a radio. The boots move away again. Are they letting us through?

No. Coming back this way. The voices are closer now, at the side of the truck, but I can't make out what they're saying.

Any second now ... Any second ...'

No, please no. Don't let them find us. Don't let them find us, don't let them ...

OK. I open my eyes and unclench my fingers. The footsteps are fainter now, somewhere off to the right. I can hear something hard being dragged across the road, and more conversation, up by the cab. What's happening?

Yes! The engine's back on. Someone shouts, 'Right you are!' and we're moving again, slowly at first, then picking up speed until we've got be doing around seventy. Ryan pulls the groundsheet away and sits up, rubbing his fingers. I must have been holding his hand tighter than I thought.

I lie there, limp with relief, staring up at the canvas top of the truck and gulping down air.

'Need a hand?' Liam's bending over me.

'Thanks.'

'Right. Now tell us what happened.'

Before I can open my mouth, Ryan says, 'She's not the one you should be asking.' He turns to Dr Brown, who's still lying on the floor next to Marcus, and pulls him into a sitting position. 'Start talking.'

Fifty-Five

Dr Brown raises his head. In the near darkness, his face looks like a skull, with black holes for eyes.

'I suppose you two have figured out a few things,' he says to Ryan and me. 'For the rest of you, these three are part of a very small sample of young people whose brains appear to be repairing themselves, who were brought to Aveney Park as part of the same research programme as you. We asked for army volunteers under the age of twenty because younger people have better neural plasticity – meaning that their brains are more flexible, if you like – than adults.'

'And you thought you'd get results more quickly.' Ryan's voice is flat.

'I wouldn't have put it quite like that.'

'Except . . . ' I think back to our first night there, what Professor Petrossian said in the meeting about keeping an open mind and the row we overheard, and Dr Brown talking about *three years later*. 'It wasn't really research, was it? Because I think you already knew what you were going to do.'

'It wasn't . . . ' Dr Brown clears his throat. 'Not . . . We didn't all . . . ' Cautious, like he's got a Jenga tower made of words and he's trying to slide them out one by one without disturbing the others. 'Omnisant – the company I work for – got the original licence to do the research because we were working in the area of immunity – helping the body to heal itself – and Dr Seagrove was one of the leaders in the field.'

'So he wasn't really an eye doctor at all?'

Dr Brown shakes his head. 'Immunologist. His plan was to clone your antibodies.'

'That's what you've been injecting us with?' asks Liam. He hasn't moved, but his face is sharp and intense. 'Bits of *them*?'

'In a manner of speaking. The antibodies have to be mixed with other substances, and we added an accelerant.'

'But you got it wrong.'

'There were some initial problems.'

'*Problems?*' Before anyone can stop him, Liam lunges forward and grabs hold of Dr Brown's tie, yanking it so they are nose to nose. 'Lee died because of your experiments. That's not *problems*, that's murder.'

Ryan and some of the others prise Liam's hands away and drag him back. 'Look out!' I shove someone's legs to keep him from treading on Marcus, who's looking even worse than before and isn't even trying to keep out of the way.

'What about Sam and Jayden and Ashley?' someone else shouts.

I'm guessing they're the blind guys that we saw in the basement, and wonder if the volunteers realise what happened to them.

'I'm sorry.' Dr Brown's eyes are glistening. 'I don't know what more I can say.'

Silence.

Sorry. I suppose it's all he can say right now, but it's pathetic.

'Also,' says Ryan, 'there's what happened to Alice, Cerys and Treyshawn. Unless that was deliberate.'

'You saw them?' Dr Brown asks.

'We saw everything, including Mr Virtanen. And he'd have seen us, only he was busy having a colour orgy with a virtual reality headset.'

'Alice?' says Liam. 'Who's that?'

After Ryan's finished explaining what we saw in the basement and how the fire started, there's more silence.

There's a moaning noise from somewhere near my feet, and when I look down I realise it's Marcus, eyes wide with horror. 'They said she'd gone home,' he croaks.

'Yeah,' says Ryan sarcastically. 'That's what they said.'

'They talk a load of shit.' Liam gets to his feet, swaying with the movement of the truck. There's a second's pause before several of the others join him. They're glaring at Dr Brown, but at the same time there's something uncertain about them, like they're not sure what to do and are waiting for a signal. The atmosphere's so tense that the air feels stretched, like it's going snap any moment.

Liam digs into the pocket of his camouflage jacket and hands something to one of the volunteers sitting next to the tailgate. There's a glint. Silver. A knife.

'Cut.' He points at the canvas. 'This one's leaving.'

Fifty-Six

The volunteer starts to slice through the material, and I imagine Dr Brown's body smacking onto the tarmac at seventy miles an hour. For a second, he looks like he hasn't understood what Liam's saying. Then he starts trying to scramble backwards, only there's nowhere to go. I look at Ryan for help, but he's still sitting on the floor, frowning like he's trying to decide something.

My heart feels like it's trying to beat itself out of my chest. I scramble to my feet, swaying and just managing to avoid standing on Marcus. 'No!' It comes out like a bleat. 'You can't. Dr Brown's the only one left who knows how it works.'

'It *doesn't* work.' Liam glares at me.

'Not now, but in time—'

'He's done enough damage. He turned your friends into *machines*.'

'I know. And I know this is messed up, and I'm not trying to defend him. I mean, we're the ones who were suspicious, right? That's why we went down to the basement. But he can help people.'

'By killing them?'

'OK, so he was part of that. But listen, you know about Franchot, right? His guys are looking for us, and if you throw Dr Brown out on the road, and they find him . . . Do you see what I'm saying?'

'He won't be able to tell them anything.'

'Maybe not, but they'll still know we've been this way, won't they?'

'So? We'll be long gone. Sit down.'

Ryan puts up a hand to tug me back down. 'He's right, Grace.'

'No, he *isn't*.' I sit down with a bump. 'What's the matter with you?'

'He didn't try and stop any of it, did he?' Ryan turns to Liam. 'And when they get it sorted, they aren't going to give it away, they're going to *sell* it. Grace figured it out.'

For a moment, the only sound is flapping canvas. I can practically hear what they're thinking: the most in-your-face example ever that the world is unfair, and why did anyone expect anything different?

Liam says, 'Of course they are.' He nudges Dr Brown with the toe of his boot. 'They're right, aren't they?'

Dr Brown makes a noise like a sob. 'I didn't know, not when we arrived. It was Anne – Professor Petrossian – who warned me. She thought she could talk Seagrove out of it, but she didn't realise they were all behind it, and—'

'Wait,' Liam says. 'Who's "they"?'

'Omnisant. The government hired them. All the governments. It's a global initiative. I knew there'd been some differences of opinion, way above my pay grade, but we were told it was all settled, and—'

Now it's my turn to stop him. 'When you say differences of opinion, are you talking about Mr Kowalczyk?'

Dr Brown stares at me, eyes wide with shock.

'Professor Petrossian was trying to get to him, wasn't she? When she had the accident – if that's what it was.'

'Hold on.' Liam turns to me. 'What are you talking about?'

I tell him as much as I know. I don't think I make a great job of it, and there's a lot of confused muttering when I finish, but it seems to calm everyone down a bit. 'She didn't know Mr Kowalczyk was dead, did she?'

Dr Brown shakes his head. 'None of us did, except Seagrove. He told me after she'd left. We knew Kowalczyk had been asked to leave Omnisant, but it was hushed up. The fraud squad were involved, I know that, but now—'

'Now' – Ryan interrupts him – 'you're saying it was a stitch-up because he was against selling the colour-vision stuff.'

'Yes. A way to discredit him.'

'Right,' says Liam. 'So, they bring down a shedload of grief on this guy's head and he kills himself, and they keep quiet about it and go ahead anyway.'

'And Dr Seagrove would get to be King Scientist,' Ryan tells Dr Brown. 'All the glory, lots of money, and the Nobel Prize. You kept quiet because you were going to be the Crown Prince – and Lee and Alice and Cerys and Treyshawn, and the soldiers who got blinded—'

'And us,' says one of the volunteers with sunglasses.

'And you. That was all just . . .'

'Collateral damage,' finishes Liam.

'And that,' says Ryan, 'is before we get on to the people who got shot back there.'

'Bastard.' Liam spits the word out. For a taut, mad second I think he's going to kill Dr Brown right there, and the others look like they wouldn't think twice about helping him.

'What I *don't* understand,' I gabble, 'is why Dr Seagrove started shooting. OK, so he'd lost a bunch of stuff, and three sources of antibodies – four, if you count Sophie – but the programme could have gone on somewhere else with the rest of us.' It's so weird, being able to just say this stuff without crying or . . . well, feeling anything, really. It's like it's nothing to do with me, and I'm just listening to myself talk.

Liam scowls like he's about to tell me to shut up, but he doesn't. Instead, he turns to Dr Brown. 'Yeah, Professor Science. Explain *that*.'

Dr Brown's voice is whiny, like a child. 'I tried to stop him. It wasn't my fault. When we heard that you two had gone down to the basement—'

Ryan cuts across him. 'Who told you?'

Dr Brown looks down at Marcus.

'I might have known it was your fault.' For a moment, I think Ryan is actually going to spit at Marcus, who closes his eyes and turns his head away. 'Always thought you were better than us, didn't you? I'd like to—'

'Don't, Ryan.' I put a hand on his arm. 'There's no point. He thought he was doing the right thing. Kieran was trying to warn us, wasn't he?' I ask Marcus. 'When Dr Seagrove shot him. He knew what you'd done.'

Marcus's reply is barely audible. 'I heard you. Kieran tried to stop me pressing my button – him and Kareem. They were worried what Seagrove would do, and they were right. I'm so sorry.'

'But you thought you were *doing the right thing*, so that's OK.' Ryan's voice is tight, squeezed out through clenched teeth. 'And a bunch of people burnt to death because of it.' He turns back to Dr Brown. 'So?'

Dr Brown looks like Ryan's just punched him in the face. 'Seagrove just ... He lost it. He was paranoid even before we came to Aveney Park – didn't want to share his findings, even with people in the company. He thought that Professor Petrossian had been spying on him. It wasn't true, but ... He just went crazy. I think,' Dr Brown's voice is a whisper now, 'that he didn't want anyone else to have you.'

'To get his hands on his valuable "human samples", you mean,' says Ryan.

'Yes, he said the pair of you were going to destroy everything. He pushed me out of the lift when I tried to follow him down to the basement and he must have done something to it to stop it coming back up. I tried to phone Virtanen, but he wasn't picking up. I didn't know what was happening until I heard the explosion, and then ... then ... ' He shakes his head. 'I didn't know what he was going to do. This was *his* project, the chance he'd been waiting for, and the pressure must have been unimaginable. We'd argued after what happened to Alice – I said the dosages were too high, but he said we needed to go ahead because everyone expected results ... He'd made all these claims, the licence had been granted, and everyone was waiting.' Dr Brown is gabbling now. 'Omnisant own five of the most important medical journals, and they spend millions of pounds advertising in all the others. They've paid experts hundreds of thousands of pounds to produce reports saying that this is the only way forward, which have been seen by the governments of all the developed countries, and no one was going to put their head above the parapet and say that it wasn't because then they'd look as if they didn't care about the fate of the planet ... And, because the consensus amongst those scientists in the know was that it was going to succeed, they'd look like idiots if they challenged it – which would mean they'd have trouble getting funding for their own research in the future. You see how it works?'

'Bunch of arseholes,' says Liam. 'Out for themselves.'

'It's not that simple.' Dr Brown rubs a hand over his face. 'People are fallible. For the politicians, there's too much at stake. They want to look as if they're in control even when they're not, and they want to be associated with good news – how we're beating this ... And they're human beings, same as the public, desperate to believe that the men and women in white coats have the answers. *I* was desperate to believe it – and maybe it *could* be the answer. Because we *were* getting there ... Mistakes were made, but *all* medicine is trial and error. That's why we know more than we did a hundred years ago.

But we don't know *everything*, and nothing remotely like this has ever happened before.'

Ryan glares at him. 'What about Franchot?'

'He was told to prevent security breaches at all costs. He had clearance at the highest level.'

'So he could kill people and get away with it?'

'They never thought it would come to that, Ryan, but . . . yes.' Dr Brown sighs. 'I'm not saying,' he adds quickly, 'that any of what I've said is an excuse, for Dr Seagrove or Captain Franchot or anybody else. I'm just trying to explain.'

Everyone stares at him.

It wasn't meant to be like this.

I suddenly remember the beginning of the greyout, sitting on the stairs and thinking that maybe nobody has ever really been in control of anything.

Turns out I was right.

Fifty-Seven

'Just now, you said "dosages", right?'

Dr Brown looks at me warily.

'They weren't vitamins or supplements, were they?'

'No.'

'Professor Petrossian didn't know about that, did she?'

'Not when she joined the project – not until we got to Aveney Park, in fact.'

'Did you?'

'Yes.' Dr Brown's voice is a whisper. 'I tried to tell Seagrove he was using too much—'

'On *some* people,' Ryan spits.

'We had to vary it, to establish the correct dose.'

'What are you talking about now?' Liam's impatient. 'Dose of what?'

'These.' I roll up my right sleeve and hold out my arm so it can be seen in the light coming through the torn canvas at the back. It's bright and sort of moonscapey out there, so I'm guessing we're still on the motorway.

Liam peers at the writing on my skin. 'Fluma . . . what?'

'Flumatoxin,' says Dr Brown quietly. 'The other one's Bemethiazide. They're stimulants. In large doses, they can cause convulsions.'

'Which was what you wanted – to stimulate production.'

'How did you—'

'The storeroom in the basement.' I cover up my arm. 'What about rhenium? What does that do?'

When I say this, I'm expecting him to look *really* shocked – like, how could I know about that – but he just stares at me, frowning. Ryan's frowning, as well, and I realise I never told him about it.

I describe what Mr Kowalczyk said, omitting the fact that I'm not a hundred per cent sure he actually *did* use that particular word because I don't want to give Dr Brown a get-out.

'Why would he say *that*?' Dr Brown sounds baffled, but perhaps he's just a good actor.

Ryan scowls at him. 'You tell us.'

'I don't know . . . Honestly. I know it's an element. A transition metal, I think, but—'

'We don't need a bloody chemistry lesson!' Liam's so loud that everyone flinches. 'How much?'

Dr Brown's eyes widen. 'How much what?'

'For colour vision. What will it cost?'

'I . . . I'm not sure. I think they were waiting to see what the—'

'You must have some idea.'

'Well, apparent self-healers like Grace and Ryan and Marcus are very rare—'

'Even rarer now,' Ryan mutters.

'But you're all set, aren't you?' asks Liam. 'If you can clone the antibodies.'

Dr Brown sighs. 'I'm afraid it isn't quite that simple.'

'Hang on,' Ryan says. 'If you can mass-produce it, then what's the problem?'

'That's what we hope to do eventually, once we've perfected the technique, but it'll take time – years, maybe – and . . .'

He tails off, and I know exactly what he's thinking, but not saying. 'And,' I say, quietly, 'even when you perfect it, why *give* something away when you can *sell* it? If Omnisant is the only company who's got it, they can charge whatever they like.'

'She's right,' Liam says. 'What about that, then?'

'Well, Omnisant *are* the only company, but obviously the politicians can regulate—'

'Politicians!' Ryan's shouting. 'A bunch of rich people getting into bed with their rich friends to make themselves even richer. That's how come we're in this mess.'

'Yeah.' Liam leans forward, his eyes menacing. 'Come on, how much?'

'Well, initially . . .' Dr Brown's voice drops to a whisper. 'A figure has been mentioned . . . five hundred thousand pounds.'

There's silence, and then everybody starts talking at once.

'There'll be loans,' says Dr Brown desperately. 'Like buying a house.'

'I don't know if you've noticed,' someone says, 'but most people can't afford a half-a-million-pound house, either.'

'Well, obviously there would have to be some sort of security against the loan. Property, or—'

'Or what?' shouts Liam. 'A superyacht? A private jet? Because we've all got those, haven't we? I've had it with this.' He jumps to his feet, hauling Dr Brown upright by his lapels and dragging him towards the flapping canvas. 'Out of the way—'

'Stop!' I reach over knees and feet to grab on to Liam's leg.

'Really? You're *still* defending him?'

'I'm not defending him, it's just that—'

'Wait!' Dr Brown's voice is a strangled scream. 'I'll give it to you. Everything that's left. I've got it here.'

Fifty-Eight

'Colour. I've got it. In my pocket – I kept some. Please don't do—'

'That shit makes people go blind!' someone shouts.

'This won't,' I tell him. 'They were experimenting before, and—'

Liam rounds on me. 'Why should we trust *you*?'

There are shouts of agreement, and then all the volunteers – even the ones in dark glasses – jump up at once, pushing and shoving, grabbing for Dr Brown's arms and legs. I try and wriggle towards him, but someone steps on my hand.

'Ow! Get off—'

'Out of the way, then.'

I look up to see who's speaking, and spot Ryan through the milling legs. Marcus is beside him, scrunched up, his hands protecting his head. 'Is he all right?'

'Yes.'

'Then why aren't you helping Dr Brown? He's going to get hurt!'

Before Ryan can say anything, the truck swerves violently, and everyone crashes down on top of the three of us.

For a moment, I'm suffocating under a scrambling heap of

elbows, knees, feet and fists, and everyone's swearing and shouting. Then the truck slows and judders to a halt.

Connor's head appears through the rip in the canvas as we're picking ourselves up. Dr Brown is curled up in a corner, hands over his face.

'Bloody hell. What's happened here?'

The volunteers look at each other. Finally, Liam shakes his head. 'It's OK. Just . . . ' He shrugs. He's slumped back on one of the bench seats and his face is a dull red. All around me, as Connor undoes the canvas and lets in more light, I can see khaki, and Ryan's purple top, and the blue of Marcus's jeans, and . . . everything. Despite what's happened, it's amazing, like a miracle. I suddenly wonder if Rosie and Kieran and Kareem got to see colours before they died. I really hope they did.

Marcus is still hunched over on the floor, but Ryan's blue eyes are shining and hungry, like he's trying to take in everything at once, and I know that he can still see the colours, too.

'Services.' Connor lowers the tailgate. 'We need fuel.'

'Right.' Liam looks at us. 'Got any money?'

Several people laugh, but Connor says, 'I think we're a bit past that, mate. Come and look.'

I let everyone scramble past me – Ryan doesn't wait, just jumps straight out – until the truck is empty except for Dr Brown and Marcus.

Dr Brown takes his hands away from his face. His tie has come loose and his nose is bleeding, red smears down his neck and on his collar. Marcus hasn't moved. His injured foot is now covered in reddish-purple bruises and looks like it's been inflated with a tyre pump.

He turns towards me when I put a hand on his shoulder. His face is a sweaty greyish-yellow, moving like he's trying to get words out but can't.

'Hang on.' I bend right over him, so his mouth is by my ear.

'I'm sorry. *Alice* . . . I'm so sorry.'

'You weren't to know.'

'If you'd told me . . .'

'You wouldn't have believed us.'

He doesn't say anything. We both know it's true. I suppose I could say that we don't even know if Alice, Cerys and Treyshawn might have been saved – as in, back to the way they were before – if the fire hadn't happened. That's true, but somehow I haven't got the words for it, or for the way I'm feeling right now. 'I'll bring you some water, OK?'

Dr Brown watches me as I get to my feet and climb out of the truck, but I ignore him. I probably ought to say something, but right now it's like I'll actually choke if I try to speak – and in any case, I never want to talk to him again as long as I live.

I'm not sure I want to talk to Ryan, either.

Fifty-Nine

Connor has pulled up on the forecourt of a service station. All the lights are on, and I can see the empty motorway stretched out beyond the barrier. The pumps seem OK, but pieces of brake light are shining like rubies on the tarmac and, beneath the bright green fascia, the plate-glass front of the shop is smashed like somebody ram-raided it. The inside is a mess of wrecked units, with a scattering of brightly coloured food wrappers, and empty cartons and cans. The soldiers are swarming all over the place, but it doesn't look like there's anything left to nick.

The land behind the shop slopes up to a service road, and behind that is one of those buildings that's like a box made out of Lego, all primary colours. A motel – but there don't seem to be any lights on and the car park beside it is empty.

Maybe the staff made a run for it when the looters arrived. I can see a light winking on the shop's alarm, but judging from what Ryan and I heard on the radio, the police would have been too busy to come. Which is good, if Captain Franchot's men are looking for us . . .

I suddenly realise that I need to pee, and head into the shop. I spot the sign behind a small café area with tables and benches. There's a television screen, too, high up: silent footage of trashed shops and crowds outside warehouses. The subtitles say, '*Scenes in London earlier today . . .* '. The world's gone mad – and Mum, Prune and Rusty are somewhere in the middle of it.

There's no one in the Ladies, thank God, just a tipped-over bin spilling out rubbish. I'm washing my hands – the soap dispenser has a Kerr + Bell logo, of course – when I catch sight of someone in the mirror above the basin: a terrified girl with messy curls and a dirty face, dressed in a stained blue hoodie and looking like she needs help.

It takes a couple of seconds to realise that I'm looking at myself.

'Hello,' I say, stupidly, watching the pink mouth frame the word back at me. 'You're still here.'

I wish Alice were here as well. I suppose I barely got to know her – although it didn't feel like that, because sometimes you just bond with people straightaway – and I never got to see her in colour. I really, really hope that she and Cerys and Treyshawn were past feeling anything and didn't know what was happening at the end.

I can't think about them now, or I'll never stop crying. I look around for paper towels to wipe my hands but there aren't any, so I go back into the cubicle for some loo roll. Something on the dispenser catches my eye: bumps on the white plastic surface. When I take a closer look, I see white capital letters.

AMARANTH.

275

The word that was on the box in Alice's room in the basement, that I knew I'd seen before.

I stare at the rubbish on the floor. Takeaway coffee cups, small food trays and disposable forks ... The government banned the sale of single-use plastics after the announcement that plastic was causing the greyout, but I guess you're allowed to finish up the existing stocks.

I pick up one of the trays for a closer look. It's transparent, with those same raised letters on the back.

Amaranth.

They made plastic things. Lots of them.

And then I remember.

The photo in the staff wing, the big board with the company names on it. Amaranth was one of them.

Amaranth is part of Omnisant.

I am *so* naive. Of course Omnisant would own a company that makes plastic. They probably own one that makes pesticides, too. Maybe more than one.

Money from creating the problem; money from providing the solution. Win-win.

Sixty

I'm at the door when it crashes open, banging against the wall. That's all I need. Ryan, with his arms full of bottles, sandwiches and bags of crisps. His clothes are as messed up as mine, and the harsh strip light is bleaching his tan to a sickly yellow.

'Excuse me.'

I move to go past him, but he drops the stuff by the basins and puts his hands on my shoulders.

'Hey!'

He lets go of me and raises his arms for a moment like he's surrendering, but he doesn't move out of the way. 'OK, but listen—'

'Why should I? You weren't exactly helpful back there.'

'I couldn't stop them, could I?'

'You could have *tried*. They were going to throw him into the road.'

Ryan shrugs. 'He's all right, isn't he?'

'Only because Connor stopped for fuel.'

'Whatever. Just drop it.'

There's plenty of stuff I want to say, but the look on Ryan's face stops me. It's the same expression Liam had when Connor asked him what was going on: confused and furious and helpless all at once. I'm angry with Ryan because (a) it's not like what happened is just Dr Brown's fault, and (b) throwing somebody out of a moving truck is not only vile, it's also pointless. At the same time, I totally get how he's feeling. This whole thing is just too *big*. It's like, if one person steals something from a shop or cheats on welfare benefits, they get punished, but a whole bunch of people can do something so massively greedy and stupid that it trashes the entire planet, and get rewarded by making a shit ton of money from it. And apparently that's all right and the rest of us have to suck it up because that's just *how it is*.

'OK . . . But, so you know, this isn't me being the bigger person. It's just that there's no point fighting about it. Plus, we need to help Marcus.' I can see Ryan's about to say something and hold up my hand to stop him. 'Yes, I *know* he's a dick. But he's a dick who's said sorry – to me, just now. I'm going to take him some water, and then he needs a hospital.'

'Yeah, OK. You're right.' Ryan picks up a bottle of orangeade and holds it out to me. 'Drink it, then you can fill it with water.'

'Thanks. Where did you get it?'

'Storeroom at the back. Some of the guys broke in.'

I don't know if it's because I can see colour again, or because I'm thirsty, or both, but that orangeade is the most delicious thing I've ever tasted. Ryan watches in silence as I slurp it down and refill the bottle with water. Then he says, 'I'm sorry Alice isn't here.'

Like he'd read my mind. I nod, surprised.

'You made friends really quick, didn't you?'

I can't resist another dig. 'I thought you were too busy hating the world to notice.'

Ryan looks sheepish. 'Whatever . . . Girls are good at that stuff.'

'You made friends with Treyshawn.'

Ryan looks surprised, then says, 'Yeah, I did. He was . . . Yeah.' He blinks a couple of times and says, 'So . . . You look nice.'

'Yeah, right.' This has to be as hard for him as it is for me – just that he's showing it in a different way. 'Are you still seeing in colour?'

Ryan grins. 'That's why I said it. Forgive me?'

He puts his hands on my shoulders again, and this time I don't shrug him off. It's not just that he's gorgeous – despite the rubbish lighting – and that fighting that, or him, is pointless. Even if he didn't defend Dr Brown, I know he's got my back, and right now I need that more than anything. All of this shoots through my brain in about a nanosecond, and by then we're so close that our foreheads are touching, and—

There's a shout and a massive crash from somewhere in the shop, and we leap apart like we're scalded.

'Come on.' Ryan gathers up the food. 'We better get out of here before they completely trash the place.' He hands me a packet of prawn mayonnaise sandwiches and I'm instantly hypnotised by the delicate pink filling.

'Earth to Grace.'

'Sorry . . . Just by the way, do you think Marcus has colour vision?'

'No idea, but' – Ryan glances in the direction of the shop – 'if he has, I think he ought to keep quiet about it, and so should we.'

'Agreed.' I move towards the door. 'And I need to find a phone.'

There's a couple of soldier volunteers crouching over a third, who's sitting on the floor beside an upturned shelving unit and rubbing his head.

I start to pick my way through the wreckage. 'There's got to be a phone here somewhere.' Ryan passes me, weaving through the mess towards the area where the cashiers sit. The door at the end is open, and the place has been thoroughly ransacked, but . . .

There's a landline, and . . . Yes! It's working.

'No point calling 999 for an ambulance, though,' Ryan says. 'They'll be swamped. Plus, they might realise who we are, and—'

'I wasn't going to.' Then, staring at the numbers on the phone, I realise. 'It's useless. I thought I might be able to remember Mum's number, but I can't . . . Or anybody else's.'

Ryan prods the keyboard of the computer. 'There's Wi-Fi, but this needs a password. Sorry. But I'm sure you'll be able to get home.'

'Are you?'

'We'll manage it somehow.'

I'm not sure I believe him, but it's nice to hear. 'Don't you want to talk to your dad?'

'No point. He'll only be . . .' Ryan stops mid-shrug, eyes widening. 'I've just thought. What if Dr Brown's got a mobile?'

'I don't think the staff were allowed to keep them, either.'

'Maybe not, but he could have grabbed it out of the safe or wherever when everything kicked off.'

'But my mum's number's not going to be on there, is it?'

'No, but he'll phone Omnisant, won't he?'

'What, so they can come and shoot him?'

'Captain Franchot only shot Dr Seagrove because Seagrove lost it. And Dr Brown said he shot the others because they witnessed it—'

'So did he.'

'Yeah, but he's got the stuff, remember? And he knows how to make it . . . Plus, he's got *us*, hasn't he? And Marcus. The gifts that keep on giving.'

Alice. Cerys. Treyshawn. Antibody machines. They could keep us like that for years, and no one would ever know.

Sixty-One

The forecourt is deserted, but the truck's still by the pumps. Marcus is lying in the back where I left him, but Dr Brown has disappeared.

'I'll find him.' Ryan tips the food over the tailgate. 'You stay with Marcus.'

'Liam and the others – you don't think . . . ?'

'I don't know. Seriously, Grace, you better stay here, OK?'

He disappears before I can answer. I clamber into the truck and help Marcus raise his head enough to drink some of the water.

'Thanks,' he whispers.

'Do you think you can eat anything?'

He doesn't look like he's hungry. His forehead's fever-hot, but he's shivering, and I'm not surprised when he shakes his head.

The groundsheet we hid under is scrunched up by one of the benches. I fold it over several times and put it under his head, then eat the sandwich – which tastes great – while I look round for anything else that might make him more comfortable. There's nothing – but a plastic tube, sealed, and small enough to fit in someone's pocket, is lying underneath the bench. I pick it up and turn it over. Clear fluid, with a label: *Antibody GEB*.

My initials: Grace Emily Ballard.

Underneath that are a load of other letters and numbers. I'm guessing those refer to whatever they've mixed with the antibodies. Below them is what I suppose must be yesterday's date.

Dr Brown must have dropped this.

I am holding a half-a-million-pounds' worth of colour vision in my hand.

I turn back to Marcus. 'What happened to Dr Brown?'

'I don't know.' He can barely speak.

'Did anyone come back for him?'

Head shake.

'He didn't say anything?'

Marcus swallows. 'Just, "Sorry".'

That useless word again. 'Can you see colour, Marcus?'

'At the moment. Comes and goes.'

'Did you tell anyone?'

'Only you.'

'Good. Keep quiet about it, OK?'

This can't wait. I don't know how you tell if someone has blood poisoning, but there was a story about it on one of Prune's favourite hospital drama series, and the person nearly died. I put the little tube in my pocket and climb out of the truck. 'Just hang in there, all right? I'm going to try and persuade Connor to take you to a hospital.'

*

There's no one in the main part of the shop now, but I can't hear any shouting, which has to be a good thing. I head past the TV, which is now showing footage of masked people hijacking a supermarket van, and make for the storerooms.

All the doors have been wrenched off their hinges, and it looks like the volunteers are working their way through the entire stock. Even the ones in sunglasses look like they can see well enough to raid the place, and the floor is ankle-deep in cartons and wrappers. I spot Kyle in front of an open fridge. 'Do you know where Connor went?'

'Nah.' He pulls out two beers. 'He'll be back, though. Want one?'

'No thanks. I'll have some water, though.'

'Still or sparkling, madam?'

'Still, please.'

'Here you go.' Kyle reaches in and picks out a bottle, but it's sparkling water.

'Uh-uh,' I say, automatically. 'The blue label.'

Sixty-Two

Shit.

'Woah!' Kyle backs away from me, staring. '*What* did you say?'

Dead silence. Now everyone's staring at me.

'You said "the *blue* label". You can see it.'

It feels like everyone in the room is holding their breath.

'No, I just . . .' I don't know what to say.

'You can see colour.'

'I . . .' My throat feels like it's closing up. I look round at their faces: confusion, anger . . . even fear.

'You didn't tell me.' Kyle sounds like I've betrayed him.

'I didn't have time. The truck came, remember? I was going to. Honestly.'

'I told her,' Kyle tells the rest of them. 'About me and the others – how it worked for a short time, because of what that doctor gave us – but she didn't say nothing.'

'I'm sorry. I would have.' I look round at the others, hoping to see a sympathetic face, but they're all glaring at me like they're going to start shouting 'Burn the witch'. As I look towards the

285

doorway, two of the soldiers move across to stand side by side, blocking it.

I'm trapped.

'You heard what Dr Brown said about how a few people might be self-healing,' I gabble. 'They don't really know yet, but they were giving us stuff, too, like we told you, so it might just be because of that, and—'

'How long?' someone asks.

'When the fire started.'

'Hours.' Liam steps forward so he's right in my face. 'Aren't you the lucky one?'

'Not necessarily.' I will myself to look at him, to sound like it's a normal conversation, not to shake. 'It might not last.'

'But you get it free.' Liam says this like he hasn't heard me. 'We'll never be able to afford it, but you . . . You just get it for nothing.' The air in the room seems to thicken with menace. What he – what they – might do.

'I didn't ask for it,' I say, desperately. 'It just happened. It could have been anybody.' Looking round, I can see I'm making it worse. It's the total unfairness of the whole thing: right now, despite the fact they know what happened to Alice and Cerys and Treyshawn, they feel like I'm part of that and they hate me.

Trying to run will make it worse, too. A lot worse. If they were prepared to throw Dr Brown out of a moving truck, then . . . The tube of colour vision feels like it's burning a hole in my pocket. Should I offer it to them? Bribery didn't work for Dr Brown, but now they've seen that Kyle's OK after he had some, it might . . .

'Get out.' Liam's voice is a growl, low and thick. 'Just go.'

What? I blink at him, astonished. 'Where?'

'Anywhere.' He takes a step back, making just enough room for me to squeeze past. 'Take the others with you.'

Nobody speaks as I make my way to the door. My legs are shaking now, so much that I feel like they're not going to hold me up. I whisper, 'Sorry, sorry, sorry,' as I slither past them, turning sideways to get between the two in the doorway, who don't move, and feeling their breath on me – beer, crisps and cigarettes – before I run for it.

I blunder through the shop in a panic, and onto the forecourt. I can't see Ryan, or Dr Brown.

Marcus.

I head for the truck.

Marcus feels like he's burning up, and he stares at me as if I'm part of a nightmare. 'I can't.'

'You've got to. I'll explain later.' He groans as I drag him over to the tailgate, feeling like my arms are going to come out of their sockets. 'You'll have to try and sit up. Put your legs over the edge.'

'No . . . Hurts.'

'You *have* to. Come on . . . '

He cries out as I shove him into the right position, then half falls onto the ground, pushing me away as I try to pull him upright. Too bad we'll have to leave Ryan's food behind. 'Stop. Wait for the others.'

'No time. I'll explain later. Let me . . . ' I get my arm round his waist and push his arm up and round my shoulders. His skin is slippery with sweat and he feels like a sack of concrete. My knees almost buckle under the weight, but I manage to stumble forward.

'Where ... going?'

Good question. *Think, Grace.*

'Over there. Motel. You can lie down.' I'm talking rubbish, but I've got to get him away from the forecourt before the volunteers come out of the shop. I don't really know why Liam suddenly decided to give us a chance to get away, but I'm not going to push my luck. It's much darker over there – easier to hide if he changes his mind.

'It'll be OK. You'll see. You're going to be fine.' I barely know what I'm saying, but I keep talking as we limp across a road and up a grass bank. It's not steep, thank God, but by the time we get to the top I'm almost on all fours, with Marcus sort of draped across my back, moaning.

Every muscle in my body feels like it's going to snap as I pretty much carry him across the car park. The sliding doors at the front of the motel open as we get near, and a fluorescent strip light blinks on in the small foyer.

Marcus winces as I lower him into a sitting position on the sofa. 'I'm going to find Ryan, OK? It'll be all right, I promise.'

He just stares, like he doesn't believe me.

I don't blame him. I don't believe me, either.

Light from the motorway spills over onto the huge car park, but with no vehicle noises it's eerily unreal, like a different planet.

No Ryan. No Dr Brown. And if Liam and the others change their minds about letting us go, Marcus won't be able to help me.

I don't dare call out.

I've never felt so completely alone.

Sixty-Three

Blood roaring in my ears, I jog past a row of dark windows to the far corner of the motel. No one here, and no cars. Just more tarmac, strewn with litter and divided by strips of baked earth with shrivelled bushes – nothing big enough to hide behind. I force myself to keep going until I turn the next corner.

A pool of light, coming from an open door halfway down the wall. A white van stands in the middle of it, driver's door open. *'Farm Fresh Fruit and Produce'* is written across the side in looping letters, a red apple with a cartoon grin dotting the 'i' of 'Fruit'.

Transport.

'Hello?' My voice echoes down the passageway. From the scuffed lino and marks on the walls, I'm guessing this is a service area. 'Ryan?'

'Grace?' A door at the end swings open, and he appears. He looks like he's been in a fight, and the knuckles of his right hand are red raw.

'What have you done?'

Ryan rolls his eyes at me. 'I'm fine, Grace, thanks for asking. Is Marcus OK?'

'No, and we're not, either. It's my fault. They know I can see colour. I didn't mean to tell them – it just slipped out.'

'What happened?' Ryan's voice is sharp. 'Did they hurt you?'

'I'm OK, but I honestly thought they were going to kill me. I think they would have, but then Liam said we all had to leave, so they let me go, and—'

'Where's Marcus?'

'Motel foyer. We've got to get out of here, and there's a van outside so there must be—'

'A driver. We just found him, and—'

'*We*? Is Dr Brown here?'

'In there.' Ryan jerks his head towards a door. Written across it in large red letters are the words 'COLD STORAGE'.

'In a freezer?'

I reach for the handle, but Ryan stops me. 'I couldn't think what else to do. Found him at the front making a call, but he legged it round here as soon as he saw me. It's OK, I got his phone off him. I'd have come straight back, but I wanted to find out about that van, and—'

'You're not going to *leave* him in there?'

'He was calling Omnisant, Grace. I heard him. They know where we are, so they'll send people to pick us up.'

'What if the motel staff don't come back? He'll die.'

'And what do you think is going to happen to *us* if we let him out?'

'Apart from being tried for murder if we *don't* let him out, we need to find out about the rhenium.'

Ryan frowns. 'He acted like he didn't know what you were talking about.'

'Yeah, but it's not like everyone's been super honest over this, is it? They could have been doing something with it that's so new it's not even mentioned on the internet, and Dr Brown didn't want to admit he knew what it was, so—'

'Bit late now, isn't it?'

'OK, but we'll *know*, and maybe – just maybe – we can do something about it. I'm sick of having shit happening to me that I've got no control over.' I go for the door handle again, but Ryan blocks me.

'You won't have control over *anything* if we open that door, because he'll tell them we're alive.'

'You said he already had – that people are coming to pick us up.'

'I didn't hear him say any names, though. Right now, they may not know *which* of us is still alive, and with the fire, it's going to take time to find out. We can give ourselves a chance by getting these off' – he taps his hospital wristband – 'but if he tells them . . .' He produces a pair of scissors from his back pocket. 'I found these in the kitchen. They know where we live, Grace. I wasn't planning on going home, but you are. Hold out your arm.'

I stare at him as he cuts off my wristband, then his own.

'Well,' Ryan stuffs the scissors back in his pocket with the wristbands. 'Aren't you?'

The thought of not being able to see my family is like a punch in the gut. 'Yes. So ... we'll just have to persuade him not to say anything.'

'Oh?' Ryan's eyes are glittering and hard. 'We're not white mice, Grace. He can't just order up a bunch more of us from a supplier. Now that Seagrove's out of the way, he's King Scientist, isn't he? And what about Marcus?'

Marcus. Who could be dying while we're standing here arguing. Ryan sees me hesitate, and says, 'Right. We're finding the key for that van, then we're out of here.'

'What about the driver?'

'That's what I was trying to tell you. He's round the corner.' Ryan gestures towards the end of the passage. 'And he's dead.'

Sixty-Four

'What happened?'

A man in green overalls is lying on his front, half in and half out of one of the storerooms. There's nothing on the shelves except a few empty boxes, but several big slugs are clustered near the guy's ear like they're trying to crawl inside his head.

'Probably interrupted the looters. Look at his hair.' Ryan points, and I see that it's clumped with blood, and there's a dark red spray across the pale tiles. 'Help me roll him over.'

'What?'

'We need to look in his pockets.'

That means touching him. 'OK. Right. How . . . ?'

'You take his legs.'

I kneel down beside Ryan, force myself to put my hands under the man's thigh, then lift and shove. As we turn him over, I spot the smiley apple, same as on the van, on his chest pocket next to a name badge: Barry.

Barry's head lolls as his face comes into view – weather-beaten skin, baggy eyes staring dully at the ceiling. A slug comes unstuck from the edge of his mouth and drops out of sight behind his neck.

'I just spotted something.' Ryan feels under Barry's shoulder and pulls out a key. 'Must have dropped it when he fell. It's OK, I know how to drive.'

'Right . . . ' Barry looks, and felt, so solid, but so empty of life. Something and nothing at the same time. I think of Sophie asking what colour death is.

Barry might have children.

So might Dr Brown.

It looked like Barry's death was quick, at least.

Dr Brown's won't be.

'Grace . . . ' Ryan's in the corridor, heading outside. 'We need to go.'

I catch up with him at the corner. 'We *can't* leave him in there.'

'But—'

'No!' I give Ryan a shove, sending him reeling back against the wall. 'I know what you're going to say, but I don't care. There's been enough death already. Do you understand? We. Cannot. Do. This.'

Before he has time to react, I run to the cold store and open the door.

Sixty-Five

'Why are there no signs?'

This van isn't exactly comfortable, and it must be nearly as old as Rusty's, but at least it's got a full tank. Ryan's belting along the motorway, with me, Dr Brown and Marcus squashed up on the front seat beside him, and I'm sweating buckets because we've got the heater on full blast.

Marcus's face really is grey now, and he's slumped against the window. Although Dr Brown's finally stopped shivering, I think he's in shock because he hasn't spoken once since I let him out of the cold store – which makes me pretty certain that he's not going to give us any trouble, at least for the moment. The army truck was gone when we drove through the forecourt, thank God.

Maybe I'm in shock, too. I feel numb, and it's like I can't believe anything that's happened. I peer down the endless chain of white lines to the vast concrete pillars of the bridge up ahead. 'There's bound to be a sign soon.'

'There better be. We need to get off this road before the next checkpoint, or they'll stop us, and then ...' Ryan takes his hand off the wheel and draws a finger across his throat. 'Take this.' He fishes Dr Brown's phone out of his pocket and tosses it into my lap. 'Get him to give you the PIN.'

Dr Brown blinks as I hold the phone up in front of him and for a moment I think he isn't going to tell me. When he speaks, the words sound thin and brittle, like they haven't thawed out. His eyes are watery as he watches me unlock the phone. 'Thank you,' he adds.

He must mean for getting him out of the cold store, but I don't respond because I honestly don't know what to say. It was the right thing to do, and he's grateful, but that doesn't mean he's on our side – and he still hasn't explained about rhenium.

I'm getting the hang of Dr Brown's phone, which is a lot newer than mine, when Ryan slaps the steering wheel. 'Cambridge! Next turning's nine miles. Can you find the hospital?'

I google the address, then look at the road again. Lines of cat's eyes, more bridges with concrete pillars, weeds and rubble on the grass verges, and the dark shapes of buildings in the distance: all as much in colour as a moonscape can be. But for how much longer?

I lean forward to look at the clock on the dashboard: 03.27. There must be about three and a half hours until dawn.

Please let me see the sunrise in colour, even if it's just one last time.

There are blue flashing lights coming up behind, and a police officer on a motorbike waves us towards the hard shoulder.

'Shit,' Ryan mutters. 'We'll have to stop. This thing won't go any faster.'

'Pretend we're lost,' I say.

'What if he asks for a driving licence? Or if *he*' – Ryan jerks his head towards Dr Brown – 'starts . . . Wait, though . . .'

As we slow down and pull over, the motorbike cop shoots straight past us, followed by a police car, and then a lorry – a huge one, with the name of a big supermarket chain written on the side. And another. And another. And another . . . Fifteen lorries in all, with police cars on either side, and more motorbikes at the end. I think of the masked men I saw on the TV in the shop, hijacking a supermarket van.

Ryan stares after the convoy for a moment, then leans forward until his forehead is resting on the steering wheel. 'Thank God for that.'

'They're not taking any chances, are they?'

Dr Brown mutters something.

'What did you say?' Ryan's voice is sharp. He didn't try and stop me when I opened the door of the cold store, but he wasn't exactly happy about bringing Dr Brown with us.

'Silicon Fen. What they call this place. Tech companies. Bio Tech, as well.'

'We don't need a guided tour,' Ryan snaps, restarting the engine. 'We just need to find a hospital. And you need to tell us about . . .' He looks at me. 'What's it called again?'

'Rhenium.' I turn to Dr Brown. 'What is it?'

'I don't know.'

Ryan smacks the steering wheel again. 'Of course you bloody know! You've been using it. On us.'

'I honestly have no idea.'

'Tell us!' Ryan shouts so loud it makes me jump, but Dr Brown looks totally bewildered.

'I can't. We didn't use rhenium.'

Dr Brown's voice is flat and definite. He's not begging us to believe him, just saying it. I stare at him. How do you know when someone's telling the truth? People always say that liars don't look you in the eye or they repeat your questions or start fiddling with their hair or whatever, but most of that is rubbish ... And besides, Mr Kowalczyk *could* have been saying something else. Just because I've sort of convinced myself they were using rhenium doesn't mean I'm right.

I can see that Ryan's about to go off on one. 'Wait a sec,' I say. 'Dr Brown, did you *really* not use it?'

'Never.'

'And you never heard Dr Seagrove or anyone else talk about it?'

Dr Brown shakes his head.

'You better not be lying,' Ryan mutters.

'Hold on, OK?' I think back. I can picture Mr Kowalczyk's face in my mind, the fear in his eyes. But ... at that point I couldn't actually hear what he was saying; I just saw his mouth move. *Ree No. Renew.*

Re ... *new*?

I suddenly think of when Ryan and I saw Mr Virtanen in the basement with the virtual reality headset. Ryan was mouthing at me, saying 'VR', but at first I'd thought it was 'The' and 'Ahh'.

JAMIE COSTELLO

Lip-reading is hard unless there's something to give you an idea of the subject, like me being able to see the actual thing that Ryan was talking about. Better to concentrate on sounds. So, something that's *not* 'renew', but *like* it . . .

I start going through the alphabet. It takes a while, but . . .

Of course.

We knew.

Sixty-Six

It's that feeling you get at the top of a rollercoaster, the second before you plunge straight down. 'It wasn't rhenium,' I tell Ryan. 'What I told you . . . I was trying to lip-read and I got it wrong.'

'So what was it?'

'I think Mr Kowalczyk was saying "*We knew*".'

Ryan jerks like he's been electrocuted. '*What?*'

'The Monochrome Effect. The people at Omnisant *knew* it was going to happen. That's right, isn't it?' I look at Dr Brown, who stares back at me like a rabbit caught in headlights. I turn back to Ryan. 'It's like this: one of their companies – maybe more than one – make plastic. I realised when I was in the loo at the services – the name on the plastic stuff in the bin was one of the names in that photo I saw at Aveney Park. For years they've been profiting from causing the problem, and all the governments just let them carry on swamping the world in plastic because no one had the will to do anything about it. Now they're planning to profit from selling a solution – and they can do that because they managed to figure out the issue with the microplastics absorbing all the bacteria and other crap before anyone else did. So now they get to be heroes and make even more money. Dr Brown, I overheard you talking to Dr Seagrove about a breakthrough you made three years ago. I know, you thought I was out, but I was awake and listening – I just didn't manage to put it all together until now.' Dr Brown gapes at me, eyes and mouth so wide open in shock that it's almost funny – or it would be if all of this wasn't so serious.

'It's how come they got all those contracts, Ryan. They'd fig-ured it out and they were already working on how to fix it before it happened. That's why Mr Kowalczyk couldn't live with himself. Dr Brown, you said they'd fitted him up because he was against selling colour vision, but it wasn't *just* that, was it? It was because he knew they *already* knew the greyout was going to happen – they'd carried out experiments or whatever – and instead of warning everybody about it, they carried on making plastic crap. And they got you and Dr Seagrove working on solving the problem, so they'd be the first ones with a result and they could make more money than anyone could even dream of. Plus, I'm guessing that people in governments round the world were in on it, because you can bet that companies with that much money and power have a *lot* of friends in high places. Which is also why Mr Kowalczyk's death wasn't reported, and why they put boards up all round his house and took everything away really quick – in case he'd left something incriminating. No evidence. End of.'

Ryan shakes his head. 'If he'd wanted to blow the whistle, he'd have emailed someone.'

'Emergency Powers, remember? They were in place by

then – and they're used to monitor stuff and censor it and shut people up.'

The silence is thick as a blanket.

Dr Brown clears his throat. 'We didn't know Kowalczyk was dead.'

'Maybe not, but what Grace is saying still makes sense,' Ryan says. 'How long *have* you been working on this?'

'Almost ...' Dr Brown is staring straight ahead like he's looking down a long tunnel. 'Five years, with Dr Seagrove. Professor Petrossian didn't come on board until a lot later.'

'Five years.' Ryan keeps his eyes on the road. 'Five. Whole. Years.'

'It's not what you think. We had reason to think that microplastics would eventually cross the blood-brain barrier, but we didn't know which part of the cerebral cortex – that's the part of the brain associated with higher functions like movement and sensory perception – they would affect. The Monochrome Effect was just one of a number of possibilities.'

'You total bastards.' Ryan's words come out between clenched teeth, like he's struggling not to hit someone. I'm not surprised. It's all so calculated it takes my breath away.

'So ...' I think of the film Mr Metcalf showed us at school, how I thought the blood-brain barrier sounded like a checkpoint with teeny-tiny armed guards. 'It might have been something else, like everyone going deaf or not being able to move or speak?'

'Possibly.'

'Could that still happen?'

'We don't know. That's the point. We were trying to be ready for whatever *did* happen, so we did a lot of groundwork, ran tests . . . We didn't want to find ourselves in a position where we'd have to start from scratch.'

'But you didn't tell anyone you were doing it.'

'It was felt – and I'm talking about the people in charge – that it would scare the public.'

'Yeah,' says Ryan. 'And mess up Omnisant's profits.'

'As I said, it wasn't my decision.'

'Oh, that's OK then.' Ryan's tone is viciously sarcastic. 'You were following orders. Fucking up the entire world is just a detail, right?'

Dr Brown sighs. 'I know you think it's a conspiracy—'

'What else would you call it?'

'It's more complicated than that, Ryan. Like climate change . . . It's hard to alter the way people think, and plastic is a huge part of everyday life. You can't just stop making something overnight when the world relies on it. Business people and scientists aren't perfect, any more than anyone else is. They convince themselves that something is OK, or that they're doing the right thing, because that's what suits them – and suits everybody.'

'Until it turns into a shitshow,' Ryan says. 'And even then, you lot find a way to come out on top.'

Apart from Marcus, whose eyes are closed now, we all stare straight ahead.

It's like there isn't anything more to say. I feel empty, like I've been hollowed out inside.

Sixty-Seven

There are no soldiers at the turnoff, thank God, just a row of cones, which scatter as Ryan ploughs straight through them and onto a side road. Darkness, apart from the headlights – just a couple of metres of tarmac in front of us and, alongside it, the edges of verges. As we drive across country, I see the night sky for the first time since I went into greyout: dark blue velvet, sprinkled with stars, and the moon, round and clean. It fills up my heart in a way I could never describe, even if I knew all the words in the world. I'd forgotten how vast it is up there. Grey sky looks like someone just slammed a colossal saucepan lid down over your head, but this ... this ... You know how people in the olden days called it 'the heavens'? Well, that thing. A great blue infinity.

People are always saying stuff is amazing, but this actually *is*. Way more amazing than figures on a bank statement, and, unlike money, it belongs to everyone. Or it used to.

I'm about to read the directions off Dr Brown's phone when he starts telling Ryan how to get there, so he obviously knows Cambridgeshire pretty well. No one else says anything as we negotiate our way through the lanes and into the city. There must have been riots here, too: glass like frost, glittering under the streetlamps, shops with grilles across the doors and windows, sirens in the distance. We pass a lot of army vehicles, and guys with baseball bats standing guard at the ends of streets closed off with plastic safety barriers. I bet Amaranth makes those, as well.

The hospital car park is full and so are all the streets nearby, so we wind up parking on the pavement round the back, next to an empty car with the driver's door still hanging open. Ryan cuts off Marcus's wristband and we bury it with ours inside a litter bin before we half carry, half drag him out of the van.

I thought Dr Brown might try to make a run for it the minute the van doors were open, but he takes my place helping Marcus hobble round to A&E.

'Right.' Ryan stops by the sliding doors, Marcus sagging against his side, and glares at Dr Brown. 'You say *anything* about any of this . . . '

'I shan't.'

'You better not, because if you do I'll tell them—'

I don't know what Ryan was going to threaten because Dr Brown interrupts. 'You have my word. I know you don't think that means much, but the most important thing right now is to help Marcus.'

'OK. But watch it, yeah?'

Dr Brown turns to me. 'You can trust me, Grace.'

'Can we?'

'Yes.'

I nod, because I don't know what else do to.

The rush of colour, light and noise as we get inside the building are almost more than I can handle, and Ryan looks like he's feeling the same way. At first, the waiting room is like being inside one of those enormous abstract pictures where it looks like the artist has flung different coloured paint all over the canvas, and it takes a few seconds before it untangles itself into individual people. The whole place smells of disinfectant, sweat, and fear. It's after 4 a.m. but it's heaving. As we steer Marcus into the only free chair, I spot clothing combinations so bizarre that the wearers must have forgotten what colour their stuff is, plus loads of socks – and sometimes even shoes – that don't match. Neither do the medical staff's scrubs: red tops with blue trousers, and all sorts. It's like a clown convention, except with nurses rushing about everywhere and lots of injured people. There are police officers hanging round the reception desk, where one woman is trying to process a long line of patients. Judging by her brick-red face and green lips, she's either lost track of her make-up or the cosmetics company mislabelled it. She's not the only one, either.

Dr Brown says he'll go with Ryan to get some help. It's a relief because my eyes are aching and my legs feel weak as ribbons, and all I can do is sit down on the floor next to Marcus's chair. He looks terrible and is slumped over like he's barely conscious. It's only when – after what seems like an hour – the two of them come back

307

with a porter and a wheelchair that his eyelids flutter. For a second I think he might be going to speak, but nothing comes out and the guy wheels him away.

I suddenly realise we were so focused on getting to the hospital that we didn't even discuss what we were going to say when we got there. 'Shouldn't we go with him?'

Dr Brown shakes his head. 'They'll do everything they can.'

Ryan takes my arm and hustles me outside, with Dr Brown following us. 'I told Marcus not to mention Aveney Park, which I think he understood, and we told the nurse we found him by the road. Don't want the police involved.'

'But they won't know who he is, or—'

'The important thing is that he's getting treatment, and he's in the best possible place, OK?' Then he adds, more gently, 'We've done all we can, Grace. It's up to him now.'

Everything's lit up blue by the revolving lights from the emergency vehicles as we stand on the concrete apron in front of A&E, staring at each other. It's weird, like the three of us are waiting for someone in charge to come and tell us what to do.

Ryan rubs his eyes. 'What's your plan?' he asks Dr Brown. 'Because you're still here.'

Dr Brown looks around as if he might find an answer to the question somewhere on the forecourt. 'I felt responsible.'

Ryan holds up the mobile, snatching his hand away when Dr Brown reaches for it. 'No chance. You've called Omnisant once already.'

Dr Brown shakes his head. 'I called a colleague – *ex*-colleague – who didn't agree with what was going on. I told him what had happened . . . And that he'd been right all along.'

'Yeah, right. Like this ex-colleague – whoever he is – could pick you up from that service station when there's no ordinary traffic allowed on the motorway.'

'I didn't ask him to. I just . . .' Dr Brown swallows. 'We'd argued, and I wanted to set the record straight in case anything happened to me.'

'I don't believe you.'

Dr Brown sighs. 'I can't say I blame you, but I'm telling the truth.'

'So,' I say, 'you didn't call Omnisant at all?'

'No.'

'Were you going to?'

'No.'

Did that come out a fraction too late, or did I imagine it? Dr Brown is shaking his head, but it seems more like it's because he doesn't know what to do than a denial. I hear an echo of my own voice from back in the summer, telling Jake we had to trust someone.

Look where it got us.

'Why should we believe you?' Ryan says.

'Phone David Parker and ask him. You can see the number on my phone, the last one I called, and the time. He'll tell you what I said to him.'

'What, and we're supposed to trust him, as well? Someone

we've never met? He could be anybody.' Ryan turns to me. 'What do you think?'

'I think ...' I have no idea what I think. My thoughts are so tangled I feel like there's no way I'll ever separate them out enough to make sense.

'Grace?'

Ex-colleague ... Right all along ... He could be anybody.

Then, as if something has shaken itself loose from the mess inside my head, I remember the other thing that Mr Kowalczyk said. The jumble of words spoken in front of the gate, that I'd only partially understood, reforms itself in my mind. I was totally wrong about the rhenium, so perhaps I was wrong about something else, as well ... 'The guy you said you phoned ... What did you say his name was?'

Dr Brown blinks, like *what's that got to do with it?* 'David.'

'David What?'

'Parker.'

Parker. Of course.

Sixty-Eight

'So what?' Ryan asks.

'There was something else Mr Kowalczyk said before he died. It seemed like nonsense, so I didn't think about it again, only the rhenium thing, but he also said something about a mistake. Then I thought he said "park a car" – but it wasn't. It was *Parker*. Maybe *Parker can't* . . . something or other.'

Ryan's sigh is dismissive. 'Even if you're right, Parker was probably . . . I don't know, his *butler* or something.'

I turn to Dr Brown. 'Would Mr Kowalczyk have known your friend?'

'It's possible. Omnisant's a huge organisation, but if David had spoken to him, tried to—'

'Wait. What happened to David?'

'He resigned and he hasn't worked since. But he would have had to sign something – non-disclosure—'

'And the Emergency Powers thing would have stopped him saying anything anyway. Come on, Ryan, you've got to admit—'

'OK.' Ryan puts his hands up in surrender. 'Fine. Where are you going with this?'

'We should call him.' I turn back to Dr Brown. 'If we do, will he confirm what you just told us?'

'Yes. He was working with us on theoretical modelling for antibody treatment and experiments using animal subjects.'

'OK – but right now, for human subjects, me and Ryan are it, right? Apart from Marcus.'

'As far as I know. We're still looking for subjects, but I've not been told about anyone else.'

'So apart from the colour stuff you . . .' I almost say 'had' but stop before I give myself away, because I've already decided I'm not going to tell either of them about what I found, at least for the moment. 'What you said you had when we were in the truck—'

'Gone.' Dr Brown's voice is flat. 'It must have fallen out of my pocket.'

'So right now, the only *useful* blood is what's inside us, yes?'

'Whoa!' Ryan takes a step back, eyes wide.

'Give me a minute, OK? I'm not the enemy here, Ryan.'

He stares at me like he's trying to make up his mind. Finally, he says, 'I'm listening.'

'The world needs colour vision, right? It's how they're planning to do it that's wrong.'

'Yeah, but if we give him' – Ryan jerks his head at Dr Brown – 'more of our blood, he's just going to turn it over to Omnisant so a bunch of rich arseholes can benefit, isn't he? If that's what you're suggesting—'

'I'm not.' I turn to Dr Brown. 'If we give you some of our blood, you and this Parker guy could keep it until you can get hold of whatever you need to mix with it. It's not much, but it's *something*. Perhaps more people will start to develop antibodies like we did, and maybe you can ask the parents of the younger kids who had colour episodes – yeah, I overheard that, too, so don't bother telling me they don't exist. Look, I don't know . . . but you've got to start somewhere, right?'

Dr Brown opens his mouth, but Ryan gets there first. 'Our blood belongs to Omnisant, remember? They'll just say it's their property, and nobody else can use it.'

'They won't know, and it has to be better than nothing.' Ryan's face is expressionless and I think I've lost him. 'Plus,' I add desperately, 'if we don't do anything, there's no possibility the remedy can exist, so Alice and Cerys and Treyshawn and all the others will have died for no reason . . . And people have to have *hope*, right? Not just a grey world where they can barely afford to eat and everybody's fighting. Don't you see what I'm saying?'

Ryan turns away for a moment, and I'm sure he's going to refuse.

'This is about the future, for everybody. *Please*, Ryan.'

'All right, I get it. Just stop . . . bouncing up and down, yeah?' Ryan flashes me a grin and I know he's OK with it. 'Where does this guy live?' he asks Dr Brown.

'Muswell Hill. The address is on my phone.'

North London. 'Did Professor Petrossian know him?'

'I'm not sure. She joined the team after he left. It's a small world, though, so she'd certainly have known *of* him.'

313

'Perhaps that's where she was heading, then.'

'It's possible.' Dr Brown chews his lip, thinking. 'She lived in St Albans, so she can't have been going straight home.'

'Ask him if she contacted him.' Ryan hands me the phone. There's a call list on the screen, with 'DAVID PARKER' at the top, and 'OUTGOING THU 02.48' just underneath.

'Nick? What's happening?'

I put David Parker on speaker, then tell him who I am and hold the phone up for Dr Brown to confirm it. He says Dr Brown was telling the truth and that he's sorry about all of it. He sounds friendly but scientific, like Mr Grice at school, which makes me want to trust him.

When I ask about Mr Kowalczyk, he says that he spoke to him a few months before he died but felt like he wasn't being listened to, and that Professor Petrossian did phone him from Aveney Park. They arranged to meet but she never showed, and he read about her death in the paper . . . and Muswell Hill is very close to Hampstead Lane, where she crashed her car, so that makes sense, too. I glance at Ryan, who gives me a thumbs up, so I explain my idea about the blood.

'Makes as much sense as anything else. Only problem is lack of equipment to draw the blood. I might be able to order it, but that would take time, and we don't want to draw attention to ourselves.'

'Could you borrow the stuff? I mean, from a doctor?'

'Not without explaining what I want it for.'

314

I look at Dr Brown, but he's frowning like he's playing catch-up, and Ryan's looking completely blank. 'There's got to be a way . . .'

I can see a blind man coming towards A&E, oldish, with his arm in a makeshift sling. He's got a woman with him who looks like she might be his daughter, and, leading the way, a guide dog. It's a golden retriever with soulful brown eyes, mouth slightly open like it's smiling. I stare at it for a moment, and then—

'I've just had an idea,' I tell David Parker. 'I'll call you back later.'

Sixty-Nine

I use Dr Brown's phone to send an email to Holly – I can always remember her address because it's a silly one – and tell Ryan that we might as well get on our way to London.

He stares at me, obviously pissed off. 'That was your idea? To email your friend and say hi?'

'Holly's dad is a vet and they live next to his surgery.' I decide not to mention Jake. No point in complicating things, and I can cross that bridge when I come to it. 'It's not that far from Muswell Hill.' I turn to Dr Brown. 'The equipment's basically the same as human stuff, right?'

'I should imagine it's pretty similar, but . . .' Dr B gives me a helpless look which makes me want to slap him.

'Then it'll have to do, won't it? Come on.' I start back to where we left the van.

It's still there, which is a relief. Ryan gets behind the wheel again and we try the radio, but it's really crackly and we end up driving in silence, eating Barry's mints. There are three family-sized packets in the glove box, so he must have liked them a lot. I think of him lying in the storeroom, and hope somebody finds him.

I think about Marcus too, and wonder, dully, what would have happened if he hadn't alerted Dr Seagrove to us being in the basement. What could we have done? Dr Brown might not have liked the idea of selling colour vision, but he was going to go along with it, wasn't he? He'd probably justified it by telling himself there was no alternative.

No point asking him. I bet he doesn't even recognise himself right now – and I know how he feels because I seem to have turned into a different person, too.

Everyone thinks they know themselves so well. People say, 'Oh, I'd never do such and such in this or that situation,' like they can be one hundred per cent sure, but all they really know is how they are when things are basically OK. No one knows how they're going to behave when the world gets turned upside down. They like to think they do – stuff that fits in with their idea of themselves as brave, noble people – but the truth is that no one has a clue.

I wouldn't have had the confidence to stand up for what I believed in before. Partly because I wasn't sure what it was that I did believe in, except generally, and yeah, this is a *really bad* way of finding out what you *can* do, but still . . . It feels good, knowing that.

I get directions to Holly's address from Dr Brown's phone. It keeps trying to put us on the motorway, but we stay on the back roads because of the soldiers. There's a breeze, and something chemical in the air – pesticides, I'm guessing.

It's slowly getting lighter, and my colour vision seems to be holding up OK. The pre-dawn light makes the countryside seem like a new world. Silent, because there are no birds, but all soft, washy greens, like in a watercolour painting, with the sky a very faint blue and cows like ghosts in the mist. It's so beautiful that I gasp a couple of times and Ryan gives me this really intense look, like, 'Watch out'. He clearly doesn't trust Dr Brown enough to tell him about us seeing colour, so I'm not going to say anything, either. But in any case, I honestly think Dr Brown's so sunk into himself right now that he'd barely notice if the van caught fire.

Every time we go through a town there's vandalised cars and barricaded shops – once, a whole row, burnt out – and litter and graffiti everywhere. It makes me wonder what London's going to be like.

London: Mum and Prune and Rusty. The feeling of wanting to be home is so strong that it's like a pain in my chest.

I know Holly's probably asleep right now, and that she might still be pissed off with me, but I wish she'd hurry up and reply.

We cross the junction with the M25, where the army are directing the traffic and the empty motorway stretches out for miles in both directions. We're passing what must be the last green fields before London really begins when the first pink streaks appear in the sky, and the sun starts to come up. It's so beautiful that I can't stop staring.

People used to go on like sunrise and sunset are these big clichés – in photographs or romantic films – but it's only when they've been taken away that you properly appreciate how lovely they are. Especially if you're wondering if it's the last sunrise that you or anyone else will ever see in colour.

I wonder if Marcus can see it, if he's awake and in a room with a window . . . If he's still alive.

Ryan slows right down. 'Chemical magic moment?' I ask.

'Still counts.' He pulls over to the side of the road and cuts the engine. There are a few more fields rolling away down a hill, and the edge of a housing estate beyond them – and shimmering, golden light on the horizon, like the sky's being touched by God. Even if Dr Brown wasn't right beside us with his thousand-yard stare, I know that neither of us would speak as we scramble out of the driver's door.

The smell isn't so bad here. Perhaps it's too near where people live to use that many weapons-grade pesticides. We lean against the side of the van to watch the sky light up like a delicate fire. We don't do anything or say anything, we just look.

Ryan puts his head back and lets out a long breath, deep as a groan. 'Ay. May. Zing.'

We look at each other, and then suddenly it's awkward, like we shared this really intimate and perfect sensation and don't know what to say next. I turn my head away and look across the fields at the housing estate: low-rise white boxes, each in their own bit of garden.

'Grace?'

'Yeah?'

319

'You're really smart.'

I don't know what I was expecting him to say, but it wasn't that. When I turn to look at him, he's lolling his head towards me, like, casual. Except it isn't. 'So are you,' I say, lightly. 'You got us here.'

'Driving.' Ryan shrugs. 'You're *smart* smart. Figuring everything out. Like how you were right about Dr Brown, bringing him with us. You could really get it together and . . . you know . . . *do* something in your life.'

He's assuming that either of us will get the chance to do something in our lives, but I don't spoil it by saying that. The world in front of us is just too beautiful not to have hope. 'Thanks.'

'It's true.' Ryan leans towards me, and immediately I'm wondering if I'm sweaty and thanking God for Barry's mints because at least my breath smells OK. But then I forget about all that because it's like when we were in the wood at Aveney Park, the first two people in a newly created universe.

I close my eyes as our lips touch. I can see the pinks and blues of the sunrise swirling behind my eyelids, and as we kiss my entire body is glowing with colours, like they're actually inside me. It's warm and tender and it feels like we're melting into each other, bright and beautiful and perfect like a book or a film or a dream – except it's not any of those things, it's here and it's now and it's *real*.

Dr Brown leans out of the driver's door, holding his phone – with all the excitement about the sunrise, I didn't realise we'd left it in the van. 'Email from your friend.'

Seventy

'Thanks.' I take the phone from Dr Brown and check to see if he sent a message or made a call, but everything is fine.

The email just says CALL ME FIRST and then Holly's mobile number, and Mum's.

'Are you OK? Why do you need Dad's help?'

'We're fine, but—'

'Who's we? And where are you? I didn't know if I should call your mum, or what, because—'

'Holl, slow down.' I think I do an OK job of explaining without going into too much detail about the really shit bits – apart from anything else, I don't feel like I could even find the words – but there's still a shocked silence at the end. I know how she feels – I mean, I was actually *there* but it hasn't really sunk in yet. 'So,' I say, 'do you think your dad could . . . I mean, the equipment's probably the same and I'm sure Dr Brown or Mr Parker could pay for it so he can replace it and—'

'Dad's at a conference about the greyout. The surgery's shut this week, and school's closed because of the riots, so I'm stuck here because Lotte doesn't want us to go outside.'

'Actually, that's probably better – your dad not being there, I mean. Maybe don't mention it to Jake, either.' I say this as casually as I can.

'It's OK, he's staying with a friend.'

She doesn't say which friend, and I'm not about to ask, but I hope it's a new relationship because that would make things a whole lot easier all round. 'Can you get out?'

'I don't know. Lotte barely leaves her room. The problem is if Freddie wakes up.'

'What about the keys?'

'That's OK. Dad always puts them in the same place.'

'We won't need any drugs, just some basic kit. Can you do the alarm?'

'Yeah, no problem.'

'So can you meet us there? I think it'll take . . . an hour, maybe?' I look at Ryan, who nods.

'I'll try.'

'It's really important, Holl.'

'Yeah, I get that.'

'OK.' I ignore the fact that she sounds a bit pissed off, like I only wanted to talk to her so she could do us a favour, and not because she's my best friend . . . OK, that's sort of true, but not something I can think about right now.

*

'Jake . . . Was that who you were seeing?'

I obviously didn't manage to be as casual as all that.

'Yeah, but it's history. Plus, he's not even there.'

'OK.' Ryan sounds wary.

'No, *really*. Apart from anything else, it's like . . . I don't know, I'm not even that person any more because so much has happened.'

Ryan frowns for a moment, then gives me a rueful, just-glad-to-be-alive grin. 'Hasn't it, though? Come here . . . You can call David Parker in a minute.'

David Parker answers at once. I'm half expecting him to argue or point out why my plan won't work, but he just says he'll see us at the surgery. It's weird, having adults just falling in with your suggestions, but I could definitely get used to it.

'All set?' Ryan's back in the driver's seat.

'I just want to try my mum.'

'OK.' He closes the door.

I call the number, but nobody answers. The voicemail doesn't kick in, either, and the phone rings and rings until I give up.

Seventy-One

All the way into London I'm thinking that even if Holl *is* pissed off with me, she'd tell me if something had happened to Mum . . .

If she knew. All the things I've been worrying about since I heard that stuff on the radio come flooding into my head: fire and chaos and our flat being trashed and Rusty trying to be heroic and getting himself killed and Mum and Prune being hurt or . . .

'Your mum's probably still asleep,' Ryan says quietly.

'Hope so.'

He reaches out and touches my hand. I don't say anything else because of Dr Brown sitting right beside us, even if he does seem to be miles away.

Or I thought he was. A minute later he says, 'How long have you two been able to see in colour?'

Ryan and I look at each other.

'You can, can't you?'

'Yeah,' Ryan says. 'Since the fire, more or less.'

'Is this the first time?'

'Yesterday as well. Both of us. Not for so long, though.'

'You didn't take anything when you were in the basement, or—'

'All we've had is the stuff you've given us. Do you think it'll last?'

I'm thinking that – seeing how I'm sitting next to him – Dr Brown might want to peer into my eyes to check things out, but he just stares at the pair of us. 'I don't know,' he says, finally. 'It might come and go, but maybe you'll get it back permanently . . . You were watching the sunrise, weren't you?'

I want to laugh. 'Yes, that's right.'

'And you could see it properly?' Really, he ought to be saying something scientific, but he's gawping at us like we've just landed from another planet.

I nod, and his eyes seem to get even bigger and his face sort of gapes. Then he bursts out into loud, ugly sobs.

I don't know why he's crying. Because he's glad we can see, or because of the unforgivably cynical get-rich conspiracy he was part of, or because he's afraid of Omnisant, or all of it? *He* probably doesn't know why he's crying, but it's like he can't stop.

Ryan doesn't say anything. I put my arm round Dr Brown because it seems like I ought to do something. It feels really awkward, what with snot coming out of his nose that he doesn't even try to wipe away. I look for tissues in the glove box, but there aren't any. I guess Barry must have liked an old-fashioned cotton handkerchief, same as Rusty. I want to tell Dr Brown it's going to be OK, because that's what people always say, even if they don't believe it, but the words stick in my throat.

Seventy-Two

I stare past Dr Brown's heaving shoulders and out of the window. Not much traffic this early, just the odd car. I can hear alarms going off in the distance, and a couple of ambulances race past with their sirens wailing.

There's litter strewn across the road in places, overturned bins on the pavements, and more parades of shops with boarded-up windows. Once, I spot thick tyre marks on the grey asphalt in front of us and a medium-sized lorry on its side in a ditch. Its rear doors are open, and plastic boxes that once held food are scattered along the verge.

By the time we've got through the outer suburbs, Dr Brown's sobs have subsided. Ryan tries the radio again – still pretty crackly, but between the bursts of static we make out that the City and the West End are closed to all traffic except essential services.

We see more vehicles and people moving about as we get properly into north London, but not nearly as many as you'd expect. I think of what Holl said about school being closed. Maybe it's the same with businesses. There's a weird sort of quietness, like everybody's crouched behind the doors of their homes, waiting.

I'm suddenly too tired to talk, or even think. I try to keep my eyes open, but the jolting of the van sends me into this sort of disembodied half-sleep where I'm stumbling down the corridors at Aveney Park, trying to get away from Captain Franchot. I can't see or hear him, but I know he wants to kill me, and I've got to find Mum and make sure she's OK. Everything's tilting around me, all the doors marked 'Private' weaving about in front of my face, the letters going up and down and merging into each other. I try to keep upright but I'm lurching against the walls and Mum isn't there and Captain Franchot's coming and something terrible is going to happen and I'm being shaken about and—

It's Ryan, trying to wake me up. I stare at him, confused and hot. The van's stopped.

'We're here. At least you didn't snore . . . Who's that?'

I look up, and Holly's little brother Freddie is dashing out of the back door of the surgery. 'Grace!' He runs up to the van and starts banging on the side.

'All right, mate, but let's keep it down, shall we?' Ryan's getting out when Holly appears.

'Sorry, he woke up – I didn't really have a choice, and—' She catches sight of Ryan. 'Who are you?'

'This is Ryan, from Aveney Park.' I clamber out of the van.

Holly looks at Ryan suspiciously, then stares at me like she's trying to work out if I've changed in any way, but she doesn't ask if I'm all right. I want to give her a hug. Apart from anything else, it's lovely to see her in colour again, even if she's not smiling, but the metre of space between us feels more like infinity. Ryan and I didn't agree not to tell her about the colour thing, although I know he won't. I hope Dr Brown doesn't say anything. I don't think I could bear it if Holly reacted like Liam and the others did.

'Who's that?'

Dr Brown's still sitting in the van, and Holl's eyes widen when she sees the state of him. He mumbles hello when I introduce them, but nothing else, which is a relief.

'Mr Parker's already here.' Holly gestures at a bicycle leaning against the wall. 'He said he could find the things he needs.'

'Thanks for this, Holl. We're really grateful.'

Still, she doesn't smile. 'I hope you know what you're doing.'

'I'm not sure anyone does, right now, but it's better than nothing.'

She seems to relax a bit at that. 'It's like everyone's lost the plot. Our corner shop got trashed, and the supermarket's like . . . ' She shakes her head.

I think of the shop in the service station. 'I can imagine.'

'I'm sorry about your friends.'

I swallow the lump in my throat. 'Thanks,' I manage. 'Can we . . . ?'

Ryan follows us through the reception and into the treatment room, with Freddie, who seems to have decided they're best friends, bouncing along beside him. Dr Brown is trailing behind, looking blank.

David Parker is busy with a bunch of vials and blood bags. The treatment room is all white – bright light and wipe-clean surfaces. I suddenly remember when we brought Parsley in here after the accident, and Holl's dad said there was nothing he could do, and having to leave without him, which makes me think about Marcus and the others, and . . .

Freddie tugs my arm. 'Are you going to cry?'

I shake my head, but I can't get any words out. It's like I've been on autopilot, and now I'm feeling a big wave of all the emotions I couldn't feel before because there wasn't time or head space.

Someone takes me gently by the arm. David Parker. Crinkly, kind blue eyes and sticky-up eyebrows like a hairy terrier. 'Come and sit down. Who's going first? Let's get started, and we can talk afterwards.'

Ryan says he'll go first, so I close my eyes and tune out for a bit. I can hear Freddie asking loads of questions, and David Parker asking Holl if she can 'rustle up' some tea and biscuits. I don't hear Dr Brown say anything. I noticed David P barely greeted him when he came in – just a nod – so I'm guessing his feelings are pretty mixed, which I can totally understand.

When it's time for my go, I open my eyes again. Dr Brown's left the room, which I guess means he's been out the back with Holl. She locked the surgery door when we came in and he hasn't got his phone, so I don't suppose he could get up to much, even if he wanted to.

Giving blood only takes a short time, but I feel quite woozy afterwards. It isn't nearly as much blood as Ms Anson took at Aveney Park, but I suppose I'm not getting any back this time. Holl gives me a cup of tea with sugar in it, and two ginger biscuits that are properly golden brown. It's like with the orangeade and the sandwich at the service station – they seem like the nicest thing you ever tasted.

David Parker asks Holl if she can find a cool box so he can take the blood away, then says, 'Nick told me everything that happened.'

'Yeah . . .' Ryan's looking wiped out.

'It was terrible.' I say it because I think I ought to say *something*, even though 'terrible' doesn't come close to describing it. I don't think I'm capable, right now, of putting what it actually *was* like into words, any more than I was earlier, on the phone with Holly. Instead, I say, 'We're lucky to be alive . . . and we can see colour. Both of us.' Ryan gives me side-eye, but I don't see that my telling him matters – after all, Dr Brown already knows.

David Parker's terrier-eyebrows go up. 'Normal colour?'

'Well, yeah . . . I mean, everything looks how I remember it. Dr Brown said it might come back permanently.'

'It's not impossible.' David Parker glances towards the door. 'How is he?'

'I'm not sure he really knows what he's doing. It's like . . . Well, we thought he'd phone Omnisant, but he phoned you instead, so . . .'

Ryan says, 'There was a bunch of stuff he wouldn't have told us, but Grace figured it out.'

'He said he was sorry, though,' I point out. 'Before that. But I think he's sort of disconnected.'

'I think we all feel a bit like that at the moment.' David Parker says it gently.

Ryan sits up. 'Yeah, but he was part of it. You weren't.'

'We argued about it a lot,' David Parker tells him. 'Sometimes people find themselves in too deep to back out, so they have to keep justifying. We were offered a great deal of money for the project, and Nick's wife was having another baby, so I think that was part of it.'

'But you didn't take it.' Ryan's voice is flat.

'No, I didn't. But – and I'm not excusing him – I have fewer responsibilities.' David Parker sighs. 'If you tell yourself that something's OK often enough, you start to believe it, even if you originally thought the opposite. And of course, nobody ever had to justify anything to the public, because the public weren't told.'

So Dr Brown does have a family. Perhaps Dr Seagrove had one as well: a partner, and maybe children and even grandchildren. Professor Petrossian might have, too, and even Captain Franchot, although I can't think about *him* for long.

'We all justify things to ourselves,' David Parker says. 'And it was – and still could be – a good solution to the problem.'

'Except for selling it.'

'Except that.'

'What do you think is going to happen?'

'I don't know, but at least I have these' – David Parker gestures at the two blood bags – 'thanks to you. It's going to be difficult – very difficult – but it's a beginning. And these may not look like much, but they're not just blood ... '

I stare at the liquid inside the bags: beautiful deep red, thick and glistening. 'No,' I say. 'They're *hope.*'

Seventy-Three

'Well,' David Parker says, 'I'll do my best.'

'It better be good.' Ryan nods at the bags. 'We can give you more when you need it.'

There's a slight pause before David Parker puts out his hand. 'Thank you.'

I shake his hand, too. It feels good, like we've accomplished something, but David P frowns. 'I'd better speak to Nick.'

We find Dr Brown in Reception, staring at a poster about rabbit parasites, and David Parker looks relieved and takes him back into the treatment room to talk. I leave Ryan and Freddie looking at a display of dog toys and go and find Holly in the little kitchen.

'Have you finished?'

'Yeah, all done.'

'Only I can't stand needles.' She leans against the sink unit. 'You must have seen a lot of them in the last few days, right?'

I make a face. 'Right.'

'I'm really glad you're OK, Grace, except . . .'

'Except?'

'Are you? I mean, *really*?'

'Yeah. *Really.*' And in one way, I am. It's like I said to David Parker about Ryan and me being lucky. But again, I have this feeling of a vast space between the two of us, because – like I said to Ryan – I'm not the person I was before. Right now, I don't feel like anything is ever going to bring the old Grace back, because you can't *un*-have experiences. It's like a cup of tea: once the sugar's stirred in – you can't take it back out again.

Holly turns away and starts fiddling with something on the draining board. 'I need to get Freddie home before Lotte notices we've gone, only I can't find the keys to lock up. I was sure I'd left them in here, but ....'

I tell her I'll help look and go through to the back, so I can be by myself for a few minutes.

I do a sweep of the storerooms and the place where animals stay overnight – now just a row of empty cages – but I don't spot anything. I'm wondering how long Dr Brown and David Parker are going to be when the phone rings in my pocket.

'Hello? It's Lizzie Ballard here. I had a call from this number.'

'Mum!' I'm yelling, instantly fizzy with relief.

'Grace?'

'Are you OK?'

'Yes, we're fine. Well, fairly fine.'

'Why, what's happened?'

'Apart from the country going completely mad? Nothing

333

specific. What's going on where you are? I thought they said you couldn't phone. Has something happened?'

'I'll explain when I'm home. I'm in Muswell Hill, so—'

'What? Why? You're supposed to be in Norfolk.'

'Tell you later. It's so great to hear your voice, you can't imagine.'

'Are you sure you're all right?'

'I'm fine! Change of plan, that's all.'

'Do you want Rusty to come and get you? Only it might take a while, because—'

'No, it's fine. Honestly. We've got a van.'

'Well, if you're sure. There's a barricade, so you might have to walk the last bit. We'll tell the guys you're coming.'

'What guys?'

'Security. Eddie from next door, and some of the others. You'll probably recognise them, but it's—'

'Grace!' It's Holly, yelling from the kitchen. 'It's OK, the keys were in Reception.'

'Listen, Mum, I'd better go. I'll see you soon, OK?'

'All right – but take care, won't you?'

'Yes. Love you, Mum.'

'Love you too.'

It's one of those things where you don't realise how much you've been worrying until you stop. I could hear in Mum's voice that she was trying so hard to keep it light, but at least they're all still there. Knowing that makes me feel like a colossal weight has fallen off my shoulders.

Freddie comes barrelling down the corridor, all important. 'Ryan sent me to find you.' He peers at me, frowning. 'You're not going to be sad any more, are you?'

'Nah.' I grin at him. 'Promise. Come on, then.'

Seventy-Four

David Parker stashes the cool box in his backpack and unlocks his bike. 'Don't worry, I'll keep this safe. I've written my number down here.' He hands me a piece of paper. 'Text me yours as soon as you're reunited with your phone. Oh, and' – he jerks his head in the direction of Dr Brown, who's standing beside the back door of the surgery – '*he* wants to come with you.'

'Isn't he going with you?'

'I suggested it, but he said he needs to see you safely home first.' David Parker lowers his voice. 'He wants to apologise to your family.'

'I could have sworn I left the keys in the kitchen, but they were on the desk.' Holly finishes locking the back door and turns to Ryan and me.

'You probably just forgot.' I give her a hug, but she stiffens and it's awkward. I suddenly wonder if she overheard us telling David Parker about being able to see in colour and was expecting me to tell her about it when we were in the kitchen.

She gives me a weak smile and reaches for Freddie's hand. 'Talk soon, OK?'

'Yeah. Course. And thanks again, Holl.'

'No problem.'

Holly locks the gates behind the van. Freddie waves like mad as we drive away, but she just stares after us. I feel like I've really let her down.

Ryan eyes me. 'The fewer people who know, the better.'

'I was wondering if she heard.'

'Hope not. Did she stay in Reception,' he asks Dr Brown, 'after she brought the tea?'

'I don't think so.'

'But you were there all the time, right?'

'Yes . . . I think she went back to the kitchen, but I can't really remember.' Dr Brown turns away to stare out of the window.

Ryan rolls his eyes at me. 'There you are, then – she can't have heard.'

Still not many cars on the road. There are more people about, but mostly they look scared and furtive, hurrying along with their heads down. Torn banners are lying on the pavement, like people were on a march and dropped them. I can see bits of clothing as well, and odd shoes, like there's been a fight or something, but I don't see a single police officer, just some men loading the shells of torched cars onto a flatbed truck.

When we stop at the lights by Highgate Station, two guys

pound on Ryan's window, shouting and trying to wrench the door open, and we all jump. It's like they've come out of nowhere, and they look insane – snarling, like dogs – and yelling after us when Ryan takes off.

'What did they want?' I ask him.

'They think we've got food in here.'

I'd forgotten about the van having *'Farm Fresh Fruit and Produce'* written on the side. 'Perhaps we have, if whoever killed poor Barry wasn't able to open the back. We're probably lucky to have got this far – although Mum said there's a barricade in our road, so we might have to abandon it anyway.'

'You spoke to her?'

'She rang me back. Sounds like she's OK.'

'Good. Keep going straight?'

'Yeah. We're nearly there.'

It's just down the hill and over the big junction. The houses here seem OK, but the garage at the intersection looks wrecked, with the shopfront shattered into a glass mosaic and the Portakabin doors hanging off at crazy angles.

The lights are green, but as we cross the junction a big SUV comes up alongside us. The windscreen's cracked and the front looks battered like it's been rammed into something. The man in the passenger seat is leaning out of the window, yelling at us and gesturing at the side of the road.

It takes me a second to recognise him. 'It's those guys from the lights. Perhaps you should stop.'

'What, so they can beat us to a pulp? *Look* at them, Grace.

Besides,' Ryan adds, grimly, 'if there's food in here we'll need it for ourselves, won't we?'

'OK, if you can just get into our road – second on the left.'

Ryan's knuckles are white as he puts his foot down and the van groans through the gears, straining to go faster. The SUV disappears behind us for a moment, and then I can see the bonnet through Ryan's window and there's a grinding of metal on metal as it tries to push us off the road.

Ryan's yelling at the top of his voice and the driver's yelling back. The van is big, but not big enough. We're being forced over, scraping the cars parked along the side of the road, and any minute now . . .

'No!' Ryan stomps on the accelerator and the van roars like a wounded animal and shoots forward. I can see our turning coming up, any second . . .

'Now!' I yell.

The van skids and fishtails as Ryan fights to keep it under control. Everything's a blur as we veer from one side of the road to the other and crash onto the pavement, crunching the wing mirror on a tree and scraping past hedges. Dr Brown's leaning so far away from the window that his head is practically in my lap as we bounce down on the tarmac again. The van tips and lurches, but Ryan practically stands on the accelerator and we take off down the road.

'Can't see them.' Ryan's teeth are clenched. 'Perhaps they overshot.'

Dr Brown's still got his head down, so I undo my seat belt

and lean over him to peer out of the passenger window. 'They're right behind.'

There's a crash from the back as the SUV rams into us and I almost go through the windscreen. As I scramble back onto the seat we get to where the road bends round and I can see the barricade – a car, a tow truck and two builders' skips in the middle – with people standing at each end. 'They'll ram us right into it.'

'Handbrake turn.'

'In this?'

'No option. Seatbelt, *now*.'

'OK.' By the time I've locked the belt into place, we're so close to the barricade that I can see the rust marks on the edges of the yellow metal skips. We're almost on top of them when Ryan's yell fills the cab as he wrenches the wheel and yanks up the handbrake. The van slews sideways in a single, violent swerve, and the air is split open by a long, harsh screech of metal on metal and a boom that makes my teeth rattle.

Seventy-Five

Someone is screaming.

It isn't one of us. Not close enough.

Hissing. OK, that's near. Steam?

A hollow ticking noise.

The van's dying, I think stupidly. *We killed it.*

I look around, trying to figure out where the noise is coming from, but nothing seems to be in focus. The windscreen is broken, a crazy starburst of cracked glass.

The passenger side of the van is hard against the skip, and I can see Dr Brown's upper body lolling away from me, half in and half out of the broken window. Both our laps are covered in fragments of glass.

I pull on his arm. 'Are you . . . ?' My voice comes out in a whisper. Are you what? I can't think of the word I want, but, to my surprise, he rights himself, nodding. He looks weirdly calm, and I wonder if he's got some terrible injury that his brain hasn't processed yet. No blood, though, except a thin trickle from somewhere under his hair.

I look to my right.

Ryan's staring down at his hands, which are resting on the steering wheel, as if he can't imagine how they came to be there. He raises his head like it's a massive effort, and looks at me blankly.

'That was amazing.'

His eyes come back into focus, and he raises his left hand in a half-salute and smiles. 'Love you,' he whispers.

'Love you, too.'

And I really, properly, mean it.

The van rocks as somebody pulls at the driver's door. Then there's some sweary shouting, and a face comes into view. Craggy. Grey hair and beard. Fisherman's sweater.

Rusty.

It's going to be all right.

I don't know how much time has passed. Rusty helped the three of us out of the van but then he went away again. Somebody put a blanket round my shoulders because I was shaking, and I heard people talking about an ambulance, although I don't think any of us are hurt – at least, not much. Dr Brown is dabbing the blood on his head with a tissue, but I think he's basically OK.

Ryan and I sit on the grass verge, arms round each other. I can see, on the side of the van, that the long gouges made by the SUV have almost obliterated the words *'Farm Fresh Fruit and Produce'*, although the smiley red apple is still visible. The wing on the far side is crumpled where it collided with the skip, and there are thick black strokes of shredded tyre across the white lines in the middle of the road.

The SUV, though. They were right behind us.

Where is it?

I try to stand up, but the effort makes me lightheaded and wobbly. All the colours – the dull yellow of the skips, the greenery, people's clothes, and the apple on the side of the van – seem to be breaking up into blotches. Ryan pulls me back down again.

'What happened?'

'Couldn't stop in time.' Ryan points across the road.

At the far end of the barricade, beyond the tow truck, I can see one corner of the rear end of the SUV. The front has smashed through the railings of one of the derelict houses, and, beyond them, I can make out people kneeling in the waist-high grass of the front garden, tending to somebody on the ground.

'Is it the driver?'

'Don't know. Someone's coming over.'

It's Prune, in her velvet coat. The different-coloured squares dance in front of my eyes, as if they're moving by themselves, carrying her along with them.

'Grace, oh, Grace . . . ' She kneels down in front of me and takes my hands in hers. As I look down at the big cuffs, the rainbow of embroidered leaves and flowers fades back to grey, and her fingers turn to mottled stone. When I look up I spot, over her shoulder, the smiling apple on the side of the van. It's glossy red for a split second – and then the colour and the grin disappear like a light going out and all I can see is a dark grey blob.

'Darling, I'm sorry . . .' For a moment, I think she must be apologising because the colour's gone, though how can she know? But when I look up at her face, I realise it's something much, much worse.

'We thought we'd come and wait for you, in case you had a problem getting through. We were over there.' She gestures towards the SUV. 'It was so quick. I thought she was right behind me, but . . . I'm so sorry.'

'No.' This can't be happening. Those people in the garden, kneeling in the grass . . . I clamber to my feet. 'Mum!'

Prune grabs me as I start across the road and pulls me into a hug. Over her shoulder I can see the people around us – faces, bodies, arms, legs – all merging into one grey mass, and beyond them . . .

'Such bad luck,' someone says.

'No! No, no, no, no—'

'Don't, love.' Prune strokes my hair. 'They're doing all they can.'

Seventy-Six

Grey people talking all around me: *Ambulance – Two hours or more – They closed A&E so we'll have to wait – You won't get through – Can't leave her here – One of those boards – Never mind those morons – Don't have a choice . . .*

Prune won't let me go to Mum. As she and Ryan guide me round the opposite end of the barricade and we stumble down the road towards home, all I can hear in my head is Dr Brown's voice: *It wasn't meant to be like this.*

I feel numb. When we get inside, everything looks the same as when I left. The kitchen's the same: grey, with a bowl of fruit that looks like it's made of stone, and snails crawling up the legs of the table. I can hear the ringing *pi-yow, pi-yow, pi-yow* noise of gunshots coming from the TV in the sitting room, like Rusty just fell asleep watching a cowboy film.

We go through. No Rusty, only John Wayne galloping across a grey desert, and a single snail sitting on top of the TV, the horns on its head like two tiny aerials.

Everything's going into slow motion. I lurch against the little table, tipping over Rusty's whisky glass, and watch as it rolls to the floor, liquid spilling out onto the rug. After a moment or two, I pick the glass up and stare at it. My mind is registering the absence of something, but my thoughts are moving so slowly that I can't figure out what it is.

This isn't happening. It's a dream.

'You need to sit down.' Ryan leads me to the sofa and sits down beside me, his arm round my shoulder.

Over in the corner, more galloping, more gunshots. Hooves in the dust.

It wasn't meant to be like this.

I don't know how much time has passed. Ryan cuddled me and Prune brought tea, but I couldn't drink it. John Wayne galloped about shooting baddies until somebody turned off the TV. Dr Brown's here now, a statue in Rusty's chair, and I blink and suddenly the room is full of people, and Mum, covered in a blanket, is being carried in on a board.

There are a thousand questions I want to ask, but she's so still that I don't even know where to start. Whatever damage was done when the SUV ploughed into her, it's beyond bad.

We move so they can lie her on the sofa, and they let me sit down on the floor beside her. Her face is white as chalk, her eyes closed. Close up, her breathing is faint but harsh-sounding, as if it's hurting her.

There's blood on the blanket. Someone asks if there's any news on the ambulance and I feel, rather than see, somebody else shaking their head.

'Mum,' I whisper in her ear. Her skin is cold and clammy. 'It's Grace. I'm here.'

'Grace.' The word is barely more than a breath. 'Hurts . . .'

Prune bends over me. 'Talk to her, love, so she knows you're there. The car went over her legs, and she may have internal injuries. We need to keep her calm . . . We're trying to find something for the pain, because it might be a while before the ambulance gets here.'

'There's stuff in the medicine cupboard.'

Prune's voice is gentle. 'I don't think aspirin will cut it.'

'Sorry, that was stupid.' I turn my head away from Mum and lower my voice. 'She's not going to die, is she?'

Prune squeezes my hand. 'Just stay with her.'

'I'm here, Mum. It's all right. We're getting help . . . Please, just hang in there . . . You'll be all right.'

I repeat this over and over again, because I don't know what else to say.

Seventy-Seven

I can hear people in the kitchen – raised voices, like frustration or an argument – but I tune them out. The words coming out of my mouth are a meaningless jumble of sounds now, like I'm not making sense even to myself. I stare at Mum, willing her to respond, but nothing happens. Surely I can reach her if I just try harder. 'Mum, can you hear me? Please show me you can hear me . . .'

A noise behind me makes me turn my head. I'd forgotten Dr Brown. He's getting out of Rusty's chair with stiff movements like an old man. If he even *thinks* that now is the time to start giving Mum some big speech about how sorry he is . . .

'You need to leave,' I snap.

His eyes lock onto mine, and it takes me a moment to realise he's fumbling something out of his pocket. 'Here.' He drops a blister pack into my lap.

'What are they?'

'Painkiller. Tramadol. It's a smallish dose, so you'll probably need a few.'

Tramadol. I know what it is: Prune was given some after she had an operation. They're opioids and very strong. Dr Brown's given me a whole strip, with none missing.

I want to ask him why he didn't hand them over before, but instead I say, 'Great. My grandma used to be a nurse, so you'd better check with her first.'

I nip to the loo while Prune gives Mum the pills and when I come back down, Dr Brown's waiting for me at the bottom of the stairs, looking like he's got a speech prepared. 'You're right,' he says. 'I should go. I'll understand if you're not prepared to give me back my phone, but—'

'I want to ask you something.'

He gives me wary look, as if I might attack him. 'OK.'

'Marcus was in agony. Why didn't you give him any of those pills?'

The silence is sharp as a sliver of glass, and I know he's trying to work out what to say. Even as he starts telling me he forgot he had the pills, my mind leaps to the vet's surgery: Holly saying she found the keys on the reception desk, where he was standing in front of the rabbit poster. And, when Ryan asked him if he saw Holly in Reception, he couldn't remember . . .

Because he didn't know.

He didn't know because *he wasn't there all the time*. Because he swiped the keys and put them back afterwards.

'You took those from the surgery, and Prune's just given them to Mum. What have you done? They're meant for *animals*.'

I push past him to get to the sitting room, but he grabs my arm. 'They're identical.'

'How do you know? Let go of me!'

'What do you think you're playing at?' Rusty comes out of the kitchen and grabs Dr Brown by the lapels, shoving him against the wall.

'Those pills he gave me for Mum, they're not for people.'

'They're the same for humans and animals.' Dr Brown's voice is a croak. 'You have to believe me, Grace. They'll help her.'

Rusty eyeballs Dr Brown. 'They'd better.'

'I swear – or I'd never have suggested it.'

'But . . . ' I'm about to ask why he stole them when I realise that I already know the answer. How he cried in the van, and then, once we'd left the surgery, how calm he seemed, how detached, and why he didn't give me the pills immediately . . .

That was the other thing the boiling-a-frog counsellor guy told me. Mum had been calm that morning four years ago when I went off to school, and I'd thought she was feeling better. Afterwards, it kept coming back to me that I'd missed something. I was beating myself up for not spotting it, but the counsellor said that often there was nothing *to* spot, if somebody had made a decision about suicide and kept it to themselves.

I'm so angry I feel as if I want to kill him myself. 'What about your wife and children?' I yell. 'Have you thought about them for *a second*?'

Rusty glances at me, confused. 'Grace, what's—'

'No,' I shout. 'I need to say this. *He* knows exactly what I'm talking about – yes, Dr Brown, you do, I can see it on your face. You can't just *leave* all this. You're part of it, and you have to help David Parker. You have to make it *right*.'

'Gracie. Calm down, OK?' Rusty's let go of Dr Brown, who's fussing with his collar like I haven't spoken.

'*Look* at me!' His head jerks up like it's on a string, and his eyes are round and stunned, like I've just slapped him. 'I know about fear,' I tell him. 'And I saw Mr Kowalczyk, remember? He was too scared to stay and face up to things, but *you* have to, because *you* can do something about it.' Dr Brown flinches as I take a step towards him. 'Have you got more pills? I want to see in your pockets.'

'I'll do it.' Ryan steps out of the kitchen, face expressionless, and frisks him. Dr Brown doesn't try to stop him – which would be impossible, anyway, with Rusty towering over the three of us like an angry giant – and he pulls out ten more blister packs and hands them to me.

'That's the lot.'

'Right.' I take a deep breath. 'And yes, you should go.'

'The phone?' Dr Brown's voice sounds small, like it's coming from a long way away.

'You won't tell Omnisant we're here?'

'I promise.'

'I deleted the number,' Ryan tells me, 'and copied David Parker's contact details into Rusty's phone.' When Rusty nods I can see he's already decided he likes Ryan. There's nothing to stop Dr Brown getting hold of another phone, of course, or getting the number for Omnisant, but still . . . I pull it out of my pocket and hand it over. 'Call your family. They need to know you're all right.'

Seventy-Eight

Rusty escorts Dr Brown out through the kitchen, and Ryan takes a long breath. 'Wow.'

My heart's hammering like I've run a race. 'To be honest,' I say shakily, 'I surprised myself a bit.'

'Yeah, well. I think it worked.'

'His choice. I need to . . .' I glance through the doorway to the sitting room, where Prune's sitting on the floor beside Mum.

'Course. I'll be in the kitchen. Call me if you need anything.'

Mum's eyes are still closed, so I sit down on the floor next to Prune. I think I'm talking really quietly as I explain everything that's happened, but when I'm finished, and Prune is hugging me, I see that Mum's eyes are open, and she's looking at us. 'Grace . . .'

'I'm here, Mum. I'm not going anywhere.'

She closes her eyes again, and drifts away.

*

352

We've been watching her for about an hour, and her breathing sounds like it's more comfortable. There's no news about the ambulance, though, and the A&E is still closed to new patients.

'Should we give her some more painkillers?'

'Not yet.' Prune's face sags with worry as she leans over Mum. 'Lizzie . . . ?'

'Better . . . ' Her eyes are still closed.

'That's good. Just take it easy.'

After a few more minutes, Mum's eyes open again. She's looking at me and Prune, and everything around us. All grey.

I feel as if the world's died. That night, when we were talking after I had the nightmare, that's what she said. And Alice, saying death was grey, empty space.

Where she went. Where they all went.

If it's going to happen, I can't stop it, but I can't let it happen like that.

I suppose it was in the back of my mind when I was in the army truck, just not like this. But now . . .

Now, I may not have another chance.

'Mum,' I say quietly, 'there's something I want to give you.'

I reach into my pocket and pull out half a million pounds' worth of colour.

Seventy-Nine

'Let her do it.' Rusty's voice makes us jump.

Prune and I have been arguing in whispers in the hall, and we didn't realise he was listening from the kitchen. Him and Ryan, in fact, because they're both standing in the doorway.

'It's my initials on the label, so we know exactly where it's come from,' I tell Prune.

'But all those other things—'

'It's been tested, love. Grace said so. And besides . . . ' Rusty tails off, and we all avoid each other's eyes.

Prune sighs. 'All right, but how? You can't drink it, can you?'

'It has to be injected,' I tell her.

'That's what I mean. We haven't got—'

'Yes, we have. Dr Brown isn't the only person who stole something from the vet's.' Ryan's eyes widen as I fumble in the sleeve of my hoodie and produce a sealed packet containing a syringe. 'I took it when I was helping Holly look for the keys,' I explain. 'Prune can give it to her.'

*

I follow Prune back into the sitting room and look round while she prepares the injection. Mum will see *us* in colour, and the furniture, and the view from the window – the house opposite, and trees and cars – but it needs to be *more*.

All the colours. Every shade we can find.

'I'll be back in a minute,' I tell her.

Ryan follows me through the kitchen and down the outside steps. 'What's going on?'

'You'll see.'

We run past Prune's garden – bare earth, criss-crossed with slime trails – and across the terrace. Ryan stops for a second to peer through the French windows at the derelict swimming pool. 'This place must have been amazing.'

'Thirty years ago.'

'What a waste. Wish I could see it properly.'

'No colour?'

'Since about half an hour ago.'

'Mine went after the crash.'

Ryan looks round at the massive tangle of undergrowth that is the back garden. 'Just have to hope, I guess.'

'Paint charts.' Ryan leafs through the bundles of cards, intoning the names of the colours: 'True Blue, Sapphire, Misty Lake, Daffodil . . .'

'Forest Green, Copper Penny, Pomegranate Red . . . Every colour under the sun. Let's take them into the house.'

Eighty

We stand round the sofa, waiting for the antibodies to begin to work. It takes about half an hour – which I suppose is because of the accelerant Dr Brown told us about in the truck – and then it starts to happen. Mum doesn't say anything at first. She doesn't need to, because even in greyout we can see her eyes brighten as she starts to see the colours. Watching her makes me think of what it was like when Ryan and I were in the wood: the tingling magic of it, and thinking that that pile of rubbish was the most beautiful thing in the entire world. Mum's whole face is shining as she stares at each of us in turn, as if that's the only thing she wants to do, for ever.

'Beautiful,' she says. 'So beautiful.'

I know what she means: the world so bright, so full of light and energy, glowing like jewels, and *alive*.

Prune props Mum's head up with cushions so she can see better, and she looks all around the room and out into the street. She even spends ages staring at the tie Rusty gave Prune to use as a tourniquet – which, I remember, is purple and orange and so hideous that we won't let him wear it in public.

Ryan and I bring in the paint charts, which we taped to some bits of old cardboard boxes so they can be propped against the furniture. I watch her gaze move across them, one little oblong at a time, and her face is so intense it's like watching someone have an out-of-body experience. It's amazing and beautiful and my heart feels like it's breaking. We stand in silence and watch as she looks and looks and looks until, finally, the day turns into evening and the ambulance comes to take her away.

Part III

Eighty-One

'Wear this one.' I take Prune's blue shirt off its hanger. 'It's gorgeous.'

Prune feels the shining silk between her thumb and finger, and sighs. 'Remind me.'

My colour vision comes and goes now, and so does Ryan's, but it's getting so it's there more than it's not, if that makes sense. I'm glad today is a colour day for both of us. In a bizarre way, it's good that we still have greyout days as well, because it reminds us of something we took for granted before: living in a beautiful world is not only an immense privilege, but it's a privilege that, like Alice said, we didn't do anything to earn. 'That iridescent colour, like a peacock's neck. It really suits you. And don't worry, I've picked out something for Rusty, too – the dark suit. He's insisting on wearing a t-shirt with it, so I chose the light green one.'

Prune nods, approving. 'Where are we with the food?'

'All sorted. Ryan's downstairs, bringing stuff in.'

*

The people who occupied the house down the road turned out to be really nice, and they're lending us their glasses and things. Well, not *actually* theirs, because the stuff belongs to the people who own the house, but, as Rusty pointed out, they barely visited the place even before the greyout, so what the hell. Trish, the woman who's sort of in charge of the occupiers, told us that the guys who were chasing us got away in all the confusion – on foot, because the SUV was a write-off. It's still sitting on the road next to Barry's van with the smiling apple, which turned out to contain quite a lot of food. We shared it out, giving Eddie-Next-Door and his mate Pavel the idea of breaking out the stocks in their boarded-up mansion's dried food stores. It's not like the owner is going to find out about it any time soon, because you can bet that right now anyone who's *that* rich is going to be holed up on a private island or somewhere like it until everything calms down ... Whenever that's going to be. One thing I do know about the future, though: it's going to feature a lot of tinned soup.

Except for this afternoon. We've managed to get together the next best thing to a banquet: because it's for Mum, everyone's donated stuff – which is great because people are starting to eat a bit more now they're getting used to food not being the proper colours. Eddie and Pavel even broke into next door's wine cellar, so thanks, Russian guy. Plus, I got a bunch of photos, something from pretty much every part of Mum's life, and stuck them on a big wooden board I found in one of the sheds. Rusty's supposed to be propping it up on the mantelpiece, but, judging by the noise from downstairs, I think he's just dropped it on his foot.

Prune rolls her eyes. 'Better go and help him.'

Sure enough, I find Rusty in the sitting room, still swearing. I help him lift the board onto the mantelpiece and we stand side by side for a moment, looking at all the pictures of Mum. Rusty puts his arm round my shoulders. 'I know . . .' he rumbles, not looking at me, 'you're not my granddaughter, but that's how I think of you. I'm proud of you, Grace.'

I feel the sudden pressure of tears behind my eyes and have to blink really hard. 'I'm proud of you, too.' I'm not just saying that for something to say. I am properly proud of Rusty, because he's stopped drinking, which is amazing. That was what was weird about knocking over his glass in the sitting room, that I couldn't work out at the time: no smell of whisky, because what I spilt was apple juice.

When we finally got back from the hospital the day of the crash, after I'd sat with him and Prune in that exact same room where the doctor told Mum and me that Dad had died – the bad flower paintings were still there – and they'd told us to expect the worst, I thought he'd get stuck straight into the Scotch, but he didn't. He made us all cups of tea, instead. He said he'd concluded that drinking all the time was like being in greyout – meaning you don't see anything as it really is. He told me about a prayer he often said, too: 'Grant me the serenity to accept the things I cannot change, the courage to change the things I can, and the wisdom to know the difference.'

I've been saying that a lot this past month, sitting by Mum's bed and holding her hand. I'm guessing Rusty has, too, because – even at the worst, darkest time – he's aced it. He's been keeping busy while Prune and I have been at the hospital, clearing away the undergrowth round Mr Zhang's pond. Amazingly, some ducks from the pond up the road have moved in, and they've been scoffing all the slugs. As a result, Prune's garden is doing way better, and we get loads of vegetables even though it's practically winter – although you wouldn't know that from the weather, which is still warm enough to be outside in a t-shirt. Rusty managed to get hold of some hens, too. He and Ryan cleared all the broken glass and crap out of the swimming pool, then put down a bunch of straw. They made cardboard nesting boxes and a wooden ramp in the shallow end so the hens can get outside and help control the slugs.

Ryan's been living here with us, and he and Rusty get on really well. He's way calmer now – I guess that's being around all of us, with nobody to wind him up – plus he understands about addiction and recovery because of his dad and the gambling.

The fire at Aveney Park wasn't on the news and, so far as Omnisant knows, we're missing, presumed dead. They sent someone round to see if I was here, but Prune and Rusty said they hadn't seen me and did such a good impression of bewildered grandparents that they soon went away again. They must have sent people to Ryan's home, too, but Ryan said that if his dad was in he would have seen them off in ten seconds flat. I wondered if they'd start asking the neighbours whether they'd seen me, but David Parker says they're trying to be inconspicuous, and I reckon he's right.

He says we need to keep a low profile for the time being, too, which is fine by us. Ryan phoned his mum, but he reckoned it was best not to contact the rest of his family. Rusty asked around, so at least we know they haven't been hurt or – which Ryan said was way more likely in the case of his dad and brother – arrested. I really hope Marcus is OK, too, but right now there's no way we can find out without being found out ourselves.

It looks like Rusty's having difficulty not tearing up, as well, so I give him a huge hug and go and help Ryan with the crockery. I'm not sure where he's going to put it, though, because practically every surface in the kitchen is covered in plates of food, all labelled so everyone knows what the flavours are.

I find him at the top of the outside steps with a box in his arms. 'Last one.'

'Great.'

'Arrived this morning.' I hand him an envelope. 'It's from Sophie.'

'*Sophie?*' Ryan looks alarmed. 'How did she find you?'

'Broke into her dad's computer. Turns out he had enough shares in Omnisant to be able to get hold of a bunch of classified information, although she swears he didn't know about Dr Seagrove's methods. She doesn't mention anything about selling colour vision, so either her dad doesn't know about that, or he hasn't told her.'

'Do you believe that?'

'I think so. He wouldn't have let her take part in the trial if he'd known, would he? And if her dad has found out about selling colour vision, that's got to be way too sensitive for him to tell *anybody*.'

'Guess so.' Ryan puts the box down. We lean on the rail, side by side, while he reads out loud. '*Dear Grace, I don't know if this letter will ever reach you. I don't even know if you're alive, but I wanted to write* it anyway. I swear to you . . . OK, so this is the bit about how her dad didn't know . . .' He scans the page, then carries on. *'Dad's information didn't include email addresses or mobile numbers and I thought I shouldn't try and contact you via social media because you might not want to be found . . .'* Ryan rolls his eyes. *'At least she figured that out. After I got into Dad's computer (which he doesn't know about) I made him tell me what happened at Aveney Park. Dad was told that some people survived the fire, but they are still examining the remains and it will take time to work out who was in there. I don't suppose the information will ever get to the media. Dad doesn't know I've written to you, and nor does anyone else.*

'I wrote to Marcus and he told me he would have died if you and Ryan hadn't taken him to hospital. His parents are suing Omnisant because he almost had to have his foot amputated, but it's all happening behind closed doors. He asked if I can give him your address because he wants to write and say thank you but I won't unless you tell me it's OK.

'Marcus said people like us don't think to question the system because it works in our favour, and he's right. Except I'm not sure it will for much longer because if the planet is dying and people losing their health because of it then we'll just be left with a pile of money that's no use to anybody.

'I really hope you're OK, Grace. You were right all along and I'm sorry I said you were paranoid. If you're reading this, please get in touch.

'Seems like she got the message.' Ryan folds up the letter. 'You going to write back?'

'Absolutely. We need to keep in touch. And with Marcus. Better stick to the post, though.'

'Sounds like a plan.'

*

We look out across the garden in silence. The ducks are sleeping by the pond, heads curled round on their brown speckled wings and Betty, my favourite hen, is pecking at something in a flowerbed. She's a Rhode Island Red with feathers like flames, and she blends in beautifully with the drifts of late autumn leaves, orange and gold, on the green grass. I don't think I'll ever get over the wonder of colour. Ryan says the same. One of the best things about him is that we can just be quiet together. It's so great to be with someone who knows how you're feeling because they've been through the same things you have. We both get nightmares and flashbacks, and although they can be awful it's good being able to talk about them, but also to have somebody who understands when you don't want to say anything at all and just need a hug.

'Better go and change,' he says, after a while. 'She'll be here soon.' He puts his arms round me from behind and kisses the top of my head. 'You know *I'm* here for you, don't you?'

'And me for you.' I wriggle round to kiss him properly – and right that second one of the ducks wakes up and starts quacking like, 'Stop that'.

'Ah, shut up.'

The duck flaps its wings and quacks even louder, like it's telling Ryan to piss off. He looks mock-disgusted as I start laughing, then rolls his eyes, picks up the box, and dumps it in my arms before loping off into the flat.

I manage to clear a space for the cutlery and line it all up, then I step back outside to wait for the guests. We couldn't invite everyone we wanted, in case too many people learn that Ryan and I are here, but Mum's best friends are coming, and Trish and co. and Eddie and Pavel. Dr Brown's coming, too. I thought he'd be angry with me when I confessed I'd given Mum the tube of colour, but he said he understood.

He and David Parker have been working together on the antibodies. Rusty and Prune have volunteered to be guinea pigs. Holly has, too. She'll be here this afternoon. Things are still a bit awkward between us, but they seem to be slowly getting better. And it turns out Jake does have a new girlfriend, which helps. David Parker talked to their dad, who said he'd be able to buy the stuff we need through his company in order not to raise suspicion, because the fewer people who know about the project, the better. I shan't mention any of this to Sophie or Marcus yet, but maybe in the future . . .

I know what we're doing isn't going to save the world overnight, however much I want it to, but it's *something*, and – most important – we want to do it so it's *fair*.

I wish Alice could be here, too. I dream about her quite often, and it's always the same: I'm in a street full of tall, thin houses painted in different colours – what she said that first night at Aveney Park. It's lovely and happy and everything's all right again and I know she made it that way so I want to say thank you, but she isn't there. Although the houses look separate from the outside, inside they're all linked up and I open door after door after door, like walking through a rainbow . . . I wish I could find her, just once, but I never do.

I lean on the rail, looking at the garden and blinking a lot until I hear the buzzer go on the gate, which means the first guests have arrived.

Pretty well everyone comes in the next half hour, and I manage to make sure that they all have a drink in their hand before Ryan takes me aside. 'It's time. Let's go down.'

He holds my hand as we stand on the verge and watch the big black car sweep round the bend and stop by the gates. Rusty, who must have got a chauffeur's cap from Eddie or Pavel at the same time as he 'borrowed' the Russian guy's Merc, gets out of the driver's seat, opens the rear door, and helps Mum out. She's pale and wobbly and using a stick to walk, but she's alive, and . . .

'Still colour?' I whisper in her ear as I hug her.

'Still colour. Don't worry, still secret.'

'Good. Save the colour chat for me and Ryan.'

'I'm looking forward to getting to know him better. And . . .' She takes hold of my elbow and steers me slightly away from the others. 'I wanted to say thank you, because you saved me. You gave me something to live for.' She catches sight of my face, and adds, quickly, 'I'm sorry. I don't mean . . . But after you'd gone to Aveney Park, it was so hard, even just those two, three days. I couldn't have carried on like that.'

'But you—'

'I know, Grace. I know I promised, and I'm sorry, but I was losing the will to live, everything just . . . draining away. I could feel it.'

'It's OK, Mum.' I hug her again. 'I understand.' And actually, I do: because if I've learnt one thing over the last few months it's that life is much more complicated than ... well, than just black and white. Mum saying she was losing the will to live isn't her saying she doesn't care about me, because that's not how it works – it's not one thing or the other.

'I love you, darling. You know that, don't you?'

I nod because I don't trust myself to speak.

'I'm so lucky to have you, Grace ... No, don't cry, or you'll set me off.'

We both sniff a bit, and she wipes a tear off my cheek with her finger. 'Now, what I want to know is what all this' – she gives me a wonky grin and waves a hand at the car – 'is in aid of. I couldn't believe it when Rusty rocked up at the hospital in that hat, but he wouldn't tell me anything.'

'Don't you remember what day it is?'

She frowns. 'I've lost track.'

'It's your birthday.'

'Oh, God. Is it?'

'For real. You're forty-five, in case you've lost track of that, too.'

She makes a face at me. 'Shut up.'

I give her a kiss. 'I'm so happy you're home.'

Ryan and I hang back, watching Rusty help Mum up the drive. I wish that someone – anyone – could tell me, honestly, that they've got this, and that everything will go back to normal, but I know they can't. It's not like there's going to be any kind of miracle, either. Really, it comes down to what it says in Rusty's prayer:

change the things you can. Because everyone has to start some-where, and this is where we are.

'Just checking for ducks.' Ryan makes a show of looking round, then pulls me into his arms. We kiss – uninterrupted this time – then go back to join the party.

Acknowledgements

I am very grateful to Simon Appleby, Veronique Baxter, Claire Billingham, Sue Bonfatti, Nick Canty, Phoebe Carney, Gabrielle Chant, Suzanne Clarke, Tim Donnelly, Nick Green, Paddy Gregan, Jane Gregory, James Gurbutt, Caroline Horn, Sara Langham, Mel McGrath, Kate Manning, Stephanie Melrose, Charlotte Stroomer, Katie Sadler, Professor David Thomson, Beth Wright, Sue Young & the Society of Authors Foundation for their enthusiasm, advice, and support during the writing of this book.